The Black Diamonds

The Black Diamonds

Clark Ashton Smith

Edited, with an Introduction, by

S. T. Joshi

Hippocampus Press

New York

Published by Hippocampus Press
P.O. Box 641, New York, NY 10156.

Permission to publish this text has been granted by CASiana,
the Estate of Clark Ashton Smith

First Edition
1 3 5 7 9 8 6 4 2

Cover art and interior illustrations by Jason C. Eckhardt.
Cover design by Barbara Briggs Silbert.
Hippocampus Press logo designed by Anastasia Damianakos.

ISBN 0-9673215-2-2
Library of Congress Control Number: 2002090073

Printed in the United States by Morris Publishing
3212 East Highway 30 • Kearney, NE 68847 • 1-800-650-7888

Introduction

The Black Diamonds is a full-length novel of almost 90,000 words written by Clark Ashton Smith (1893–1961) around 1907, when he was fourteen. It is remarkable that so youthful a writer could have produced such an extended narrative, with numerous clever plot-twists culminating in a satisfying resolution; but it is only the most substantial of a number of surviving texts of its kind.

Smith attested that around 1905 he began producing a number of tales of Oriental adventure, based largely upon the *Arabian Nights*. Among the works found in his papers (now in the John Hay Library of Brown University) are stories—some of them fragmentary—with such titles as "The Brahmin's Wisdom", "The Curse of Runjat Singh", "The Emir's Captive", and several others, many of them written in a distinctive purple ink. Smith notes that he discovered William Beckford's *Vathek* in 1908, but *The Black Diamonds* does not appear to bear any influence from that work, hence its provisional dating to 1907.

The Black Diamonds is, to be sure, not a literary masterwork in its own right, but it is a rousingly entertaining narrative that keeps the reader's interest from beginning to end. Unlike Smith's later work, it is almost entirely non-supernatural; the only suggestion of supernaturalism occurs in the episode in which the Fire-Worshippers' "Lake of Fire" appears to exhibit miraculous curative properties. Even here, though, the leader of the Fire-Worshippers maintains that these properties "are within the realm of nature", although he fails to elaborate upon the claim. But *The Black Diamonds* does not require the supernatural to maintain interest: its bewilderingly convoluted plot is sufficient for the purpose.

Readers familiar with Smith's work will be curious to know how *The Black Diamonds* relates to the four early tales that Smith published in 1910–12: "The Malay Krise" (*Overland Monthly*, October 1910), "The Ghost of Mohammed Din" (*Overland Monthly*, November 1910), "The Mahout" (*Black Cat*, August 1911), and "The Raja and the Tiger" (*Black Cat*, February 1912). There does not appear to be much of a connexion, as these latter tales are manifestly written under the influence of Rudyard Kipling's Indian stories. (Smith had in fact conceived a volume entitled *Tales of India*, and stories from this uncompleted collection constituted early versions of three of the tales he published at this time.) The Kipling influence is entirely absent from *The Black Diamonds*.

Lovers of weird fiction may perhaps regret that Smith virtually gave up fiction-writing from about 1911 to 1929; but in this period, of course, he produced—largely under the guidance of George Sterling—some of the most remarkable poetry in all American literature, and much of this poetic work readily falls within the realm of the weird. While *The Black Diamonds* and the other tales of this period reveal surprising precocity and promise in prose narration, no one should regret Smith's decision to master the craft of poetry—and master it he did.

It is not untoward to ask the indulgence of readers and critics in evaluating *The Black Diamonds*. As the product of a fertile young imagination; as an experiment in extended narrative; as the single longest work of fiction Clark Ashton Smith would ever write—in all these ways and more it should earn our admiration; its implausible incidents, its stilted dialogue, and its wooden character portrayals can be easily forgiven. Not the least engaging of its features is its charming naïveté, and there are many scenes or turns of phrase that suggest the slow emergence of a boy into young manhood. The highest tribute that a reader can pay to *The Black Diamonds* is to regard it as its author himself very likely wished it to be regarded—as just an entertaining story.

—S. T. JOSHI

New York City

A Note on the Text

The Black Diamonds survives in a manuscript of 243 foolscap (7¾″ × 12½″) handwritten pages or 122 leaves written on both sides of the sheet. The first sheet has been damaged around the edges, and omissions are indicated in square brackets: [. . .]. I have tried to follow the text as literally as possible, but have corrected occasional instances of inconsistent or erroneous spelling and punctuation. Moreover, Smith's use of quotation marks is so erratic that I have systematised his usage for the sake of readability. Pages 167–70 of the manuscript (occurring at the very end of Chapter XVII) are missing, and it is not certain whether these pages are simply lost or were deliberately omitted by Smith; the chapter does end a little abruptly, but there is no real gap in sense or plot.

The text as presented here appears to be the first draft, although it bears some pencil corrections of a later date. However, it may not in fact be the first draft. There is a confusion within the text as to whether the date of the events is 1650 or 1585, leading one to suspect that this draft might be a revision of an earlier version. (The former date seems to be the one most frequently used, and I have made emendations accordingly.) Smith attempted to rewrite the novel several times, and several fragmentary versions of later drafts exist in the Clark Ashton Smith Papers at the John Hay Library; but these drafts rarely amount to more than a few pages, and this draft is the only one that appears relatively complete. The text seems remarkably free of revisions, so that it is either a generally uncorrected draft or a fair copy.

—S. T. J.

The Black Diamonds

Chapter 1

In the middle part of the seventeenth century there liv[ed] in the city of Bagdad, Turkey, a wealthy young man named Must[apha.] His parents and relations were dead, but his father had left him a [large] and well-furnished house,
many servants, and the supreme cont[. . . . .] a rich merchantile establishment, which consisted of man[y ware]houses in which silks and tea and
other things imp[orted] from foreign lands were kept and sold to those who
wished to buy them, by men under Mustapha's control.

The house in which Mustapha and his servants lived was situated outside
the walls of the city near the banks of the river Tigris and was surrounded by a
garden, in which palm trees, flowers of all kinds, and other trees were grown.

Mustapha himself was somewhat handsome and was always well dressed
though he was not at all vain. At most times he wore a silk turban upon his
[head], with a golden crescent, studded with jewels, to hold it together, for the
crescent had a clasp behind it which held the turban and kept it from unrolling
and eventually dropping from its owner's head and falling to the ground. A
jeweled scabbard was always at his left side which contained a short scimitar of
the best Damascus steel, very rare, for the art of making these swords was then
almost extinct, and those who were fortunate enough to be the possessors of
such weapons were generally envied by both their friends and enemies. The
hilt of the s[word] was studded with the most costly of gems and glittered in
the [sun] like a silver sky studded with brilliant hard stars [. . . . . . .]

Mustapha was always kind to those under his control. But a light slum-
bered in his [. . . . . .] which showed that he would be a person to be feared if
he so [desire]d. He was athletic in his habits and was almost six feet in height
[and wa]s very strong. Unlike his associates, who were [. . . . .]s and addicted to giddy pleasures, he was studious, and would [rather] read than go off
on a frolic with his companions. Yet, as I [have a]lready said, he possessed
athletic habits and devoted a large portion [of h]is time to walking and other
exercises, but he always performed them in [a] serious manner.

Mustapha was twenty-two years old and it was time for him to marry, for
most Turkish youths married before they reached such an advanced age. His
friends were the first to advise him in this matter, and some said that a certain
woman would be a good wife for him, while others spoke of another. As
Mustapha was not in love, he did not wish to choose rashly. He knew a great
many young women with whom he was friendly yet he knew not which to
marry, though any of them would have readily consented had he asked her to
become his wife.

It was in this state of perplexity that one day he happened to be walking
through a bazaar on his way home.

Many people were advertising the wares they had for sale at the top of
their voices and one of them stepped up to Mustapha and showed him a large

black stone which glittered as brightly as a diamond, for it appeared transparent to a great degree.

"Would you like to buy this, sir?" asked the man, who was very shabbily dressed and evidently poor.

["W]hat is it?" asked Mustapha, after contemplating the stone [for sev]eral moments.

["It is] a black diamond," answered the shabby man.

"Where did you get it?" This was said rather suspiciously.

"At any rate, I did not steal it, sir," said the man, indignantly.

"Did I accuse you of doing so?"

"No, sir."

"Then answer my question—and tell me where you got it."

"It was given to me by a man who said that he came from a faraway land. I think he said Brazil."

"Ah! probably it came from the mines of Peru or Mexico."

"I think it did, sir."

"How much do you want for it?"

"I will sell it to you for the small piece of gold you have in your pocket, sir."

"Pocket? How can you tell what I have in my pocket? You cannot see!"

"No matter, sir. I know that it is there. Will you give it to me."

"Well, this is a strange matter. It savors of occultism and Black art and other Hindu sciences; but I will take the diamond. It is a small price to pay and I wonder that you do not charge more. Here is the coin," and Mustapha handed it to the shabby man and received the black diamond in exchange.

Then the shabby man walked away without even a "Thank you, sir," and was soon lost in the vast crowd in the bazaar.

"He is rich and I am poor, but I have him within my clutches now," thought the man to himself. But we will leave him now and return to Mustapha who is much more deserving of our attention.

After buying the diamond as related above he went home and forgot all about it. He did not remember it till the next day and then he took it to one of his friends, who was a sorcerer, or pretended to be one, and showed it to him and asked his advise about what had best be done with it.

This sorcerer was a Hindu and was proficient in Black art, mesmerism, jugglery and such-like things. He was able to make people believe in what he did; for in those days people were very superstitious and credited what we now know as nothing but sleight-of-hand, as magic, and magic of a very marvelous kind. Nowadays most people know that Black art is a very clever piece of trickery and that mesmerism consists only in getting hold of the senses of your victim so as to cause him to do what you wish him to, but in Mustapha's time people did not know this and of course were easily deluded by those more clever than themselves. If your will is stronger than the will of another person your will can control the will of said person. This is mesmerism, but is sometimes known as hypnotism. Black art consists of having a background all in black for your performance and having some of the performers dressed in black and some in white.

"Would you like to buy this, sir?"

Those who are dressed in black cannot be seen by the audience because their background is of the same color, but those in white can plainly be observed. Here is one of the tricks. A table with two goblets upon it is shown to the audience. A performer holds up the goblets so that all may see that they are empty. Then he sets them upon the table again and waves his wand. The goblets are again held up for inspection and are found to contain pieces of cloth and various other articles. This is the explanation of the trick. The man clothed in black is in the room though those watching cannot see him, and when the magician waves his wand, he places the articles in the goblets. All this is very simple, but there are other tricks much more difficult of performance.

The sorcerer whom Mustapha had visited took the diamond and examined it closely for several minutes.

At the end of these minutes he went to a small table in the room and seated himself at it, and taking up a pen, dipped it in an ink-well, and began to write something on a large sheet of parchment.

Mustapha would have drawn near to see what he was writing, but the man beckoned him to keep away and went on again.

In about an hour he stopped, folded the parchment, wrapped it in another piece which was blank, made the whole into a parcel, handed it to Mustapha, also giving him the diamond, and said:

"Do not read what I have written until you reach your home. It is very important that you should do this, for it is the only thing that will save you from a great danger. Remember, do not read until you get home. Now go."

"But would you not tell me what it is about?" asked Mustapha, pausing upon the threshold. "I am afraid that my curiosity will overcome me if I do not know."

"My telling you would only make you more curious," said the sorcerer with a sigh, "but as you request me to let you know what the contents are about, I will. They tell you some important secrets about the man who sold you the diamond and about the diamond itself."

"I will do as you say," said Mustapha and bidding the man good-bye he left and walked towards his own home. He did not notice that three men had been standing near the sorcerer's home and had heard part of the conversation between Mustapha and the magician.

Neither had the sorcerer himself seen them, but if he had he would have entertained grave suspicions concerning their intentions.

These men carefully noted the position of the sorcerer's house, its architecture and surroundings, and then followed Mustapha, being careful to keep far enough behind him so that if he turned and saw them he would not surmise that they were watching him.

Street after street was passed, Mustapha passed through many bazaars and market-places where great crowds of people were assembled; but still the three shadowed him.

At last Mustapha reached his house and went in. The three walked past it, as if they were nothing but ordinary travelers and did not stop to gaze at it as they had done the sorcerer's home for many servants were within sight and busy in the gardens, and they feared that they might attract the attention of these and arouse suspicions.

But they took note of it even then, and when they were satisfied that they could recognize it at any time they passed on finally returned to the city by another route. We had best leave them there and find out what Mustapha is doing.

As soon as he reached his home he immediately went to his private room, and bidding the servants admit nobody until he gave them orders to do so he sat down and opened the parcel and took out the large piece of parchment. Let us look over his shoulder and see what is written upon it. These were the contents:

"To thee, Mustapha, who are one of my dearest friends I send greeting on this day, June 21st of the year 1650.

"On this very day you brought to me a black diamond and asked my advice concerning it. I did not tell you in words but sat down and wrote to you this answer.

"You say that you purchased the jewel from a shabbily-dressed man in one of the large market-places. From his willingness to sell it to you for the small price of one piece of gold I gather these facts: Yesterday I learned that a black diamond extremely valuable was mysteriously stolen from a very rich man who, nevertheless, is very wicked. He was one of your father's worst enemies and tried to ruin him many times but did not succeed. He is one of the most notorious thieves in the city of Bagdad, yet there is not sufficient circumstantial evidence to warrant his arrest.

"I have obtained information from an acquaintance of mine that this man did not obtain the diamond honestly. The story is that one night he happened to be passing through a lonely street when he perceived the jewel lying in the mud. He picked it up, and was about to pocket it when a man rushed up and claimed it, saying that he had lost it. Several other people coming up maintained this and demanded that the rich man give it back to its rightful owner.

"This he refused to do and putting his back against the wall of a house drew his sword and waved it above his head.

"The rightful owner rushed forward to regain his property, but the robber struck him down, and during the confusion that followed, escaped and reached his home in safety.

"For many days he did not dare to leave it, and finally when the affair was entirely forgotten he entered the streets again, but always wore a disguise for fear that he might meet some of those who had seen him, and recognizing him they would have him arrested for murder.

"Now, Mustapha, the description of this black diamond coincides exactly with the one you possess, but I will go on and tell of the disappearance of the jewel and give you my conclusions afterwards.

"Three days ago this rich man, whose name I will not reveal to you now for reasons of my own, placed the diamond in a large casket which he concealed in a vault far down under his house where he kept various other jewels and a large quantity of money.

"One day he entered this vault and upon opening the casket was astounded to find that the jewel was not in it. He searched every part of the box thinking that the diamond might have got caught up in the cotton in which it was wrapped. It was not there.

"He knew that the only person in the world that had a key to the casket was himself and upon finding that the keyhole had not been tampered with he grew more mystified than ever. Besides, who could have entered the vault? It was securely locked and the door could only be moved by pressing a concealed spring in the wall. Even his servants and family knew nothing of the existence of the vault, so the mystery grew deeper and deeper.

"He examined the other jewels in the vault but they were all in their accustomed places, and the thief, whoever he was, had evidently disdained them.

"Not even a coin was missing and the casket was in the very same place that it was in the last time he had seen it. He looked at the roof of the vault, but there was no indication of an opening and it was the same with the floor. The secret spring that moved the bolts had not been touched as far as he could see by examining it, and, in fact there seemed not a single clue to how the diamond had disappeared.

"Much disturbed in his mind by this strange occurrence the man went to bed, but during his sleep he murmured broken sentences which one of his servants heard, and coming to me yesterday he told me all that he could remember from which I have derived the foregoing facts.

"I swore the servant to secrecy and then sat down to think the matter over. This morning you came to me to ask my advice, and at that time I had some of my conclusions formed and what you told me verified them.

"The black diamond you possess is evidently the one that was stolen. The eagerness of the man who sold it to you plainly indicates that he was the thief and that he was afraid he would be caught and thus wanted to get the thing off his hands.

"Perhaps you thought it very strange, Mustapha, that this man knew of the piece of gold in your pocket. I admit that it was rather remarkable to you, at least, but it is easily explained. The man was probably a Hindu sorcerer like myself, but from his shabby looks I take it that he was poor and that his occupation did not bring him a large income. Now to explain why he knew that the gold was in your pocket. One who is an adept in the art we call magic is able to tell by noting even the smallest and most insignificant expressions and gestures everything that he wishes to know about you. The said pocket probably bulged a little in the place where the gold was and from the shape of the bulge he concluded, small as the evidence was, that there was only one piece in your pocket. When he offered to sell the diamond, you must have looked toward the top of one of the mosques which is of gold, right near the market-place you were in. From this action he concluded that you were thinking of gold and thus hazarded his guess. Partly by luck, I think, he was right, for the coin you had might have been silver instead of the precious yellow metal.

"He might have had other intentions in selling the diamond to you and I will hazard a few guesses as to what they are. He is very cunning I think and therefore you must beware for he has you in his power to a certain extent. I know that the rich man I spoke of has many men ferreting through the city searching for the black diamond. The reason why I did not want you to read this upon the street is that one of these men might look over your shoulder and see my first reference to the jewel and then waylay you in some alley and compel you to tell him what you know of it. He would search you and finding the jewel in your pocket would think that you were the thief and would have you arrested.

"You would think that what I have written on this parchment would save you but I will tell you that it would not. This man would read the rest of what I have written and seeing that it would prove your innocence he would be cruel enough to destroy it. You ask why he would do this and so I will explain. The rich man has offered a large reward to the man who catches the thief and recovers the diamond. That is quite plain, so you see why you would not prove that you were innocent. If you told the whole story from beginning to end you would not be believed and what evidence I could give would not save you.

"I will now explain why the shabby man has you in his power. He probably knows that I am your friend and that you will come to ask my advice and if he is as cunning as I suppose him to be he will know that I will trace the matter as far as I have already done. Knowing that you will be arrested if the diamond is found in your possession he will come to you and offer to place the diamond in the casket from which he stole it if you will pay him a very large sum of money and swear to keep the transaction a secret. Thus you see, to a certain extent he has you in his power.

"As to how the shabby man stole the diamond I do not know but it must have been done by natural means.

"The best thing for you to do is to destroy this parchment as soon as you have read it and come tome tomorrow with the diamond and then I will give you further advice and would now, but I must think the matter over more and tell you the rest of my conclusions when I meet you again.

Thy Faithful Servant,

Akmat Beg, Sorcerer."

Chapter II

"It is all very strange," said Mustapha to himself after reading the foregoing letter. "I have no means of ascertaining how the adventure is to end but I hope it will end well."

Then thrusting the parchment into a brazier of burning coals which stood in the room he watched it burn slowly until only a small portion was left. Then leaving the room he went downstairs to give some orders to his servants and did not return until night.

Two hours after he had gone any one who had happened to be in this room at that time might have seen a cloaked figure leap from behind a drapery and search the place from end to end; but as no one was there he was not seen.

As I said the man was cloaked and he also wore a mask which covered his entire head, neck included. His cloak was black and reached from his shoulders to his ankles and a turban of the same hue was upon his head.

Finally, after searching the room and thinking his search futile his glance fell upon something white upon the floor. Picking it up he found it to be a small scrap of parchment with writing upon one side. A wind had been blowing through the window and had blown it from the brazier before it was consumed; for it was the piece I mentioned before.

The man then began to read the writing. It was part of the beginning of the sorcerer's letter and these were the words upon it:

"On this very day you brought to me a black diamond and asked my advice concerning it. I did not answer you in words but sat down and wrote to you this answer."

"This is important," said the cloaked man to himself. "I cannot find the diamond itself, but this writing proves that Mustapha Dagh has the jewel in his possession and it is likely that he was the man who stole it from my master. The writing tallies with what the sorcerer said to Mustapha Dagh, so I know that it's important. At any rate I will take it to my master. I only wish that I had the rest of this parchment, for then the whole affair would probably be revealed. As it is I must content myself with what I have already found," and with these words the stranger stepped behind the drapery and disappeared.

Early the next morning Mustapha arose, dressed himself, ate his breakfast, pocketed the jewel and set out for the magician's house, arriving there an hour after his start.

As before he was followed by the three men, but as usual did not observe them. He found the sorcerer all agog with impatience for his arrival, and that person immediately began to chide him for being late.

"Why, I am not late," said Mustapha. "I arose as early as I ever did and walked very fast to reach your house."

"You must be accustomed to rising late," said the sorcerer, "but I suppose it was my impatience."

"What are you going to do," said Mustapha after a few moments of silence.

"Well, come into the next room and I will tell you," replied Akmat and he led the way. In said room Mustapha perceived two suits of clothes lying upon a table. They were clothes like those of a common laborer. Almost before he knew what the fellow was about the magician began to remove the clothes he wore beckoning Mustapha to do the same.

Then Akmat assumed one of the laborer's suits and told his friend to put on the other. When this was done he said:

"I know you wonder, Mustapha, at my action in doing what I have done and having you do the same. I will explain: As I told you in my letter, if the black diamond was found in your possession by any of the men this rich man has employed to search for it you would be arrested. My plan is that we two should, after assuming those clothes, take the diamond to him and tell him that we found it and wished him to find its owner for us. He would believe us and you would be cleared of all danger of arrest."

"But why should we wear these clothes?" asked Mustapha.

"That I was about to explain," said the sorcerer. "If we went in our real clothes the man would recognize us and as he is one of my worst enemies as well as the enemy of your dead father, he would not credit our story."

"Your reason is an excellent one," replied Mustapha, "but will you now tell me those conclusions you promised me you would. I doubt if you can tell me how the shabby man stole this black diamond. If you can I will be greatly astonished."

"Most assuredly I can," replied the magician. "I think that my theory is the only possible one, so I will tell it to you."

"Well!" said the other. "If you can explain that you are certainly a sorcerer as you say you are."

"I did not find the answer to the riddle by astrology or any other such piece of humbug; but I found it by everyday reasoning and no magic or anything else belonging to the same class."

"Why!" said Mustapha. "I always thought that you sorcerers found out things by astrology and other arts belonging in the same class as you say. I know that other sorcerers do so in that manner. How is it that you do not so?"

"Because there is no truth in such things," said the other calmly.

"But I always thought that there was, and I am sure nearly everyone else believes the same."

"Probably they do, but I will tell you now, my friend, that all those things that appear so marvelous to you and everyone else who knows not our art are nothing but tricks!"

"Tricks? Kindly explain why they are tricks."

"I will," replied the magician. "I know very well that I endanger my reputation as a necromancer by doing so, but I trust that you will not reveal what I am about to tell you."

"I will not," said Mustapha. "I would be a poor friend indeed if I did. Go on."

The sorcerer went on thus:

"You have probably seen exhibitions of Black Art so I will not stop to ask you if you have. You saw that the background and the floor of the place upon which the exhibition was given was all in black. You also saw that the performers were dressed in white and you thought they were the only ones performing. When the performer waved his wand, you saw things appear and tables and chairs move and other things. You thought this very wonderful but it was not at all so. I intimated that there were other performers in the room.

These performers were dressed in black and could not be seen against this background because it was of the same hue."

"I understand," said Mustapha as the light dawned upon him, "but will you explain how it is that you can control the will of a person, and cause him to do what you please?"

"That is easily explained," said the sorcerer, "so I will tell you in a few words: My will has been trained so that it is stronger than the will of an average person. When the will of a certain person is stronger than the will of another certain person the will of certain person can control the will of the other certain person."

"Ah! I see it now!" said Mustapha. "All the other tricks of your art, such as astrology, have similar foundations, I suppose."

"Yes," said the magician; "they can all be explained in the light of natural reason."

"But now you must tell me how the diamond was stolen," said Mustapha.

"Mustapha," replied his companion, "I will not tell you now but will reserve that for another time. Perhaps you will find out when we reach the house of the rich man."

"But what is this man's name? You might have told me in your letter but you said that you had a reason in not doing so."

"Abdullah Houssain," said the sorcerer, "is his name."

If a thunder-bolt had struck Mustapha as he stood there he would have not been more astonished. The cause of his astonishment is easily explained: This Abdullah Houssain had been his father's worst enemy and the sorcerer had said as much in his letter. Abdullah had attempted to ruin Mustapha's father financially but had been frustrated in his plans, and had then conceived a violent hatred of Mustapha who was then seventeen years of age. It was believed that he had attempted to assassinate the boy, but there was no real evidence, and the story was thought to be an absurd rumor, but still some believed it, and among these was Mustapha himself.

"I speak the truth," said the sorcerer after contemplating his friend's astonishment for some time in silence.

"I did not say that you lied," said Mustapha. "Now I wish you to explain why you did not reveal this man's name to me in your letter. When you said that he was one of my father's enemies I little thought he was Abdullah Houssain."

"I thought that you would be very angry if I told you then," said the sorcerer, "and as I did not wish to upset your feelings at the time—I refrained from mentioning the fellow's name."

"It is all plain to me now," said Mustapha, "but is it not time for us to start upon our journey?"

"It is," said the sorcerer, and he left the room and told his companion to follow him. Once outside the house he said:

"I am sure our plan will be successful. Abdullah will believe our story and accept the diamond without even a suspicion of the truth."

The three men who had dogged Mustapha's footstep heard this and nod-ded to each other. They were lounging about before the door of the magician's house like any group of idlers and the sorcerer and Mustapha entertained no suspicions concerning them.

"Nevertheless," said Mustapha in reply to his friend's last speech, "I have strange forebodings. I think that our journey will end in disaster."

The magician laughed. "I did not think you were so superstitious as that," he said.

"I am not superstitious," said Mustapha, "but I think that my foreboding will turn out to be true. At any rate we can be cautious."

"Perhaps you are right," said the other soberly; "but as you say we must be careful and not run any unnecessary risks in the accomplishment of our pur-pose."

By this time they were out of sight of the magician's house, having turned a corner very close to it so the three watchers had not heard the last speech.

As soon as the two were out of sight, one of the three turned to the oth-ers and said:

"Come, we know where they are going, so let us precede them and tell our master what we have heard. He will be on his guard then and will frustrate these schemers. Besides, we will be well rewarded for our services."

"Of course we will," said the other two, and making for an alley they en-tered it and by some means or other reached Abdullah Houssain's house long before Mustapha and Akmat.

After an hour's walking the sorcerer stopped before a large house sur-rounded by a small garden. Walking up to the door he pressed a spring and it was opened and he and Mustapha walked in.

A servant advanced to meet them and said:

"Sirs, will you please give your names?"

"Yes," said Akmat acting as spokesman. "My name is Akbar and this man who is my brother is called Cogia. Our father's name is Harun Pasha and he is a laborer like ourselves, as you can plainly see by our clothes."

"What do you want?" was the servant's next question. He was a tall Afri-can slave and was dressed in very rich clothing. He was also very ugly to the sight and his voice had an unpleasant ring.

"We wish to see your master on very important business," said Akmat.

"I will find our if he will admit you," said the African and he left the room and did not return for several minutes.

While he was gone Mustapha and Akmat seated themselves and waited as patiently as they could for his return. When he came back he bowed to them and said:

"My master is not busy and says that he will grant you an audience. You will please follow me," and he led the way through a hall and several other rooms to a room where a richly dressed man was seated at a table reading some letters.

As the two entered he turned and looked at them. He was a middle-aged man and was rather handsome, but his face was marred by a cruel look that showed that he was subject to fits of extreme temper, and that he ruled his subordinates with a heavy hand.

"What do you want?" he said curtly.

"We wish to see you upon an important errand," said Akmat.

"Well, can't you see me?" said Abdullah. "I look rather handsome, don't I?"

"Yes, you do," said Akmat, "but I would not like to be one of your servants."

"Why? I am sure I pay good wages. What is your reason?"

"Whatever my reason is it is none of your business," said Akmat.

"None of my business? For a person of your rank it seems to me that you are very impertinent. Do you not know that I could have you arrested for your imprudence?"

"Perhaps you could, but I don't think you will," replied the sorcerer.

"Well, I am anxious to hear what that business of your is, so I will forgive you this time."

"This," said Akmat and he took from his pocket the black diamond. Before entering Abdullah's house Mustapha had given the jewel to the sorcerer so its presence in his pocket is explained.

"Where did you get it?" said Abdullah looking at the stone. As he knew that they were about to return it to him he was not astonished by its sudden reappearance.

"We found it in the street," said Akmat, "and not knowing who the owner was we thought that we had best bring it to you and ask you if you could find its owner for us as we wish to return it to him."

"Oh, you do?" said Abdullah with sarcasm bubbling in his voice. "How am I to know that you did not steal it? You might have been pursued so closely that you thought you could get out of the scrape by returning it through me. What are your names and who are you, anyway?"

"My name is Akbar and this man is my brother, and his name is Cogia. Our father is a laborer and is named Harun Pasha."

"Well, if you wish to know who this diamond belongs to I will tell you: I am the owner."

Mustapha and Akmat feigned astonishment and Abdullah laughed at them. "Well," said he, "I am glad to see my diamond again. I will reward you for bringing it back to me. I have no money with me so I will call a servant to bring me some."

With that he arose and touched a spring in the wall. No sooner had he done so than five men armed to the teeth sprang from behind a curtain and rushed upon Mustapha and the sorcerer.

Akmat saw in an instant that some one was in possession of their secret, and so he leaped against the wall and drew his sword. Mustapha followed him and did the same. Escape by the door was utterly impossible, so they prepared to defend themselves.

Abdullah approached until he was just out of their reach and said mockingly: "Now you see that your plot is discovered. You," he went on, pointing at Mustapha, "are Mustapha Dagh, son of Cogia Dagh. And you," pointing at the sorcerer, "are Akmat Beg, a magician. By some marvelous means you stole from a secret vault under my house this black diamond," and he pointed to the stone which was lying upon the table.

"You lie!" shouted Mustapha. "We did not steal it."

"I am quite convinced and I am sure you will too when I show you part of my evidence." Crossing to a little shelf upon the wall he took from it a small scrap of parchment, which had the appearance of having been part of a sheet which had been burned. From it he read these words:

"On this very day you brought tome a black diamond and asked my advice concerning it. I did not answer you in words but sat down and wrote to you this answer."

"That proves that you are guilty," said Abdullah after he had finished reading.

"It does not," said the sorcerer and Mustapha echoed him.

"Does this writing not prove that these men are guilty of stealing this diamond from me?" said the rich man turning to the five armed men who were standing near.

"It does," said they in one voice.

"How did you get this?" said Mustapha, pointing to the scrap of parchment.

"That is none of your business," said Abdullah, in a mocking tone.

This was more than Mustapha could stand and he rushed at the man with uplifted sword. That person stepped back a few paces and stamped upon the floor with his foot.

Instantly a trap-door opened and through it went Mustapha. The sorcerer sprang at Abdullah but he too fell into the trap.

Far below him, as Mustapha fell through the air, he saw the glint of inky black water and knew at once the fate that had been prepared for him. It became evident to him that he was falling into an old well under Abdullah's house.

But he had little time to think and almost before he knew it he was in the water. He was unable to swim and was sinking beneath the surface when a hand grasped him and he was drawn into a small cave in the side of the well. At the same moment the magician struck the water and before the hand could pull him out he had sunk out of sight and the only thing that showed that he was there was a number of bubbles rising to the surface and the rippling of the water.

Finally all these sounds subsided and Mustapha heard the sound of the trap-door as it was closed and the voices of the servants and their master far above.

Then, before he knew it, he sank into a deep swoon from which he did not recover for many minutes.

When he revived from his swoon he found himself in a small cavern in which a light was burning. A man was standing over him pouring water onto his chest and head and somehow or other the face of this man seemed familiar but Mustapha was too faint and dazed at this time to recognize it. It was all he could do to get his scattered senses together to remember where he was, and this caused him so much effort that he swooned away once more.

When he awoke from this second swoon he felt much better and was able to recognize the man who had saved him. The recognizion was a shock, for the man was the shabby man who had sold to him the black diamond.

The man saw that he was recognized and taking Mustapha by the arms he raised him to a sitting position and said:

"My friend, I saw you come to this house and heard part of your conversation with the magician. I preceded you and hiding myself here I heard Abdullah and his servants plotting to entrap you and cause you to fall into this well. They believed that you and your friend stole the black diamond, and so they planned to take it from you when you attempted to return it and then get rid of you in that manner.

"I have saved you however, though I regret that I could not save your friend. It is no matter how I got here, but I will tell you that I have you in my power. If you do not promise to pay me 5,000 pieces of gold I will throw you into the well and you will be drowned. If you promise I will save you and all will be well."

"Scoundrel! I will not accept your terms," cried Mustapha and springing to his feet he seized the man and threw him to the ground. Over and over they rolled, fighting, each for the mastery, and finally they reached the edge and fell into the well and the water closed over their heads.

Chapter III

In a little-frequented portion of Bagdad there stood, at the time of our story, a small tailor-shop kept by a man named Emir Beg. He was tall and slim, and was about forty years of age. His eyes were black and seemed to tell you that their owner was cunning and that he could not easily be fooled. This testimony was correct, for a craftier man than this tailor never lived.

He had few patrons, but these were mostly rich people and always paid him well for his services. Nobody could make a suit of clothes better than he, and the reason he had so few customers was, as I said, he lived in an out-of-the-way part of Bagdad.

Back of the tailor shop was the tailor's house. It was large and roomy and well furnished and furnished in the latest styles, for even a Turk or a Hindu does not like to get behind the times.

Emir's wife was a pretty woman of thirty years, which is an age where most Oriental women lose their beauty, but she had not. They had one child, a daughter named Fatima who was twelve years old. She, too, like her mother, was very beautiful, though, of course, her beauty was like the bud of a rose, which is much prettier when it has fully blossomed.

In a room in the tailor's house a man was reclining upon a divan drinking sherbet. He looked to be thirty-five years of age and though not very handsome was not at all ugly. His eyes were black and his face was very dark. Any one seeing him would know at once that he was a Hindu. He was dressed in a plain suit of clothes which were not unlike those worn by the tailor. In a chair near the divan lay articles of soiled finery consisting of a gaudy turban which wore the appearance of having once been stained with blood, and in a fold of it a place showed where the cloth had been sewed together, a silken cloak and trousers of the same material and a pair of badly soiled shoes which had once been beautiful.

The Hindu seemed to be thinking deeply, and as he knitted his brows a huge scar now healed was more plainly shown. A close observer would have noticed that it was of the same length as the cut in the turban.

His meditations were suddenly scattered to the four winds by the entrance of the tailor himself.

"How are you feeling this morning, my friend?" asked Emir.

"I feel much better," was the reply of the Hindu. "And now I must thank you for your kindness to me."

"You are not yet well enough to be taken to your home," said Emir, anxiously, seeing in the man's reply the intention of leaving. "It will be a week before you will be completely recovered."

"Perhaps it will," said the Hindu, "but I do not wish to encroach upon your hospitality any more than is absolutely necessary. I should think that you would be heartily tired of having a wounded man upon your hands for more than a month. And besides, what reward is there in it for you?"

"I have the reward of my conscience," said the tailor. "If I had passed on when I found your body lying in the gutter and not attempted to help you, I should have been tormented by the recollection of what I might have done, for the rest of my life."

"That is one reward," said the Hindu, "but I intend to bestow upon you a much more substantial one. By the clothes you found upon me you can plainly see that I am not poor. Search that cloak," pointing to the one in the chair, "and whatever you find in it keep for yourself. There is nothing there that I want."

"I should not like to do such a thing," said the tailor hesitantly. "And besides I desire no other reward than the one I have already gained."

"Then I shall leave the cloak at your disposal and you can do whatever you please with it, except return it to me."

"Well," said Emir, "you will have your own way so I will see what is in it. I will not keep the things for myself but will bestow them upon the poor."

The tailor took up the cloak in his hands and began an inspection of the pockets, taking out every thing and placing it upon a small table. The contents were as follows: in one pocket he found three pieces of gold and a small leather purse containing two solid gold rings set with large turquoises. In another pocket a short Spanish stiletto was found, and also its scabbard which was of leather of a very rare and beautiful kind. A third pocket brought to light a large purse containing thirty pieces of silver and fifty of gold. The fourth pocket contained nothing except a small gold chain about six inches in length.

After placing all these articles in a large leather wallet the tailor withdrew from the room and placed it in the hands of his wife, bidding her distribute the things among the poor people of the neighborhood, which she did as soon as possible.

Then, donning his turban Emir left the house for his customary walk around the city which he never missed.

After walking about a mile through the streets he entered an alley and suddenly came upon the bodies of three men lying in a large puddle of milky water which appeared to have come from an opening under a large warehouse.

The heads of these men were just out of the water, so he plainly saw that they had not drowned. One was a young man of over twenty and was dressed in the clothes of a common workingman. The second was somewhere in the thirties and was dressed in the same manner. The third was about the same age as the second and was rather shabbily clothed. The latter two were evidently Hindus, but the first was a Turk.

"Well!" said Emir to himself, after looking at the bodies for awhile, "I wonder what I had best do? The only right thing for me to do is to take them to my home and take care of them until they recover. I suppose they will not recover from their swoon for several hours, and as it would not do to leave them here, I will have to carry them home. But how can I do it? There are three of them, and strong as I am I cannot carry more than one at a time. I am in a predicament, indeed, and the only way out of it is to call for help. Well, here come a couple of young men whom I know, so I will ask them to help me, for they live not far from my house." As he uttered the last sentence two young men, rather plainly dressed, walked up to where the tailor was standing, watching the three bodies.

"Well, friend Emir," said one of them, accosting the tailor, "what have we here?", and he pointed to the men in the gutter. He was rather plump and good-looking, though he would not have been accounted handsome, and was evidently of good family. In fact, he and the other were two brothers, who lived with their father and three servants in a house not far from that of the tailor. They were fruit-venders by trade, and had a very profitable business, making more than enough to support themselves and their father.

"I know not who they are," said Emir in reply to the question. "A minute ago I came walking through this alley and suddenly came upon them lying in this puddle of water. It is strange how the water got here, too, and how they came to be lying in it. It is evident that they were not hurt by any weapon as you can plainly see," and he dragged the body of the Turk from the water and inspected it closely, his comrades doing the same. Not a mark was found except a slight gash upon the fellow's forehead, and a scratch or two on his hands; but it was evident that this could not have produced unconsciousness.

There were no wounds on the other bodies, so the tailor and his friends grew still more mystified.

"The mystery must lie as it is," said Emir, "and now I think that you might help me carry them to my home."

"We will," his friend assented and one picked up the body of the shabby man, the other the body of the second Hindu, and Emir the body of the Turk.

"I think they will soon recover," said the tailor, "for this fellow's heart is beating vigorously," and thus talking they proceeded on their journey. Of course people they met were curious to know what was the matter, but Emir waved them aside and in due time they arrived at his home and carried their burdens within and laid them upon a large rug.

"Now," said Emir, "you have aided me greatly in helping bring these men to my home. I suppose you would like a reward." This, of course, was addressed to the two young men.

"No, no," said they, "we wish no reward, and we must be going or our good father will become anxious concerning us," and without saying farewell they ran out of the room and started towards their own home at a rapid pace, and reached it soon, I daresay.

When they were gone Emir turned to the bodies on the rug. The two Hindus were just beginning to show signs of life and their hearts were beating more strongly than before. In a few minutes they sat up and stared about them like men in a dream; and before long the Turk recovered and did the same.

"Where are we?" asked one of the Hindus, the shabbily-dressed man. Before the tailor could answer the Turk said:

"I'm quite sure I don't know."

"You are at the home of a tailor," said Emir.

"But how did we get here?" asked the Turk. "I dimly remember starting off on a journey with another man, and I think it ended in disaster. My mind is a blank as to what happened since then."

"No wonder," said the tailor, "I found you and your comrades lying unconscious in a stream of inky-black water which seemed to have flown through an opening under a house not far off. From then, with the aid of two friends I carried you here, to my home."

"Inky-black water," said one of the Hindus, the man in the clothes of a working man; "that sounds familiar to me. It seems to me that I fell through an opening in a floor, into a well of water of that color. I distinctly recall now that, being unable to swim I sank to the bottom and had no sooner done it, when I heard a roaring, sucking sound close to me, and an irresistible force seemed to be drawing me towards one side of the well. I held my breath and just as I expected to touch the wall with my hands, I was thrown violently forward by the force of the water and found myself struggling for life in a raging stream. For one moment I saw light, and then darkness came upon me and I heard close by a sound as of steel striking against rock. Slowly very slowly I found myself losing all sensation and then suddenly I lost all sense and sank into unconsciousness. It may have been hours while I found myself losing sensation and physical feeling, but it may have been only seconds. In such a predicament as I was in a minute seems an eternity, so I will not attempt to guess at the length of time."

The Turk had been listening to the narration with the closest of attention and at its end he said, very calmly:

"My friend, your name is Akmat Beg. Mine is Mustapha Dagh and I remember going through an experience almost identical with yours."

"Mustapha, my friend," said the other with a sudden burst of recollection—"I never expected to see you on earth again when I sank beneath the waters." He was greatly agitated with an uncontrollable emotion and talked in starts.

"I now remember everything that passed since we set out to return the black diamond to Abdullah Houssain till the time I fell into the well and went through an experience like yours. You," Mustapha went on, turning to the shabby man, "are the fellow who said he would save my life if I would give him five thousand pieces of gold."

"You are right," said the other, "I am the man, and I am also the man that stole the diamond from Abdullah Houssain's vault. As to how I did so I will enlighten you if you would be so good as to listen to my tale."

"We will listen," said the others and Emir, the tailor who was becoming greatly interested in the story drew near and listened too.

As it will do no harm, we will also do the same. The shabby man waited till they were all ready and then went on with his story thus:

"As you would probably wish to know who I am I will give you a brief sketch of my life up to the time I stole the diamond and then give a full account of that occurrence afterwards. I am thirty-five years of age and was born in the year 1615, in the country of Hindustan not far from the city of Calcutta. My father was a rich farmer named Ahmed Beg, and my own name is Cassim Beg. My mother died a few days after I was born and I never saw her so as to recollect her face. I had three brothers, and all three were older than I. My brother Akmat is thirty-six years old this year if he is alive. Emir is thirty-seven years of age if he is alive, and Harun is 38 if he yet lives. When I was twenty years old I, my brothers and my father came to Turkey where we scattered and I have never seen any of them since. With me I brought a very valuable diamond black as night, which had been given to me by a lama. He told me its history which was a very curious one; but I have not time to relate it now, but must go on with my tale.

"This same lama had also taught my brother Akmat and me Black Art and all other sorceries, by means of which we made a living.

"When I left my father and brothers, I came to Bagdad with five hundred pieces of gold in a leather bag and the diamond, and a good [ ] of clothes on my back.

"I took lodging at a certain Khan and leaving most of my money and my diamond there I set out to find a place where I could give an exhibition of magic.

"But not a house could I find that I could engage for even a single night. So I went home, tired but not disheartened and set out the next day to try again.

"When I was about in the center of a great crowd of people in one of the largest bazaars in the city, I felt the bag in which I carried my money jerked out of my hand and when I turned to catch the thief he was gone and chase seemed fruitless. Having no money with me I went home and set out the next day with all the gold I had remaining. When passing through another bazaar this money was also stolen and I found myself friendless and with nothing but my diamond in a great city.

"When I got back to the Khan I went to my room and flung myself upon my bed completely disheartened. I must have fallen asleep for a few moments and when I awoke I saw a man just leaving my room with the black diamond in his hand. He was dressed in the clothing of a common man and the only thing peculiar about him was his manner of walking. He took short steps like a man who is hypnotized and I instantly concluded that he was. I sprang after him, shouting for help but before I could catch him he was out of the Khan and running like the wind towards a tall man who seemed to be awaiting him.

"I instantly concluded that this man was the hypnotizer and ran the other way to get out of danger. When I stopped I saw that they were out of sight, but all the same I followed them and soon came near enough to see them, but I kept out of sight and did not let them see me.

"Before long they entered a small house and soon emerged, but this time they soon emerged, and I saw that the thief was now very richly dressed.

"All the same I knew that he was the thief, and I was quite certain of that when I saw that he was still walking in that peculiar way.

"I followed them till they entered a large house which I concluded was the home of the richly-dressed man.

"From people who lived nearby I found that his name was Abdullah Houssain. I also found that he had employed a number of men to dig a cellar under his home, and after earning a little money by dint of hard work, I brought a disguise and went to ask him if he would give me work. Seeing that I had a strong body, he told me that he had not enough men working on his cellar, so he would employ me.

"Of course my purpose in doing this was to recover the diamond. I made several expeditions into his house to search for it at night, but the first three attempts I met with ill-success. At any rate I was not discovered, so I tried again. This time I entered his bedroom and found him asleep. I had suspected that he had the diamond concealed in some vault under his house and my suspicions were confirmed by what I found. On a small mantel on the wall lay two peculiarly shaped keys near them was a small iron box fastened to the wall with another key lying on top.

"Instantly the truth flashed upon me and I was almost stupefied with joy at my success. During one of my nocturnal expeditions I had found a door of iron in the floor with a keyhole to it shaped just like the key I had now found. I instantly concluded that this door was the door to some secret vault where the diamond might be hidden.

"What the other key was for I had no method of ascertaining but I took it with me and made my way to the iron door. My surmise was correct for I instantly opened it and found myself on a flight of stairs. I lighted a candle which I had with me and went to the foot of these stairs when I found myself confronted by a massive steel door which I soon found to be bolted. Here indeed was a predicament, so what was I to do? I sat down upon the steps and began to think, and before long my mind hit upon the solution of the problem. I arose and began to examine the wall of the left-hand side of the bolted door; and before long my fingers touched something which yielded, and instantly the door itself swung open. I had found a spring concealed in the wall, and that was the solution.

"The door made absolutely no noise whatever in opening, so I stepped within and found myself in a vault made entirely of iron. Gold coins and jewels lay heaped upon the floor but I passed them by and turned to a small casket which I suspected contained the black diamond.

"The other key I had found opened it and I took out the jewels and placed the the cotton that it was wrapped in in its original position, and then locked the casket. I had not moved it while opening it so I felt sure that I would leave no trace of how the robbery had been committed.

"Then I quietly walked out of the vault and pressed the concealed spring and the door and its seven great bolts closed behind me without the slightest sound. Then I ascended the staircase and locked its door behind me, went to Abdullah's room, placed the peculiarly shaped keys in the iron box and locked it with the other key. Then I placed this one in the pocket of his coat and left the house with the diamond in my pocket. I soon found that men employed by Abdullah were searching the city from end to end to find the thief.

"Then to get rid of the diamond I sold it to a young merchant for a piece of gold. The reason why my clothes are shabby is quite obvious, for I had to work hard in digging the cellar and Abdullah did not pay me more than enough money to buy food and lodging. The rest of my tale you probably know."

"Yes, I see now what happened," said Akmat, "and all my surmises are correct. I suspected that you stole the diamond in that manner and I think I understand how Mustapha and I escaped death when we fell into the well. The men who were digging the cellar must have dug against the side of the well near the bottom and when I sank to the bottom I was sucked through the hole that had been made by the force of the water. It must have been the same with you and Mustapha."

"Part of your statement is wrong," said Cassim, "so I will correct you. You were quite right in saying that you were sucked through an opening in the bottom or side of the well, which had been caused by those who were digging the cellar, for that is precisely what happened. But your statement that this happened to Mustapha is not really correct. I surmised that you and Mustapha would attempt to return the diamond and I discovered that Abdullah knew of this. In digging the cellar I dug against the wall and made a large opening in its side a few inches above the water. I soon found that there was a trap-door at the top of the well and surmised that Abdullah would first gain possession of the diamond and then anger you by some remark and then you rushed at him he would open the trap-door and you would be precipitated into it. I did not tell the other men who were digging in the cellar, which by the way, was a very extensive one, that I had run against an old well, but kept them away from where I was working, so they did not find out what I had done.

"Then, on the day that you came to Abdullah's house I heard you talking with him and prepared to save you should you fall into the well. Before long I saw the trap-door open, and you, Mustapha came falling through it and struck the water. I pulled you into the small cave I had made, but I was unable to save you, Akmat. Mustapha became unconscious and when he recovered, I, knowing that he was a rich man, told him that I would save his life if he would give me 5,000 pieces of gold. I should not have done such a thing, and I am sorry that I did it, but at the time the temptation was strong, and fight as I would, I could not throw it off.

"Mustapha became angry, and sprang upon me and together we rolled into the well and sank to the bottom. Of course, the rest of my story is similar to yours, Akmat."

"Ah! I see now," said the sorcerer, "and you are my brother, Cassim. I remember your face very distinctly, and your face seems very familiar too," he went on, turning to Emir.

"I am your brother, Emir," said that person, and the three embraced each other in silence. From their earliest age they had been taught not to display their emotions, and so their greeting each other, with such calmness is explained. But underneath this mask of coldness they loved each other as most brothers do.

"Well I am of no use here," said Mustapha to himself, and he was about to leave the room when the sorcerer turned and said:

"Mustapha, I should like to speak to you in private about some very important matters."

Chapter IV

Mustapha and the sorcerer went into another room and the others stayed behind.

"What is it asked the young merchant when they were alone.

"Mustapha," said his friend, "your father was a Hindu and was my father's brother. We are cousins."

"Cousins!" echoed the other; "why didn't my father tell me that before? I did not know that he had any relatives."

"Of course he did not tell you," said Akmat.

"But why didn't he? and why didn't you."

"For reasons that are not obvious to you at present but soon will be. As to why I didn't tell you, I didn't know it myself till yesterday."

"And why didn't you tell me yesterday?"

"Because I did not wish to excite you too much."

"Ah! That is plain. But from who did you get this information?"

"My father. I met him yesterday morning before you came to my house."

"Why did he not tell you before?"

"That I know not. He probably had reasons of his own for not doing so. I expect he is at my home now."

"Well! Everything I have heard is very strange but I see no reasons for not believing it."

"There are absolutely none."

"Do your brothers know that we are cousins?"

"No. They do not. I am going to tell them now."

"Well, well," said Mustapha to himself as Akmat left the room, "I wonder if I am dreaming."

A vigorous pinching of his ears soon convinced him that he was not.

It is needless to say that he was greatly astonished and excited, for such words could not carry a correct impression of what he felt.

In a few moments he became calm and quietly awaited the return of his friend. In the other room he could hear the three brothers talking in low tones but he could not understand what they said, for they were speaking in Hindustanu, and that was a language he did not understand.

In about five minutes the sorcerer reentered the room and beckoned Mustapha to follow him. Mustapha had never seen Akmat so excited before, but he was soon to hear the cause of his excitement.

He followed the sorcerer into the room where the three brothers had been, but he saw nothing of them.

They then entered another room, and saw lying on a divan, the Hindu with the scar on his hand.

Emir and his brother were talking to this individual in Hindu and all four seemed as much excited as Akmat himself.

Emir turned as they came in and addressed Akmat in Hindustanu. Akmat then turned to Mustapha and said:

"We have discovered that this man is our brother, Harun."

Mustapha did not show the least sign of astonishment so the sorcerer went on:

"He, like Cassim, has a wonderful tale to tell. He is now going to relate it."

Mustapha and Akmat drew nearer to Harun and he began to speak in Turkish. His tale was as follows. It was somewhat similar to the one told by Cassim.

"I was born in the land of Hindustan, in the year 1612. My father's name was Ahmed Beg and he was a very rich farmer and lived not far from a great city. I had three brothers, one named Akmat, one Cassim and the third Emir. My own name is Harun.

"When I was 34 years of age, I my brothers and my father sold all our property and came to Turkey.

"Akmat and Cassim had learned Black Art from a priest and this priest had given Cassim a very valuable black diamond which possesses a strange history. He also gave me a duplicate stone, but mine was not genuine and he told me so.

"When we reached Turkey my relatives and I scattered, and I went to Bagdad where I soon became, by a stroke of good fortune, a very prosperous merchant.

"I heard nothing of my brothers and father, but as we had not told each other where we were going, I had no idea where they were.

"One day while walking through an alley I lost my diamond and started out to hunt for it. Some people came up to me and informed me that a certain man had found it and I went towards this man supposing that he intended to return it to me, but I was soon to be disillusioned.

"He was tall and richly-dressed and wore a sword by his side. I did not like the look on his face for it was a look that showed him to be relentless to those in his power and cruel to his subordinates. In fact he looked like a man who is accustomed to have all persons do his bidding.

"'I hear you have found my diamond,' said I walking up to him. 'Would you please return it to me, for I am in a hurry.'

"'How am I to know the diamond belongs to you?' he replied.

"'If you will come with me to my home I will prove it,' I answered rather angrily.

"'I have no intention of giving it to you,' he said by way of reply.

"'Then I'll take it from you, you thief!' I yelled and rushed forward to regain my property. He drew his sword like a flash of lightning and I felt a dreadful pain in my head and then insensibility came upon me and I knew no more.

"When I recovered I found myself lying upon a bed in a large room. A man entered that told me that he had found me lying in a gutter in a certain street, with an ugly cut on my forehead. He had carried me to his home and there I have been ever since, regaining my strength.

"And now this man who has helped me has turned out to be my brother Emir and two other men who are my brothers Cassim and Akmat have been brought to me by a strange stroke of fortune."

"All that has happened is remarkable, and now I have something to say," said Akmat when his brother Harun had finished speaking. "Cassim, the diamond you recovered from Abdullah and then sold to Mustapha, may have been the false one. Both diamonds, the real and the false are in the hands of this schemer and robber. Do you think he would have stolen jewels in such remarkable ways if he had not had other purposes than the wealth he would gain? I tell you the man has some object in doing such things, and as he has wronged us greatly, it seems to me that it is our business to ferret out these objects, prevent their accomplishment, and bring him to justice. Have I not spoken well, brothers?"

"You have," replied all four, in which number we must include Mustapha, for he had been wronged as much as any of them.

"Brother, it is time to eat," Emir broke in, and they all followed him into another room where the tailor's wife had prepared a very substantial supper.

The meal was soon eaten, and after chatting a while the brothers and Mustapha went to bed. Emir explained everything to his wife, and though she was greatly astonished she did not show her astonishment.

The next morning all arose early and after eating their breakfast set out for Akmat's house which they reached after walking about an hour and a half.

They found Akmat's father waiting—as Akmat had said, and you cannot imagine his astonishment when the brothers told him of all the strange adventures that had befallen them.

He was about fifty-six years of age but his hair was as black as night and there was not a gray streak in it. In fact he did not look to be more than forty-five and he was as strong and active as a man of that age. He was almost six feet in height and was correspondingly broad. His face was rather handsome though very dark as all Hindus are, and his beard was only about four inches in length, and it was as black as his hair. He was rather plainly dressed and did not appear to be very rich in worldly goods. But appearances are sometimes very deceiving as we shall soon see.

"Now father," said Harun after they had finished telling him their adventures, "you must tell us what has happened to you since we last met."

"That I will," replied Ahmed and he began his tale.

"After we parted, my sons," he said, "I bought with part of my money a large farm at the outskirts of the city of Bagdad. I had very good luck with my crops and earned twice the sum of money I had paid for the place inside of two months. With some of this money I built a large inn nearby and in a few days was deriving a very substantial income from that source.

"Two days afterwards I invested 510 pieces of gold in a good supply of silk just brought by caravan from China and made 3,000 pieces of gold from the sale of this silk.

"I then set up a large merchantile establishment in the city, built myself a handsome home, employed several servants, and have been doing well ever since."

"Your tale is not so long as mine, father," said Cassim, "but you have had much better luck."

"Now," said that person, "I wish you would sell your house and come to live with me, Akmat."

"But I will not be able to earn a living if I do," said Akmat. "I have all my equipments for exhibitions of Black Art and magic here and if I sold them where would I be. I would be pennilles and depend upon you would you let me go on practicing my trade."

"Akmat," said his father gravely, "your nerves have been strung to the highest notch by recent events and you are completely tired out. I desire you to rest for awhile before you do anything more."

He was quite right, for at that very moment the sorcerer collapsed in a heap, and it was at least five minutes before he awoke from his swoon.

"Do you see?" said Ahmed. "As I said you are all unnerved and unstrung."

"Yes, father, you were right," said Akmat. "I must have overextenuated my strength. I shall do as you say hereafter."

"I say that all of you come with me to my home. It is not more than a quarter of a mile from here."

"But is it not time for me to return to my own home?" said Mustapha. "My servants are probably anxious about me by this time for I told them that I would be back within half a day when I left home yesterday."

"Perhaps you had," said his uncle. Cassim will go with you." Cassim himself had thrown off his ragged clothing and was dressed in a suit belonging to Emir.

The party went along together till they reached Ahmed Beg's house. It was large and roomy and well-built but showed signs of having been recently made. It was surrounded by a rather extensive garden in which could be seen many different varieties of flowers and fruits.

At this point they separated and Cassim went on with Mustapha. As they entered a street not far from the latter's home they saw smoke rising, and upon reaching his house they found it all afire. The fire had taken hold of it so well that the walls fell with a great crash as they approached. Within five minutes all that was left of a once magnificent house was a few burning embers and great piles of stone from which smoke was still coming.

Quite a crowd of people had assembled, and the two found it hard to make their way through this crowd. At last they did so and found themselves standing quite close to the smoking ruins. They then entered the garden and found all the servants there.

"What is the matter? How has this happened?" asked Mustapha pointing towards the ruins.

"I don't know, master," replied one of the servants.

"Then tell all that you do know. You must know something."

"All that I know is to the effect that the fire suddenly broke out in one of the upper rooms. No one knows the cause and all that we could do was to rescue ourselves and several bags of gold from the vaults," replied the servants.

"Bring the gold here," commanded Mustapha. This was done and he then said.

"Count it and tell me how much there is." Several of the servants did his bidding and finally, after much counting announced that there were 10,000 gold coins all the same size.

"Where have you been, master?" said one of the servants who had done the counting. "We have been very anxious concerning you."

"I have no doubt you were. I was detained by urgent business and couldn't return till this morning."

"What are you going to do?" asked Cassim. "Your house is destroyed and only part of your money has been recovered."

"The vaults are safe enough. I don't think the fire could have penetrated there. At any rate the gold could not have been destroyed. As to what I am about to do I will tell you. I will have a new house built, of course, but first I am going to find out the cause of this fire. I strongly suspect that Abdullah Houssain has a hand in it. It certainly does look like a piece of his work. It is said that he has done such things as this before, and I think that most of the stories are true."

"Ah! I think you are right. At any rate we'll find out if there is any possible way to do so. We'd better return to my father's house, I think."

"Undoubtedly we had, Cassim. But I must tend to this gold first."

He turned and spoke to two of the servants telling them to gather the gold together and follow him. He gave the others money to buy lodging for the night and then he and Cassim and the two servants and what they carried set out for Ahmed Beg's house.

After an hour's walking they reached it and went in. Cassim explained what had happened to his father, and after depositing their burdens in a vault under the house the two servants were told to make themselves at home for the time being.

Ahmed then called his sons and his nephew into a certain room on the second floor and ordered the servants to admit nobody without orders. They were also told to keep in the lower part of the house. Ahmed then locked the door and placed the key in his pocket. He seated himself in a chair and motioned the others to do the same.

"What is about to occur next?" thought Mustapha to himself. "Nothing can surprise me now though, for I'm getting accustomed to surprises and they will begin to seem ordinary if such things go on much longer."

"My sons," said Ahmed, "you do not know what I wish to speak to you about. I will soon tell you though. Two diamonds, the ones given to you by the lama have been stolen from you by a man named Abdullah Houssain, you tell me. One of these diamonds is false and the other is genuine, but they are just alike and the difference cannot be found except by the eye of an expert. Abdullah Houssain must have had a definite purpose in stealing these jewels in the manner he did, for how did he know that you, Cassim had brought one with you to Bagdad? He must have heard of them and having heard of them, wished to possess them for the fulfillment of some plans of his own.

"Of what these plans consist, we know not, but it is obviously our duty to discover them and prevent their fulfillment. Have I not spoken well?"

"You have," the others replied, "and we will do just as you wish us to do."

"The first thing to be done is to scare this man out of his wits. Could you write a play, Harun, a play in which you would portray a number of crimes similar to those this man has committed, with the death of the man who committed them at the end?"

"I think I see your idea, father," replied Harun, "and it is a good one. Yes, I can write a play, for I used to write them when I lived in Hindustan."

"You write this play," his father went on, "and Mustapha and Akmat will supply the crimes to be portrayed, and you supply the punishment of the man who committed them. Make it a punishment at which the blood will run cold! We'll act it ourselves and invite Abdullah to see it, and at the end we'll tell him who we are, and he'll think Mustapha and Akmat are ghosts come back to haunt him."

"It is a very good plan," said Mustapha, "and rather original. Where and when shall we give its performance?"

"As to where, I'll tend to that; and as to when—whenever it is finished."

"Well, we had better begin now," said Mustapha and he went to a table whereupon a great many sheets of parchment were piled, and also an ink-well and a couple of quill pens.

Harun seated himself at this table and Akmat and Mustapha stood on either side of his chair ready to give advice. Ahmed left the room and gave them the key before doing so. They locked the door when he was gone and then Harun began to write.

It was Akmat who suggest the title and several of the incidents of the play. When finished the whole was as follows:

Revenge: A Tragedy of Bagdad.

Dramatis personae: Abdullah, a rich merchant; Cogia, a magician, a number of servants, Omar and Yusuf, two brothers.

Scene I Act I. Scene, Garden of the two brothers.
Enter Omar and Yusuf.

Om. So you have heard that Abdullah is our enemy. It seems strange for the last time I met him he was very friendly.

Yus. Of course he was. He was trying to deceive you; and I warn you that he means harm.

Om. From whom did you learn that he hated us?

Yus. From Cogia, the magician who is our best friend.

Om. Ah! If so he said, we must believe him, for I never heard that Cogia told a lie to his friends.

Yus. Of course he would not lie to us, though he might to an enemy.

Om. You are right, brother, and now please to tell me the nature of this warning.

Yus. That I will, my brother. It appears that Abdullah hates us because we have chances of becoming richer than he. You remember the merchant's offer? Well, Abdullah has heard of this and has become envious of our good luck. Thus, you see, it is to his profit to get us out of the way.

Om. And how learned Cogia of this?

Yus. A servant of Abdullah's heard his master plotting with another merchant to kill us and gain this other merchant's offer. He went to Cogia and told him to warn us for he has no liking for Abdullah.

Om. And what did he say we had best do?

Yus. Flee from Bagdad as soon as possible. He will be here this noon and give us further advice.

Om. If so he will, we had best not flee till we have seen him.

Yus. Quite right, quite right; you speak the truth, brother. And now I think we had best retire till he comes. (Just as they are about to enter the house, Abdullah and two armed men enter the garden.)

Ab. Why are you going within, so soon, my friend?

Om. Why do you enter my garden with two armed men?

Ab. For my own purposes, young man, and it does not behoove you to ask.

Om. Why not? I am in my own garden.

Ab. So you are, but I am much older than you, and age must be respected. Ask of me no more questions.

Om. Pardon me if I was imprudent. I was hasty and meant no harm.

Ab. Well, I will, if the two of you will come with me for a walk. I brought these armed men with me for our protection.

Yus. You did, eh? It is to my mind that you brought them to kill us. Cogia the magician has heard of your plot and he has warned us. Your artifice is very clumsy, I must say. Why is it not a better one?

Ab. Come, now no fooling. You know well enough that I am your friend and mean no harm. I take it that you are jesting with me.

Om. No, false friend, we are not and we will not go a-walking with you either.

Ab. Ha, ha, ha, you are jesting again. Please to hurry.

Om. I am not jesting, but am in earnest. Leave this garden immediately sir, or I will call my servants to turn you out.

Ab. Well, this is the best joke I have heard within three months. He, he, he. (By way of reply the two brothers drew their swords.)

Om. Now, if you do not leave, we shall force you to at the point of the sword. If ever you come here again you will be in danger of death.

(Abdullah and the two armed men leave the garden murmuring threats of vengeance.)

Yus. We have ventured into the lion's den this time, but I hope we come out unscathed. (Exeunt.)

Act II Scene II. A room in the house of the two brothers. Enter Omar, Cogia and Yusuf.

Om. What say you we had best do?

Cog. Flee from Bagdad in the morning in disguise and go to Constantinople. I will give you a letter of introduction to a friend of mine who lives in that city and do you stay there till I send for you. I will see that your property and business is well taken care of during your absence. Think you my plan is good?

Yus. It certainly is, Cogia, and if so you say, it must be best.

(At this point a great commotion is heard below, and two masked men rush into the room and strike the two brothers down, with their swords. Cogia hides behind a tapestry and they do not see him. They pick up the two bodies and rush into the street and Cogia follows them through several alleys till they stop in front of a gloomy-looking house. Cogia is a small man and manages to slip in behind them and they do not see him. He has time to hide behind a curtain and listens to what is going on. Abdullah enters the room and asks the two men if they have succeeded.)

1st man. Yes, master, here they are.

Ab. You did not kill them, did you?

1st man. No, master, we only knocked them senseless with our swords so as to prevent them struggling.

Ab. It is well. Now see if you can make them recover from their swoon.

(The men go through various operations and at last the two brothers sit up.)

1st man. They are al-right now my lord and you can speak to them as much as you like.

Ab. (turning to the two brothers.) You know very well why I have taken you prisoner. You are now to meet your death.

Om. You can do your worst, you rascal. Kill us if you wish.

(Here he stamps upon the floor and a trap-door opens. Omar looks through it and sees water about twenty feet below him.)

Om. Yusuf, they will throw us into this well and drown us. Let us resist as much as possible. (The two men advance to throw them into the well and a short but furious struggle follows. The two brothers are flung bodily into the well and the trap-door is closed. The wicked merchant and his men then leave the house. Cogia then rushes from his hiding-place and picks up a coil of rope. This he fastens to the door-knob and opens the trap-door and lets it drop into the well. He climbs down and after much difficulty brings out the two brothers who are hanging onto a ledge just above the water. At this moment Abdullah ren-enters the room after something he has forgotten and sees the two of them standing there. He thinks the two brothers are ghosts and rushing to the brink of the well leaps into it. The two brothers and the magician then close the trap door.)

Om. We have had a narrow escape, my brother and we are indebted to you, Cogia, for saving our lives. If it were not for you we would be lying at the bottom of this hidden well.

Yus. Cogia, you have done us a great service and we wish you to have the reward you want. Whatever it is we will give it to you if it is in our power.

Cog. I wish no reward except your friendship, and now I think we had best go to our homes.

Yus. We had, Cogia, and we had best hurry before Abdullah's men come to see what has become of their master. I warrant you he will be dead before they can rescue him, and I am not sorry for he attempted to kill us. (Exeunt.)

Chapter V

Early that evening Abdullah received an invitation to come to see the per-formance of a play at a house not far from his. A number of other people had been invited too, so he went. Of course the play was the one given in the last chapter and the actors were those who wrote it and their relations, and about two other people hired for the occasion. Mustapha and the sorcerer were the two brothers and Ahmed was the magician. Harun played the part of Abdul-lah, and Cassim and Emir and the others were the ten armed men. Three of these, however, asked to be the armed men in the first act.

Abdullah saw nothing suspicious about the play till it came to where the two brothers were thrown into the well. This startled him at first, but he set it down as mere coincidence and the rest was not so alarming. But as the curtain went down after the last act, it was soon raised again and he was frightened out of his wits, for right on the stage in front of him stood Mustapha Dagh and Akmat and the others.

"Ghosts!" he shrieked and rushed from the house, but the others who had bewen invited to the play were all his friends and seeing that he had been frightened by the actors rushed to these persons and demanded an explanation.

"I don't know what was the matter with him," said Mustapha. "It puzzles me as much as it does you and I cannot explain it."

"At any rate he was frightened at you," said one of the questioners and he dealt Akmat a blow with his fist. Some others rushed at the other actors, and a melee followed in which several people were knocked senseless. Over and over on the floor the combatants rolled scratching, yelling, striking, one on top and now the other.

Akmat was knocked down by a big hulk of a fellow who then proceeded to sit on him with his knees on his chest. Akmat's face was turned toward the man and in a few moments he rose to his feet and tottered, then fell to the floor, and began to move like a rhinocerase. Of course the sorcerer had caused him to fall asleep by means of hypnotism and he proceeded to do the same with another man that rushed upon him. The others were mystified by what had happened and throwing off Ahmed and his sons and the other actors rushed from the house thoroughly frightened. The two on the floor soon awoke and left also, without speaking a word.

Two of the actors who had acted as the armed men in the play had been knocked senseless during the melee and they did not recover until restoratives had been applied.

When this was done they and the others were paid for their services and withdrew. Ahmed, his sons, and Mustapha then went home and ate their supper, as they had not eaten before the performance.

"The plan worked rather well," said Mustapha after supper had been eaten.

"Yes, it did," said his uncle in reply. "It would have been better had that fight not occurred. We are now liable to arrest, though I hardly think Abdullah would feel like trying to have us arrested after the fright we have given him."

"You are right, father," said Emir, "and I think that when he recovers his senses he will begin to make investigations, and I think the men we fought with will inform him that we were much more substantial than ghosts."

"By the way, Emir," said his father, "don't you think you ought to bring your wife and child to live with us? You remember that you left them at your old home. You had best dispose of your tailor-shop and house and I will supply you with a better one. You wish to go as will your business."

"No, I am tired of being a tailor, father," said Emir and I would like to enter the trade of a merchant."

"Then you shall. I can procure you a position as soon as you wish it."

"Thank you, father, you are very good to me."

"And you, Akmat. I think you said you still wished to retain your trade of sorcerer?"

"Yes, father, I would. I disposed of my home today and received 200 pieces of gold for it. Was I not lucky? The man who bought it happened to be a magician too, and said it was just to his taste."

"You certainly made a good bargain, Akmat, and now is it not time to go to bed?"

"Yes," said the others and they retired, little thinking of the strange adventures that were soon to befall them.

Early the next morning Mustapha awoke and dressed himself. He slept in a room on the second floor, and in the room next to his Akmat and Emir slept. He entered their room and found them still asleep. A chair stood near Akmat's bed and on this chair lay a piece of parchment on which something was written. He picked up the parchment and proceeded to read the writing which was in Turkish. It looked as if the writer had been in a hurry and it was with much difficulty that Mustapha made it out. The contents were as follows:

"Akmat Beg, you who are my enemy, escaped from the well in which I threw you and your friend Mustapha Dagh. I know not how you escaped, but at any rate you and some friends of yours played a fiendish joke upon me yester evening. At the time I thought you were ghosts and was greatly frightened. I was soon disillusioned by my friends, and I caution you that I will take revenge. I have ample reason for killing you and your brothers, who I have learned are living with you at this time. I have in my possession the two diamonds whom your brothers Cassim and Harun brought to this city when they came here about fifteen years ago. These diamonds were given to them by a lama and one is false and the other genuine. I do not know yet which is the genuine one, but I shall soon find out.

"It is very important to me that I possess the genuine diamond and I am going to use any means to drive you and your relations from this city. I give you three days to leave and if at the end if these three days I find that you are not gone then I shall kill you.

"I have hundreds of men in my employ and all the soldiers in Bagdad could not save you from my clutches. I remain thy enemy,

"Abdullah Houssain."

"Well," said Mustapha to himself, "of all the impudence I have ever heard or seen this is the worst. I wonder how this came here? Ah! there must be a servant in the house under Abdullah's employ. How else could it have got here? Akmat! wake up. Emir! wake up."

At this the two brothers awoke and rubbed their eyes.

"What's the matter?" asked Emir, staring at Mustapha in surprise.

"This is the matter," said Mustapha handing the parchment to Emir who, looking at the name at the bottom instead of reading the contents first, leaped out of bed as if he had been shot and then proceeded to read the first words.

In less time than it takes to tell this he had read it all and tossed it to Akmat who went through the same performance.

"Where'd you get this?" he shouted breathlessly to Mustapha.

"I came in here to wake you up and found it lying on the chair. It's my opinion that there's a servant here who is in Abdullah's employ. What do you think?"

"I think you must be right," said Emir beginning to dress himself. "We'll make an investigation as soon as we've had some breakfast."

The parchment was then shown to Ahmed and Cassim and Harun and Mustapha's opinion was told to them. They soon said that it was the most likely one and after a hearty breakfast called all the servants together. Not a one was missing, and their faces all expressed astonishment at the queer conduct of their masters.

Their masters debated among themselves for awhile in whispers and then gave the parchment to the nearest servant and asked him to read it aloud as well as he could. He stumbled in reading many times, for of course the writing was scarcely legible, and the same happened with every servant till the last one. This man read it off rapidly without hardly looking at the writing. From the way he read a close observer would have thought he had read it over before.

"I was right," said Mustapha to the others, and then to the other servants: "Arrest this man and await further orders." His command was obeyed and the man was arrested and bound hand and foot with rope. When he had heard Mustapha speak of arrest he had attempted to get away but had been prevented from doing so by the others. Now he lay at full length upon the floor glaring at Mustapha and his other masters.

Mustapha talked to Akmat for awhile in low tones and then said to the servants: "Bring this fellow into my uncle's private room."

He led the way and the man was brought in. Ahmed and his sons followed wondering what Mustapha was about to do, but not interfering with anything he did.

Once in the room, he told the servants to loosen the fellow's bonds a little so he could stand up. This was done, and the fellow himself demanded what was the matter and why he had been so rudely treated.

"You are a spy in the employ of Abdullah Houssain," said Mustapha, "and I had you arrested for bringing an insulting letter from him and placing it on a chair beside Akmat Beg's bed last night."

The man's face paled a little but he soon recovered his self-possession and said: "Sir, you have lied. I know nothing of a man named Abdullah Houssain. I have never heard the name before. I cannot imagine what has prompted you to treat me thus."

In reply Mustapha turned to a servant and whispered some words in his ear. The man instantly left the room, and did not return for five minutes; when he did so he brought with him a spade in which lay some mud. On this mud was footprint of a man.

Mustapha took the spade and placed it upon the floor holding it so that the mud could not fall off.

"Place your foot in that footprint," he said to the man under arrest. Trembling with fear the man did so, and it was found that his foot just fitted the print. The markings on the bottom of his shoe were also identical with those in the mud.

"Your guilt is proved now," said Mustapha. "Is his guilt not plain?" he said turning to the others. They were beginning to comprehend what he was about and answered in a chorus:

"He is guilty! He is guilty! There is not a doubt about it."

"I don't quite understand you, master," said the accused servant. "Would you kindly explain?"

"I don't see there is anything to explain. I gave orders that no servant was to stir from the house, and here I have found footprints exactly like your own in the mud outside the house. Did you follow the footprints far?" he said turning to the man who had brought the mud in.

"I did," said that person, "and they led straight to Abdullah Houssain's house. I found the return ones too," he added with a grin.

"Now do you see?" said Mustapha turning to the man under arrest whose name was Cogia.

"I'm not guilty," growled Cogia, "and I think you are very foolish to try to convict me of being a spy with such hare-brained evidence. Why, the footprints might have been those of another man," he added hopefully.

"Positively, they couldn't," said Mustapha. "The tracks led from this house to the house of the merchant Abdullah and back, and positively nowhere else. This servant has told me and if you do not believe that he speaks the truth you may go out and see the footprints for yourself, though of course you will be accompanied by an escort."

"Let me see the footprints for myself," said Cogia hoping to gain time, for time was just what he wanted.

"You may see them," said Mustapha and everyone following they left the house and the servant who had brought in the mud showed them the tracks. These tracks led in the direction of Abdullah Houssain's house and tracks of the same kind led back to Ahmed's house.

Two servants were holding Cogia as he viewed these tracks in dismay. He saw at once that the proof against him though seemingly slight was overwhelming when closely viewed. His brain worked quickly and he looked at the knots that tied his legs together and studied them for a few seconds. He knew that they were but loosely tied and that if he could only escape from his captors a few moments he would be able to slip them off and escape if he could outrun those who would pursue him. One thing quickly made such occasion and a simple solution of the problem flashed into his brain like lightning as he stood there.

"A fire! A fire!" he yelled suddenly pointing to a house at a great distance. For about the space of twenty seconds his two captors released their hold on him to stare in the direction he indicated. The others looked that way, too, and while they were searching for the fire with their eyes he had quickly slipped out the bonds that bound his legs and was running swiftly down the street in the opposite direction before they saw that there was no fire and turned to look at him.

He quickly slipped the ropes from his hands as he ran and when Mustapha recovered his senses and set off in pursuit Cogia was more than a hundred feet away. The rest of the party set out in pursuit, led by Mustapha, but he evaded them and was soon out of sight.

The pursuers returned sadly to the house and went in.

"Now we've done it!" said Akmat. "This fellow will tell his fiendish master everything he knows and then there'll be trouble to throw to the dogs. Why didn't we watch the fellow more closely. We should have known that his words were but a ruse to distract our attention and give him time to slip those infernal bonds from his legs. Well, it's done now, and there's no more crying over spilt milk. The best we can do is to watch Abdullah's house and prevent him from getting there. I'll send some servants to do it now, for he can't possibly have made a detour in this time."

"You speak the truth, my son," said his father, and he turned to the servants who were in the room and counted out eight of the strongest and trustiest of them and lined them up and told them what they must do explaining everything to them. Then they left the house on their mission and Ahmed turned to his sons and went on talking.

"We are in a pretty fix," said he, meaning the things that had just happened. "I wonder why this Abdullah Houssain takes it upon himself to meddle in our affairs? There must be something behind all that he has done, and that something, as I said yesterday, we must make our business to discover."

"Quite right," said Mustapha, "but how shall we do this much?"

"That I haven't decided yet," replied Ahmed. "He said in that insulting letter that he would give us three days to leave Bagdad, and that if at the end of those three days we were not gone he would drive us from the city by force. What think you we had best do, Mustapha?"

"Stay here," said Mustapha. "I don't think he can do us any harm. I think that what he wrote was mere bluster, and that he only intended to frighten us and bully rag us into running away. He's full of such little tricks as that, and yet he generally keeps his promises. It won't hurt us to keep a sharp lookout, for he won't remain inactive long."

"I think you are right," said Ahmed. "It won't hurt to keep our eyes open for any trickery that he may be up to. What's that?" An animated discussion seemed to be going on between the servants in the next room and some stranger who appeared to want to see their master.

"What's the trouble?" said Mustapha looking through the door.

"A man wishes to see your uncle, master," announced one of the servants. We thought you were all busy and refused to let him disturb you."

"Bring him in," said Emir, joining his cousin at the door.

A very tall, but poorly-dressed man entered the room and bowed to Ahmed who had risen to his feet.

"What do you want, sir?" he asked quickly, but in a kind tone.

"I wish to see you alone and on important business, sir," said the man, in a voice that showed his health to be poor.

"Well, come into the next room, sir," said Ahmed leading the way. Once within he shut the door and turned to the stranger.

"Well, now tell me your business," said he.

"I am very poor, sir, and have a wife and children to support," the man began. "Lately I have not been able to earn enough money to buy food for them, and as I heard that you were very kind, I have come to you to see if you will help me. Will you?" The man spoke in such an imploring voice that Ahmed cradled his hand over his eyes and then said:

"Why certainly my friend I will help you. I and my sons will come with you to your home and see what you want."

"Ah! thank you, sir," said the man in a very thankful voice. "When can you come?"

"Right now," said Ahmed, and going into the next room he informed Mustapha and the others of what he had been told. They at once donned their hats and followed him and the man into the street and to a house about a mile away. This house was very shabby and dingy in appearance and appeared as if it would fall down at any moment, so rickety was it.

The man went in at the door of the house and the others followed him without the slightest suspicion of what was to happen. The fellow led the way up a rickety staircase and into a room where a light was dimly burning. There was nobody in the room and when Ahmed and the others were staring about them, he quietly closed the door and locked it. Then he whistled a low whistle like that of a bird and the room suddenly became alive with armed men who sprang up as from nowhere. They had been hiding behind the curtains in the room and the whistle was the signal for them to make their appearance.

"What does this mean?" said Mustapha slowly backing against the wall.

"It means," said the man who had led them there, "that you are in the power of a man named Abdullah Houssain who has employed me to decoy you here and into the hands of these armed men."

"Why didn't I suspect a trap before?" groaned Mustapha.

"Because there was nothing to cause you to suspect," said the fellow with a fiendish grin. He no longer appeared weak and poorly fed, but stood up strong and able. The others had put their backs against the wall also, when they saw Mustapha do it, and now they all drew their swords.

"What shall we do?" whispered Harun to Akmat.

"Don't ask me, brother," replied that person. "All that we can do is to defend ourselves till we are captured by main force. I warrant you I shall hurt one of these men before they take me prisoner."

At a signal from the decoy the armed men drew their swords and advanced upon those against the wall and demanded that they surrender.

By way of reply Ahmed made a sudden rush at the decoy who was standing near the closed door and struck him as hard as he could with his scimitar once—twice—thrice—and the man fell to the floor without a cry, stone dead.

Then pandemonium seemed to break loose and a fierce fight raged all over the room between Ahmed and his sons and nephew and the armed men. In this fight swords were used freely and several of these hirelings were badly wounded. Harun received a severe cut upon his left shoulder, and almost killed the man who had wounded him in his rage. Then, from loss of blood he sank senseless upon the floor and the desperate combat raged on. Ahmed and Mustapha were both wounded and they, too, sank senseless upon the floor from loss of blood. Emir and Akmat fought on like demons, and wounded quite a number of their enemies, but they could not hold out forever, and eventually they too, succumbed from loos of blood. The only man killed during the fight was the decoy and I do not think that his death was much lamented by his friends.

Two or three of the hirelings set to work to bind up the wounds of those they had wounded and before long these sat up, feeling very weak.

In about an hour the door opened and Abdullah himself walked in and saw what had happened.

"Well done! Well done!" said he clapping his hands at seeing the success of his plan.

"Yes, we've got them, master," said one of the men. "They fought well and wounded several of our number as you can see," he went on, pointing to the wounded men. These had also been attended to and most of them were sitting up or standing according to the severity of the wound or wounds each had received.

"Now," said Abdullah, "bring the prisoners and the wounded to my house as soon as you are able to remove them. You had best wait till night, however, and then you will be quite safe."

Mustapha's heart beat with joy when he heard this, for he knew that if they were removed to Abdullah's house, they would certainly be rescued by those watching it.

He did not try to speak of this to his comrades, however, for their captors were watching them closely to prevent all communication, and as it was it was not necessary to impart this information, for his friends had also grasped the same idea upon hearing Abdullah's words.

Hour after hour passed in that dingy room, and Abdullah left to return to his home.

"He'll be stopped by the men," said Mustapha to himself. "They will think that he has been to speak to that fellow who has been spying upon our plans and placed that rascally letter beside Akmat's bed last night, and who escaped us by a simple ruse." Contenting himself with this thought he turned over and went to sleep, and his comrades followed his example. He was rudely awakened by shouting and the clash of steel, and jumping to his feet, found that he was unbound, and that a fierce fight was taking place in front of Abdullah Houssain's house, between the servants who had been watching it and his captors.

All was dark except for the light of the moon which was just rising and a few stars. Stiff as he was he drew his sword, which had not been taken from him, and sprang forward to take part in the combat, though he could scarce distinguish friend from foe. He found that Akmat, Cassim, and Emir were also free, and fighting desparately. Two servants whom he recognized were cutting the bonds that bound Ahmed and Harun, and in an instant these two sprang to their feet and joined the fray.

For about five minutes the fight went on, and neighbors began to look out of their windows to see what was the matter. Three of Abdullah's hirelings were badly wounded and two of Ahmed's servants received slight scratches, but beyond this nobody was hurt during the battle.

So good was the swordsmanship of both parties that, as I said, no harm beside that already mentioned was inflicted. Abdullah soon found this out, and seeing that the three of his men who had been hurt were the worst swordsmen in his employ, he blew three times upon a whistle, and the whole force ran from the scene and were soon out of sight.

Before he could follow them his enemies had sprung upon and thrown him to the ground, and then they bound him securely and gagged him so he could not possibly shout for help. Then, carrying him with them, they proceeded down the street and before long reached Ahmed's house and went in. Utterly discouraged was Abdullah when he found himself in the house of his worst enemies, but he kept his brain busy trying to form a plan of escape.

Chapter VI

It was about 8 o'clock when Mustapha, the others, and their prisoner reached home and entered. They found that the servants had been rather anxious concerning them and that one of Mustapha's servants was there with a report of how much gold had been rescued from the scene of the fire.

According to his account twenty thousand pieces of gold was the amount recovered.

"Well, that's better than nothing," said Mustapha, "but it's only half the amount lost."

"Yes," said the servant, "but when I left from the ruins they were digging up more. I think that by morning the whole amount will be at your disposal."

"Well, return and tell them that I am in no hurry. I don't need the money at present, so it is not necessary that they work so hard."

The servant departed on his mission, and Mustapha and his comrades turned to their prisoner as if expecting him to speak.

As he did not, Ahmed said:

"Will you kindly enlighten us, my friend, in regard to what has recently occurred? For instance: why did you steal two black diamonds from my sons?"

"That I won't tell," said Abdullah, haughtily. "It's none of your affairs, anyway."

"None of our affairs! Well, that would seem strange, indeed. It certainly is our business, as you stole these diamonds from us."

"You insolent!" Abdullah began, but stopped short, realizing that he was in the hands of enemies, and that it would be no use whatever to insult them, as it would only make matters worse for him. His arms, which had been folded on his breast, now drooped hopelessly at his sides, and he eyed his captors with fear in his face.

"I think you were about to call me an 'insolent' something, were you not?" said Ahmed. "Would you kindly finish your sentence?"

Abdullah hesitated at the unexpected question and then said:

"It is absolutely uneccessary for me to finish my sentence, and besides; what would be the use? I'm quite sure words would never express my contempt of you and your sons," he added bitterly, throwing aside all caution.

"Perhaps words would not express your contempt of me, but I can get higher than that. I tell you now, Abdullah Houssain, deeds could not express my contempt of you!"

"No, I don't suppose they would, but when are you going to let me return to my home? My servants will be anxious about me. I have formed a regular habit of not staying away from home after 8 at night."

"So you think you will get away from here to-night, I suppose?" said Ahmed.

"Of course I do," said Abdullah assuming an air of bravado.

"Well, my friend, I'll tell you now that you won't leave this house to-night, or for many nights, if you don't reveal to us the reasons you had in robbing my sons, and promise to return the diamonds to us, and never cross our path again."

"Oh, you'll threaten me, will you!" yelled Abdullah in a rage. He sprang at Ahmed and would have attacked him with his bare fists had not Mustapha and Cassim intervened.

Seeing now what a fierce temper they had they took precautions against further occurrences of the same kind by binding their captive's hands together, so that he could not do more mischief.

"Oh, you rogues!" he yelled at them when they had finished the operation. "You are nothing but Hindu cowards! You have to tie my hands behind me when I try to take a little exercise. If ever I leave this accursed house alive I'll give an account of your cowardice to the whole world, and you won't dare to show your faces in the street for many a year afterwards. I'll make your names bywords for the vulgar and untutored to yell at their foes."

"What if you don't leave this room alive? What will you do then?"

"I won't do anything. I'll be dead and in Paradise, which is a place none of you will ever enter."

"You are very venomous, my friend," said Ahmed, ingnoring the insult. "Where did you get your hot tongue from? It must be flavored with the venom of the cobra. I wonder if you have fangs."

Abdullah gritted his teeth in fruitless rage.

"You'll regret this sometime!" he roared.

"The 'sometime' may never come," said Mustapha, entering the conversation at this point.

Abdullah appeared to notice the taunt and said:

"As you say, the sometime may never come, but if by some strange twist of Fate it does, then you will have enough cause to regret it."

"Stop your blasphemy, father and cousin," said Cassim. "We had best come down to business," he added, turning to Abdullah.

"Are you going to tell us what we want you to, or not?"

"I will on certain conditions," said that person.

"Name them."

"They are as follows. First, you must give me my liberty and allow me to keep one of the diamonds, which one you must allow me to select myself. Second, you must leave this city after selling all the property you own and move to some other town, which town must be at least a hundred miles from Bagdad. Third, you must never come within fifty miles of Bagdad, and you must never cross my path if I should happen to come to the city where you are located. If you will not comply with these conditions I will not give you the information you desire, torture or maltreat me as you may!"

All were staggered at the enormity of the demands, and Ahmed said: "I am sure it would be impossible for us to comply with your conditions. If you would kindly change a few of them they might be acceptable. If you will make a few changes in the whole three of them we might give them some consideration. You must return both diamonds to us and tell us why you stole them. That is the change I would suggest for the first. You should change the second in this manner. We shall not leave this city nor will we sell any of our property in it. The third should be changed thus: We will never cross your path and you must never cross ours."

"I won't submit to such demands," said Abdullah. "I will accept the second and third, however, if you will allow me to keep one of the diamonds, that one, as I said, to be selected by myself."

"It would be impossible for us to give you one of these diamonds as they do not belong to you. As it is, I think that our conditions are the most lenient possible, under the circumstances," said Ahmed.

"Those diamonds do not belong to you at present, Ahmed Beg," said Abdullah. "They are in my possession at present, and you may never see either of them again!"

"That is quite true, my friend," said Akmat, "but I think that if we searched a certain secret vault under your house, we might find one of them."

Abdullah's face turned pale.

"What are you talking about?" he gasped. "There is no vault under my house."

"Yes, there is," said Cassim. "If I went with you to your house I could show you its exact location. In fact I have been within it, and from a small casket there I took one of the black diamonds. I was unable to find the other, however, as I did not hunt for it, not knowing that it was in your house."

Abdullah's face turned two shades paler than before.

"You lie!" said he, hoarsely.

"What I speak is the truth," said Cassim. I will also inform you that I was one of the laborers who dug your cellar."

"How did you get into this vault?"

"Ah! then you admit its existence, then?"

"It would be almost useless to deny the charge," said Abdullah hopelessly.

"Yes, it would. Now I will tell you the whole story." Then Akmat related to Abdullah the tale of how he had found the keys, what he had done with them, and all the rest up to the time they had played a trick on him with their play all of which you know.

Abdullah listened with great interest to the recital of events and did not draw a full breath until it was finished.

"Well!" he gasped, "of all things this is the most astonishing."

"Then you admit that you stole the diamonds?" said Ahmed.

"Yes," replied Abdullah, "I admit that I did, and I had very startling purposes in doing so. Perhaps I will accept the terms you have offered me, but you must give me till morning to think the matter over. I think you are all hungry, so you might have supper served. After that I will retire and think the matter till bedtime. You may place a guard before the door, too, if you wish," he added with keen sarcasm. "You know, I might escape if you give me the opportunity."

"Your demand that you be allowed to think the matter over, is quite reasonable," said Ahmed, "and I am sure we grant it with pleasure." He ignored the sarcasm and Abdullah said nothing more of that character.

After supper was eaten Abdullah retired to another room and began to think over whether he had best grant the demands of his captors or not. He fully expected rescue before evening of the next day, so he determined to ask Ahmed, when morning came, if he could have all day to consider in, as he had been much excited the night before and had not been able to arrive at a definite conclusion. That they would grant this request he was certain so after thinking over some other matters, he undressed and went to bed.

About midnight Mustapha was rudely awakened by a glare and the crackling of flames in his room. Springing away from his bed he found that part of the room was afire. He dressed as quickly as possible, shouting for help as he did so.

In a few moments Akmat joined him saying that the whole house was afire and that escape was almost impossible. Many of the servants had escaped as the alarm was given but all the rest were shut in, and caught like rats in a trap.

By the time he had finished dressing Ahmed, Abdullah and the others joined them, followed by the panic struck servants.

Together they crowded to the window of the room and looked out. The flames raged quickly below them but the only room in the house it had reached was Mustapha's.

Escape by this window was impossible, so they rushed from the room, Ahmed leading the way to a room on the opposite side.

Mustapha saw that if they had a long rope they might escape by way of the window, and while a servant went to fetch one he observed closely the street below.

The light of the flaming house lit it up in many places but there were dark corners on the other side of the street, which was not illuminated but remained in shadow.

Now, Ahmed's house was isolated from the others nearby by its garden behind and on the side and by the broad street in front, which was the broadest in Bagdad, so it was apparent that no other house could be damaged by the flames.

Across the street several windows were already opened and heads peeped out to see what all the noise was about.

But what interested Mustapha most was the figures of several men who appeared to be awaiting somebody. They were in the shadow of a large house but he saw them plainly. They appeared to be armed, but for what reason he could not think, though he was soon to know.

In less than two minutes the servant returned with the rope and it was lowered from the window, and one of the servants was told to descend. This he did and the rest of the servants did the same. Ahmed went next and was followed by Abdullah, whom he guarded closely. Mustapha descended after them and the brothers followed. In less than five minutes they had thus safely escaped from the burning dwelling, and were now out of danger.

They made a strange group as they walked down the street and entered another. Mustapha led the way, strong and resolute, and the rest followed.

As they entered the second street they heard a great crash and upon moving back to see what was the matter they found that the burning house had collapsed in a heap of ruins.

Mustapha now thought he saw many men creeping along seemingly followed them, but he said nothing of this to the others.

"Where shall we go?" said Akmat as they journeyed along.

"I'm not certain," said Mustapha, "but we will go on till we reach an inn or the house of some person with whom I am acquainted."

"Well, I know a man not far from here," said Abdullah. "He would give us shelter until morning."

"Then, lead us to his house," said Mustapha. "And if you try any tricks on us when we get there, there will be trouble."

"Very well," said Abdullah and he led them to a house just across the street. The owner of the house happened to be a man with whom Mustapha was acquainted so he had no fears that the fellow was someone in league with Abdullah.

In response to vigorous knocking a sleepy servant opened the door and bade them enter. Mustapha explained matters to him and told him he need not awaken his master. Ahmed's servants found accommodation in the servants' quarters, but their masters did not go to sleep, but sat up talking over all that had happened.

They had been engaged in this occupation when a knock was heard at the door and Ahmed went to answer it. Now, the door at which the knock had been given was in a crooked corridor outside the room, so the others could not see what went on.

Ahmed did not return, so Mustapha went to the door. The others waited awhile, but he did not return. Cassim went next, but he did not come back. Harun followed to see what was the matter but he also did not return.

"What can be the matter?" thought Emir to himself. "Why do they not come back?"

"Have you anything to do with this?" he said turning to Abdullah. "Have your men captured my brothers?"

"I know nothing," replied Abdullah carelessly. "Why don't you go to the door and see?"

"I am going, but you're going to come with me and you're going to go first too." Abdullah seemed very unwilling, but Emir forced him to go, and together they entered the dark corridor at the end of which the door lay.

Emir saw that it was half open and that outside all was darkness. As Abdullah neared the door, he shouted:

"Don't strike me, comrade," and made a sudden break to get out of Emir's grip. He was successful in this and as the tailor turned to pursue him he (Emir) was suddenly grasped by the back of his neck and swung through the air until he lost all sense of feeling and swooned.

When he recovered he found himself lying upon a couch with someone pouring water on his face and chest. He was in a large and well furnished room, and on the floor he saw his friends lying with several men dressed as servants performing the same operation upon those as the one of them had on him.

The man who had poured water on his face and chest left the room when he saw that his patient had recovered and soon returned accompanied by Abdullah.

"Well you rascal!" said Emir, "where are we now?"

"You are in my house," said Abdullah. "My men turned the tables on you last night. They followed us and set fire to your house a little before midnight, knowing that we could all escape by means of a rope. I was just about to suggest such a plan when it occured to Mustapha and he surprised me."

"Then we're your prisoners," said Emir taking in the situation at once. "I see now how you turned the tables on us. Your servants followed us to the house of that man where we were going to stay for the rest of the night. All the rest is so very simple, so I won't go over it."

"You are quite right, my friend," said Abdullah. "You've defined the exact position of affairs as well as I could have done myself."

"What are you going to do with us?"

"Keep you prisoners until I get ready to dispose of you."

"And what will you do with us then?"

"I shall probably sell you as slaves to a certain ship-captain in my employ who is about to embark on a voyage to China for the purpose of obtaining silks. You'll see some of the world then," he added with a coarse laugh, and left the room. Emir's comrades had recovered, the servants followed suit, and he explained matters to his brothers and father, and Mustapha.

"Slavery!" said Mustapha. "Well, we can do our best to escape on board ship. What else can we do?"

"Nothing," was the universal reply and then, tired and sleepy, they laid themselves down and went to sleep. When Mustapha awoke, and he awoke sooner than any of the others he found that it was night, for several lamps were burning in the room.

A few moments later two servants entered bearing food with them which they set upon a large table, and then left.

Mustapha awoke the others and they made a hearty meal off what had been set before them.

The meal consisted of goat's flesh, which was exceedingly well-cooked, a large jug of cold water, goat's milk, and several courses of fruit, and vegetable soup.

Almost before they had finished Abdullah entered, and informed them that their rooms were ready and they might return as soon as they wished.

A servant conducted each to his room and they went to bed and were soon fast asleep.

Early that morning Mustapha arose and dressed. The sun had not yet risen, and the servants were just arising for he could hear by the sounds that they had not yet begun to prepare breakfast.

He went to the window of the room and looked out. Would it be possible to escape? It was at least fifty feet to the street below and as he had no rope he could not escape in that way. No, it was plain that he could not get away by way of that window, so he did not try.

He went to the bed and threw himself down upon it to think. He then arose and began to search the room for what he wanted. At last he found it, and going to the table, he seated himself. He had found an ink-well half full, an old quill pen and a large sheet of papyrus.

With these materials he began to write a letter to one of Ahmed's servants, a man whom he liked, and had been slightly acquainted with. If this man should pass under the window at any time before Mustapha was sold into slavery it would be dropped at his feet and he would thus be able to tell the other servants where their masters were and then Ahmed and the others and Mustapha himself would be rescued.

And if any other person whom Mustapha knew was to pass under that window or up and down that street, he would drop the sheet of papyrus.

Mustapha didn't want to drop it to anyone whom he did not know for the person in question might be a friend of Abdullah's, and thus worse trouble would be caused.

It was hard to write with the old quill pen, and the ink was so thin it could hardly be distinguished upon the papyrus, and the papyrus itself was not in its prime.

But these materials were all that Mustapha caould find so he had to be contented with them.

Hardly had he finished the letter when a man leaped from behind a curtain and snatched it away, and then left the room.

The man was one of Abdullah's servants, and Mustapha recognized him. It was the negro who had admitted he and Akmat to Abdullah's house on that memorable day when they had attempted to return the diamond.

Mustapha now saw the system, by which his every movement was watched, and he saw that any attempt at escape would be futile.

He stepped out of the room by the door which the African had left open in his haste and caught a glimpse of that person's legs as their owner rushed them one of the rooms below.

"Well, he'll show what I've written to his master," he thought, "and then there will probably be trouble. I wish that I had not written that letter, anyway."

About five minutes later, Abdullah entered the room half-dressed and demand what Mustapha meant by trying to inform other people that he was a prisoner.

"My reason is very obvious," said Mustapha, "and your question quite unnecessary."

"Yes, quite," replied Abdullah. "I had the ink, pen, and papyrus placed there on purpose to find out whether such a strategem would occur to you. It will be of no use for you or your friends to try to escape, for you are watched day and night. Your breakfast will be sent to you in your room if you so desire."

Abdullah then went downstairs, and an hour afterwards Mustapha's breakfast was brought to him in his room. He scarcely ate but passed most of the time in thinking. Fifteen minutes later Akmat entered the room accompanied by Harun and all three sat down to talk.

Chapter VII

"It is quite plain that we have not the slightest chance of escaping," said the sorcerer. "Therefore," and here he leaned forward and whispered in Mustapha's ear.

"Therefore," he whispered, "we must submit to be taken aboard the ship he speaks of and watch our chance of escaping."

"You are right," Mustapha whispered in return. "It is the only rational thing for us to do. You have doubtless discovered that we are spied upon constantly by concealed men."

"Yes, I have. I wrote a letter on a piece of parchment that I found intending to drop it out to the window to the first person passing, whom I knew, when a man sprang out from behind a curtain and snatched it away from me, ran from the room, doubtless to tell his master."

At this point in the tale Africans sprang from behind the tapestry, and bowing to them said:

"Sirs, you may talk aloud all you wish but you must not whisper. My master ordered me to inform you of this. I beg, therefore, that after this you will say nothing that cannot be heard." With that he stepped behind the tapestry and they saw him no more.

"The impudence of him!" said Akmat. "He acted as if he were our master. If he interrupts us again I'll give him a piece of my mind."

"If you do," came a voice from behind the tapestry, "I will report to my master and he will not allow you to be together."

"It would be exactly like him!" retorted Akmat.

There was no reply to this and the two cousins went on talking, speaking of various trivial matters.

Finally Akmat bade Mustapha good-bye and left the room to return to his own.

Mustapha sat thinking long after he left. "Can there be any possible way to escape?" was the question he asked himself over and over again, and the answer always seemed the same: "There is none." "There must be," he would answer to himself and fall to thinking again. All the forms of escape he had read of in books passed through his mind, but none seemed acceptable. Bribery was utterly impossible for he had no money and besides he knew that Abdullah had provided against such an emergency. If he had not, Mustapha did not know his man.

"Yet nothing is impossible," he quoted to himself. "There must be some escape, and if there is I'll find it."

Then he wondered if his servants would attempt his rescue. No, if they did it would be of no use, for Abdullah would surely learn of it and lead them into a trap, or else throw them off scent.

Just then a servant entered the room with a piece of papyrus with writing on it, in his hand and handed it to Mustapha. It read as follows:

"Follow wherever the bearer of this note leads you, and know that I have good reason for your removal from the room where you are at present.
"Abdullah."

Mustapha darted to the window, with a suspicion in his brain which was justified in a moment. Up the street a number of men were coming, among them several whom he recognized as his uncle's servants. There were at least forty of them and each wore armor, and was fully armed with swords, spears and other weapons of the time.

Only for a moment did he contemplate these people, for the servant sprang upon him and threw him to the floor. Several others entered at that moment and they bore him from the room, kicking, biting, scratching, hitting, and everything else in his power to free him from them.

His struggles were ineffectual, however, and realizing this he asked them to let him stand upon his feet and walk, promising that he would make no attempt to get away. After some talk among themselves in a language he did not understand they allowed him to do this and then, with that, proceeded upon their journey, Mustapha in their midst.

They went through many rooms, richly furnished, and at last came to a heavy iron door. This door was unbolted and they went through and found themselves in a dark corridor in which a few torches gleamed faintly.

This corridor proved to be about forty feet in length and at its end they came to another iron door similar to the first. This was unbolted and they entrered another corridor, which proved to be very short and at its termination they came to a flight of stairs. At the bottom of these stairs was another door which was opened and they found themselves at the top of a winding staircase which seemed to go down indefinitely.

It was lighted by rows of torches, but they could not see the end of these rows. The staircase itself was of stone, and in many places was slippery with slime and water. Above them all was darkness and off to the side nothing could be seen. Weird and strange was this sight, and Mustapha was almost frightened at the seeming vastness of the place they were in.

Imagine for yourself the scene that lay before them and you will probably have a better idea of it than all my word-pictures could give you. Imagine a narrow staircase lighted by torches winding down into darkness and finally disappearing from sight, and nothing else to be seen *except* darkness and you may be able to picture to yourself what they saw.

The staircase was not more than six feet wide and there was no obstruction on either side, nothing to keep a man from slipping in the water and slime with which it was partly covered, and falling into eternity, and add to this the air was just the least bit foul and evil smells reached Mustapha from far below.

These smells were of such a nature that he could not even guess at their cause at the time, but they resembled something burning coupled with a scent of stagnant water more than anything else.

He soon found out, however, that the burning smell was that of the torches which were made of pine coated with something like phosphorus mixed with some other inflammable material.

Mustapha was surprised because his guides did not proceed, but stopped at the head of the staircase, as if watching for some one; but he was soon to learn the cause.

In less than five minutes the door opened and half-a-dozen servants appeared with Akmat, Ahmed, Cassim, Emir, and Harun in their midst.

"Where are they going to take us?" asked Mustapha eagerly.

"To the ship," was Ahmed's astonishing reply.

"Yes, and I know the reason," rejoined Mustapha, and he related the story of how the servant had come to his room with a message from Abdullah, and all the rest, with which you are familiar, so I will not repeat it.

At this moment Abdullah came through the door accompanied by a tall man dressed in the garb of a sailor.

He was tall, as I said, and was also rather handsome, though his face was disfigured by a scar running the full length of his left cheek.

"We will proceed upon our journey," said Abdullah stepping forward to lead the way. With infinite care they picked their way down the stairs, being careful not to step on any wet or slippery place. The torches which were fixed in small brackets fastened to the sides of the stairs lighted their way most satisfactorily but were a source of danger; for if a man should make a misstep he might fall against the flames of one and be set on fire. And they also seemed to be a source of protection for if a person slipped and avoided the flames he could save himself by grasping the stalk of the torch, which was strong enough to support the weight of a full-grown man.

These torches were situated about four feet apart, however, so it was not likely that they would prove a source either of danger or protection.

After ten minutes of very slow walking the party reached the foot of the stairs and found themselves in a large cavern. Three of the servants had each removed a torch from the last three brackets of the staircase, so they had plenty of light going through the cavern, which was not lighted as the stairs had been.

Water dripped upon them in many places and little streams flowed at their feet. The water was collected in pools in many places, and this explained the stagnant smell that had greeted Mustapha.

As they traveled on the air became a little fouler and occasionally the torches flickered as if affected by it.

Finally the end of this cavern came and they found themselves in a much smaller one. There was also much more water in this and the odor of it was almost unbearable. To Mustapha it appeared to have lain there in pools for hundreds of years gathering its stagnant smell.

Suddenly they heard a faint hiss in the darkness ahead and upon advancing a few steps the light of the foremost torch glittered upon the scales of a hideous reptile. It was coiled to spring and its eyes were fixed upon the tall man dressed as a sailor. It was a cobra of the most deadly variety, which somehow or other had gotten into the cavern.

Before anyone could move a muscle the head of the snake swelled, its body stretched its opened jaws, revealing its death-dealing fangs, then sprang straight at the sailor.

Mustapha, who had been watching all the movements of the serpent with a deadly fascination, stood nearer to the man than anyone else, and in fact he was almost at the man's side, sprang like lightning forward and gripped the reptile around its neck while it was still in mid-air.

Then, as quick as a flash he broke its back with a dexterous twist of his hands and flung it aside. It was about three feet in length and was covered with curiously shaped marks, much in the shape of hooks.

The sailor cast him a look of gratitude but dared do no more, for he saw that Abdullah's eye was upon him.

"You did a good action that time," said Abdullah turning to Mustapha with a smile. "You are one of the quickest young men I ever saw, and I tell you, it takes dexterity to catch a snake in the right place when it is in mid-air."

"I need none of your compliments, no matter how flowery they are," said Mustapha in his coldest tone. "What I did might have been done by anyone with a quick eye, quick body, coupled with presence of mind."

"Perhaps you are right," said Abdullah, "but at any rate I should be proud of such an action, had I possessed the opportunity of doing it."

"No doubt you would," was the icy rejoinder. "It would be exactly like you. I can see you now, in my mind's eye, relating your exploit to a circle of admiring friends, and so puffed up with pride, that it would seem that you would burst at any moment."

"You have a sharp tongue," laughed Abdullah. "I wouldn't mind possessing one like it."

With that the incident was closed for a time, but little did Mustapha dream of what influence it would have in his destiny.

About half an hour's more walking and they beheld a faint light far ahead and the air seemed to become purer all of a sudden.

Three minutes more and they gazed upon the surface of the river Tigris. They were in the mouth of the cavern not five feet from the water, which bathed the beach in front of them.

Above them bushes of some sort grew and shaded their heads from the sun, which was now only a few hours above the western horizon.

"Well, when are we to be taken aboard the ship?" asked Mustapha.

"When it arrives," said Abdullah. "It is due here at sunset and you will be taken on at night. Its cargo will be unloaded in the morning, and the unloading will not take more than four or five hours, so you will start on your voyage at noon of the next day."

"You said that it was going to China for the purpose of buying silks. What city is the ship bound for, then?" said Mustapha.

"Pekin," was the reply and all sat down to wait for the arrival of the vessel.

Once in a while boats would sail by, but only once did they see a ship go down the river and that was just before sunset. She was very large, this ship, and carried all sailor set. A wind was blowing, and so she went along very rapidly and her crew did not notice the men in the mouth of the cave.

Beautiful beyond expression was the setting of the sun a few minutes after, and never before had Mustapha beheld such a scene.

Across the river were many farms and green woods and hills; and these were illuminated in the light of that sunset, in gorgeous colors, pink, salmon, and crimson being the predominating ones; but it is beyond the strength of my imagination to describe them adequately.

And in the light of the setting of the flaming orb Mustapha behind a ship sailing up the river, and toward the mouth of the cavern.

When within a hundred feet of the cavern, a boat was lowered from its side and this boat rowed by three sailors came toward where they were.

In less than two minutes it grated softly upon the hard, sandy bank and beach and the men stopped ashore bowing to Abdullah.

"Step aboard," that person said to Ahmed and the others, and they obeyed his command. Then he and the man dressed as a sailor entered the boat. The two rowers did so too, and began to row toward the ship.

"You may await till I return," said Abdullah to the servants who were now left standing in the mouth of the cave, knowing not what to do.

As they neared the vessel Mustapha, who had a fair knowledge of the architecture of ships, observed that it was not of Turkish or oriental build. He saw that it was of European make and looked stranger than the Turkish vessels he had seen.

He quickly concluded that Abdullah had employed European workmen in building it, giving them directions to build it in their own style.

The name of the vessel was painted in Turkish characters and possessed what to Mustapha seemed an unlucky name, namely "The Serpent."

The ship, though apparently a merchantman, carried heavy European cannon of the most deadly variety known at that time.

Mustapha's surmise that "The Serpent" was of European workmanship was quickly verified by what Abdullah said.

"She is a fine ship, my friend, for I had her built by Genovese workmen."

"She certainly is," said Mustapha, "but it seems to me that the name is unlucky. I have read of many ships going to the bottom of the sea and meeting with other calamities because they possessed the names of reptiles. For instance, there was the case of a large merchantman bound for China. Her name was 'The Cobra.'

"Off the coast of China, about three miles distant from it and no more, some Chinese saw the crew very plainly working at their tasks on deck.

"Half an hour after the same ship was seen by other Chinese and the same distance from the shore, but not a man of the crew was to be seen on board and the ship acted as if managed by a shrunken crew or no crew at all.

"Curious as to what might be the matter a boat was launched and manned by several Chinese. Upon reaching the ship and going aboard they found that not a man was on the ship. In the crew's quarters the tables were found already set for a meal, but no food had been eaten. In the officer's and the captain's quarters the same state of affairs prevailed.

"Not a thing on deck was out of place and the ship's boats were in their right places. What had become of the crew? No one can answer that question and it probably never will be answered. It was found afterward that fifty men had been on board at the last port at which 'The Cobra' had touched, but where the ship had originally sailed from and where she was bound was never known. It was probable that Pekin was her destination, but who can tell. The mystery of 'The Cobra' is one of the unexplained mysteries of the sea."

By the time Mustapha had finished telling this little tale they had reached the ship's side and were now ready to go aboard. The story had made Abdullah quite thoughtful, but he did not voice his thoughts so Mustapha did not concern himself as to what they were. If he could have looked into Abdullah's mind at that time he would have been greatly astonished, but as he could not he did not concern himself about that, either.

When they were on board Abdullah called the captain of the ship and gave him instructions in a low voice.

The captain then turned to Abdullah and the others informed them that they might go below and that they could stay there till they were called on deck.

A sailor showed them where they were to sleep during the voyage, and a wretched place it was, not over 15 feet in length and 12 feet in width. There were six berths there on each side of this little room and a door at one end.

But it was not the size of their accommodations that irked them so much but it was the evil smell that filled the whole apartment. This smell was probably caused by those who had occupied the room before.

"They must have been dirty," said Mustapha to himself. "I don't believe they knew what a bath was."

The bed cloths were dirty and very thin and scanty and the berths were as hard as blocks of iron.

All were very hungry, having eaten nothing since morning, so they concluded that they would soon receive food.

It was so, for a few minutes after, a negro boy entered the room with a large and steaming platter in his hands. Its savory smell reached Mustapha's nostrils, and he saw at once that their meal consisted of meat and vegetables, boiled into a sort of soup.

The negro laid the platter on a small table in the center of the room, which by the way was the only movable article of furniture there.

Then he left and soon returned with a jug of water and a cup which he set on the table likewise without speaking and then left.

All six attacked the meal with a ferociousness born of hunger. They drank the water from the jug and in less than ten minutes had eaten every scrap of their supper.

Another negro came in when they had finished and removed the empty platter and the jug, and after that they were not interrupted.

"We won't be treated like this, once we are on our voyage," said Akmat. "They'll serve us like this in the morning, but by noon when the ship sails, they'll treat us like any slaves."

Then, feeling rather tired they lay down and slept till morning, when they were awakened by the negro with a similar meal.

After dressing themselves they ate their breakfast and the boy came and took away the platter and the jug, but this time he was not silent.

"This is the last good meal you'll get on this ship, slaves," said he.

"Why?" asked Mustapha who was inclined to be inquisitive.

"You'll soon know 'why,'" said the negro, and was gone.

On deck they could hear the sound of unloading, and knew that the ship's cargo was being taken ashore.

At the end of the room opposite from the door was a small, round window through which fresh air came to them helping to drive away the smell which had annoyed Mustapha so much.

Through this little window they could see the green shore on the side of the river opposite from the city. It was obvious that the sun had risen for old

Sol's rays lit up the hill and meadows, and glittered upon the waters of a small brook, floating into the Tigris and upon the Tigris itself.

Several hours passed by, and then they heard the rattle of chains as the anchor was drawn up.

Then they felt the ship begin to move and looking through the window saw the foam on the water as the ship plowed the waves.

"We are on our voyage," said Akmat a few moments later. On and on they sailed, and before long they heard a voice at the door saying:

"You may come on deck now."

Chapter VIII

I need not tell you that they complied with the order, for they rushed from the room found themselves in a corridor or gallery at the end of which was a stairway leading to the deck.

They found the speaker to be the sailor whose life Mustapha had saved the day before.

He escorted them to the deck of the ship, where they found men busy at work on various tasks.

"What is your name?" asked Mustapha of their escort.

"Alzim Khan," replied that man. "You must not speak to anyone in that way, though," he added, "for you must remember that you are slaves, and indeed you are the only slaves on board this ship."

"Oh!" said Mustapha. "Sir, could you kindly give me the captain's name?"

"That's better," said the sailor. "That's the way you should speak to your superiors. The captain's name is Baber Yataghan."

"A yataghan is a long dagger," observed Mustapha to himself. "I wonder if the captain turns out to be as sharp as one of them."

Just then the captain came up to where they were standing and viewed the slaves critically. He was accompanied by another man who appeared to be some inferior officer.

"Well, they look strong, Kerrim," said the captain turning to the other. "They'll make good workers when they get used to the work. Abdullah gave me instructions to give them easy tasks at first. Now," he went on turning to Akmat, "you and your brother Harun and your cousin Mustapha are to aid the cook in whatever he wants you to do. Alzim Khan, whose life you saved yesterday, is the cook. Alzim will now conduct you to the gallery and give you your tasks for the day."

Alzim conducted his three assistants away, and Baber turned to the others.

"Ahmed, Emir, and Cassim, you are to be at the disposal of myself and my friend, Kerrim Beg. You are to do whatever we want you to do. Ahmed, you go below to the cook's gallery and give Alzim this piece of papyrus, which contains a list of articles I wish him to cook for my dinner. Cassim, you come with me to my private cabin and receive lessons in keeping it in order from one of the sailors, who is already there awaiting us. Emir, you are to do anything that Kerrim Beg wishes you to do. Kerrim, if you have any errand give him instructions concerning it."

At the end of this speech the captain went below to his cabin followed by Cassim, Ahmed departed on his errand and Emir turned to Kerrim.

"What do you wish me to do, master?" he asked.

"Keep out of mischief," replied Kerrim, shortly, and stalked away to look over the bulwarks at the green bank of the river several hundred yards away.

"Well, as there's nothing he wants me to do, I might as well employ my time watching the sailors at my work."

Five minutes after Kerrim turned from the worthy occupation of doing nothing and saw Emir following the occupation of watching two sailors carrying a large box from one place to another.

"Here, you lazy Hindu!" he roared, "why aren't you at work?"

"Because you didn't tell me what to do," said Emir in a perplexed tone.

"Don't you talk back to me!" yelled Kerrim. "You find something to do mighty quick, or I'll make you think you're standing on your head!"

"What is there that I can do, sir?" asked Emir as politely as possible.

"Don't ask so many questions. Get busy."

"But I don't know what I could do. Haven't you some errand for me to perform?"

"None at present," said the irascible Kerrim. "You can find something to do if you try very hard. Don't bother me about it any more."

"But really I don't know what sailors have to do."

"Then find out. If you pester me about it any more I'll knock you overboard."

"You might give me a suggestion, sir," said Emir in his politest manner.

"I don't give suggestions to slaves. See here, didn't I tell you not to pester me any more?"

"You did, sir, but I forgot."

"Forgot, hey? Well, I'll give you instruction in memory training. I told you I'd knock you overboard if you bother me any more, and you've heard it twice since then."

"I'm sure I didn't mean to, sir," said Emir keeping his temper remarkably well under the circumstances.

"That's the third time. I won't stand any more of your idiocy. You need a good drubbing to brush the dust from your brains."

Kerrim doubled his fists and rushed at Emir. Emir stepped quietly aside and his antagonist's right fist struck the mast near which they had been standing.

Kerrim now lost all control of his temper and rushed again at Emir, with the blood dripping from his fist.

Emir saw that he must defend himself or receive a sound thrashing, so he fell to his knees as his foe rushed upon him and pulled that person's legs from under him in the twinkling of an eye.

Kerrim alighted in a very undignified position—namely the top of his head—and turned a complete somersault, striking both his feet against a large box.

By this time quite a circle of sailors had collected around them, and some were for stopping the fight and others for letting it go on till one or other of the combatants was thrashed or the captain came on deck.

Before the sailors could come to a settlement Kerrim was on his feet again and made ready to rush at his foe.

Emir watched him and calculated just what would happen when the attack came.

It came soon, for Kerrim rushed at Emir in less than twenty seconds from the time he gotten to his feet.

Emir dodged him as he came and managed to get behind before he could stop running. Raising both hands he grasped his opponent's neck with his fingers around the man's throat and his thumbs pressed into the most vulnerable part of the back of the neck, that is, in the hollow.

Kerrim gasped for want of air and from the pain caused by the hands but Emir did not let go till he had almost choked his foe into insensibility.

Just then the captain came running on deck. A sailor had gone below and informed him of what was taking place.

He ran to Emir and said:

"What does this mean?"

Emir related the whole story from beginning to end telling everything that he had said to Kerrim and everything that Kerrim had said to.

The captain stroked his beard awhile as he had a habit of doing while in deep thought:

"Did any of you hear the words that passed between these two men prior to the fight?"

Three men stepped forward.

Kerrim had risen to his feet by this time, and he was about to rush at Emir, when the captain laid a hand upon his arm, saying:

"Don't be so rash, Kerrim. You had no right to get angry because of what Emir said. His words were not in the least offensive, and naturally he knew little of what sailors have to do. You should have given him some task to do, but instead you only told him to 'keep out of mischief. Perhaps the only thing to blame, however, is your temper. I don't think it would do you harm to take a few lessons in controlling it. For instance: let a man slap your face and try to refrain from striking back. That would do for the first lesson and others similar to that could easily be devised.

"I don't care whether Emir is a slave or not. You had no right to strike him. Even the slaves on this ship are under my protection and I shall not allow my officers to molest them without cause."

If a streak of lightning had struck him leaving him unharmed Kerrim could not have been more astonished, than he was at the captain's speech.

"Now you may go to your room and consider the matter closed," said the captain to him. "None of the six slaves are to be under your control hereafter. You are not fit to be their master. If you command one of them to do anything for you, they will be justified in not doing it. One who cannot control his temper is not fit to control men."

Kerrim went below greatly astonished at the captain's treatment of him. Finally, being tired he lay down to take a nap, and was soon sound asleep.

The captain turned to Emir.

"You may go to the cook's gallery and tell your brothers I wish to see them. Come to me about fifteen minutes later and I will have something more for you too."

Emir did as directed, and his two brothers and Mustapha went on deck to see what Baber wanted them for.

Emir related his adventure with Kerrim Beg to the cook, Alzim, and Alzim listened attentively till the end, and said: "My friend, you want to look out. You've stirred up the most malicious, hot-tempered, cruelest, and revengeful man in the whole of Turkey. Abdullah does not belong in the same class with him."

"I don't doubt you're right," said Emir. "But, sir, could you tell me why Abdullah has sent us (meaning himself, his cousins, and his uncle) as slaves on a ship bound for China."

"I'm strongly inclined to tell you," said Alzim. "If Abdullah or any other person should discover that I am revealing such a thing to you, I would be killed. This is what the captain told us last night. Abdullah had sent you on board as slaves because he wished to get you out of the way concerning a pair of black diamonds. He gave instructions to the captain to have the lot of you thrown overboard some night in the China sea. The captain was disgusted at this, but said nothing for if he had Abdullah would have had him killed.

"He told Abdullah that he would do as he was instructed and Abdullah was satisfied. You were brought on board last night little dreaming of the horrible fate your enemy had been preparing for you.

"The captain told all of us this but told us to keep it quiet. This we agreed to do on condition that he would spare you and gave you a chance to escape. He said that this was what he intended to do, so we were satisfied.

"He didn't tell Kerrim this, however. Kerrim is one of Abdullah's spies and such a thing would be fatal. There are two other spies on board. They've been confined to their rooms since midnight because they both accidentally fell overboard. Of course Baber didn't tell them either.

"The captain will have to treat you a good deal as if you were slaves, but you can be assured he won't give you too much work. He'll let you off every chance he gets.

"You want to keep an eye on Kerrim. He'll be sure to report everything that's happened and that will happen, to Abdullah if he gets a chance, but the captain has plans to get rid of him and the other two spies.

"He'll get them ashore in China some day before we leave there on our return voyage, and then sail for him. He will probably put you off in the Bay of Bengal or somewhere in Persia from which you can easily return to Turkey.

"It would not be safe to bring you up the Tigris for you might be discovered then. The captain has so much money that he thinks he can leave Abdullah's employ and live comfortably upon his earnings, so he will request Abdullah to discharge him, and then he'll take ship for Siam, which is his native land, though his parents were Hindu.

"Abdullah will discover sooner or later after that how he has been tricked, for the spies will get back to Turkey quickly enough. They'll either wait for a ship to take them home or return to Bagdad overland. The captain will tell Abdullah when questioned as to what happened to the spies, that they were accidentally drowned, and all will end well. But see here, we've been talking at least fifteen minutes so you'd better report to Baber. Good-by."

Emir went on deck feeling somewhat dazed. His mind was in a whirl of astonishment at all the things Alzim had told him.

He soon met the captain and the captain said:

"It is noon now, so you may go below to the sailors' quarters and eat your dinner. When you are through come to me and I will give you something to do.

"I've told your brothers all about your fight with Kerrim Beg. I think you'll find them below too."

Emir found his brothers, his father and Mustapha eating their dinner with the crew.

They were treated kindly by the sailors and soon made friends among them. The dinner was not varied and consisted only of two articles of food—meat and bread, but at any rate these two with good water added are all that a man really needs.

When dinner was over all six went on deck to look for the captain. As the captain had not come on deck yet they strolled around to take in the structure of the vessel.

Mustapha wandered away from the rest and counted the number of cannon the ship carried. There were three on each side, making six, and there were two at the bows and one at the stern, and an additional one which could be placed in position at any time, making a total of ten.

Mustapha thought of all he had read of pirates in the Eastern seas, and concluded that the ship had good reason for carrying such a formidable armament.

Many sailors had now come on deck and he watched them curiously. Each man had a singularly upright carriage and walked with a martial step. They were swarthy and bronzed to a darker hue than most Turks, so Mustapha, putting all these points together, concluded that they had once been soldiers.

He had scarcely finished the inspection of all this when the captain came on deck, and gave orders to the sailors, who instantly set about their tasks.

Then he came up to Mustapha and the others and bade them follow him below to his cabin.

They did so and found themselves in a room 15 feet in length by the same in width. On one side was the captain's berth, in the center was a table at which he and the other officers ate.

Mustapha expected that the captain was about to give them some little task to do, but he was not correct in his surmise.

"I have brought you here to give you advice," said the captain. "You, Emir, have stirred up the ire of a man named Kerrim Beg. He is not a sailor, but is a man much trusted by my employer, Abdullah Houssain. Abdullah put him aboard this ship to watch you and your companions. There are two other spies, who are his cousins. Their names I will not give you now, but I will give you a description of each of them.

"The oldest you will know by his beard which is about six inches in length and black as night. He is forty-three years of age and is the tallest of the two being six feet in height. You cannot possibly mistake him for one of the sailors because he is dressed in the most costly and beautiful clothes.

"The second is utterly unlike him in almost every respect. He is thirty-five years of age and has a pair of mustachios on his upper lip that give him the appearance of some kind of demon. He has no beard at all. His nose is as aquiline as that of a Jew, and his eyes are the fiercest you ever saw. They are like orbs of fire in the dark and in the daytime they glitter almost as much. He is very short though not fat, and is not over five feet five inches in height. He does not dress as richly as the other but there is one thing you can never mistake him for another man. He has the strangest turban I ever saw. It is made entirely of the skin of a huge African snake, hideously mottled and striped in every conceivable color, and the head of this snake is stuffed and its eyes are diamonds, and the stuffed head with its diamond eyes glares at you from the spy's forehead. That is the description of the men who are now your enemies.

"The short man, however is the most dangerous and cunning of the three. You had best beware of him. Kerrim will relate his experience to this man and the short man will instantly do anything in his power to injure you. He will bribe the sailors if he can and failing in that he will himself deceive and mislead you into errors as much as possible!"

"I believe you are right, sir," said Emir when the captain had finished giving them his advice concerning the three spies.

"We will keep our eyes open for any moves on the part of these men," said Akmat. "Trust me to fool them if they try any tricks, sir. But now will you kindly tell us what we are to do in future?"

"As to what you are to do," said the captain, "I will give you instructions in regard to that matter right now, so you will no longer be perplexed concerning that in future. You, Mustapha, Harun, and Akmat, are to be Alzim's assistants in future, as I told you this morning, so you see you are not exactly slaves, except that you will not be paid for your services. Cassim, Emir, and Ahmed, you are to be my servants, and I assure you your duties hereafter will be no harder than what I required two of you to do this morning. You may even have leisure time, if you work well, and I will supply you with good books, and good clothes to wear. I will have your room cleaned out this afternoon, and a lamp and a good supply of oil placed there for you. I will also supply you with pens, parchment, and ink if you wish. You might keep a diary of what happens to you during the voyage. I will also have a board covered with cloth fastened to the wall at the end of your room just under the window upon which you can keep the books and other things I give you. I will also give you four stools to sit on when eating, reading, or writing, for it is very inconvenient to have to do any of these three things without anything to sit on.

"Just before you came aboard there *were* four stools; then I saw Kerrim go below, and I suspect that he was going to meddle with something.

"The negro boy who served you with your supper last night told me of the deficiency of stools, but I forgot about it and thought nothing more of the matter until a few moments before. You will also find other commodities to night when you retire, but I will not mention them now."

"You are very kind, sir," said Ahmed. "I expected treatment fit only for a dog during my voyage as a slave and was prepared for such, but the way you have treated us is exactly the reverse."

"Oh, well, that is nothing. I suppose the spies won't like it but I'm going to treat you as much like gentlemen as I can under Abdullah's order. Now go to your work, and don't take up my time any more unless it is absolutely necessary."

Mustapha and his two cousins went below to the gallery and related what the captain had said while they washed the dishes, though rather awkwardly, I might say, for they had never had any experience in that most interesting art, except the broom he had given them that morning.

"It's just about what I expected," said Alzim. "Baber is one of the kindest men I have ever met. He'd treat a slave like a gentleman if the slave had done a good action or had performed the work faithfully."

"You are right," replied Mustapha. "He is also the kindest man I have ever met."

"I agree with you," said Harun.

"And so do I," said Akmat.

And I think you and I can do the same. At least it will do us no harm, and most likely we will agree with Mustapha and his two cousins.

"And what do you think of the captain's description of Kerrim's two confederates?" said Alzim. "You may be sure that he was quite right in saying that the short man was the most dangerous of the two. I wonder that he didn't give you their names but he has a purpose in not doing so. I could tell you in an instant, but I'm sure that Baber had a good reason in not doing so, so I will follow his example."

Chapter IX

That evening, in their room, the six discussed the events of the day together. All that the captain had promised them was there. Mustapha sat down at the table to write. He intended to begin a diary and the first words were these:

"March 27, 1650. I, Mustapha Dagh today begin an account of my daily life on the Turkish merchantman, 'The Serpent.' This day was a very memorable one as I had a fight with one of the spies of the villian Abdullah Houssain; but he started the encounter and Baber Yataghan the captain pardoned me and gave the fellow a severe scolding. Baber is one of the kindest men I have ever met. I and my cousins and uncle are slaves, yet he treats us almost as well, as he does the sailors, who are all freemen.

"The spy, Kerrim Beg by name, has two confederates on board whose names I do not yet know. The captain has promised to let us know however."

Mustapha read this to the others and it was said by them to be good enough, though the writing might have been better. Mustapha was naturally of a nervous disposition and the events of the day had added their wear and tear upon his nerves, so such a result is not astonishing.

Hardly had this been done when a sailor entered the room with a heavy package in his hand. This he laid upon the table, and at an invitation from Akmat, seated himself. His face was bronzed and darkened from much exposure to southern suns, and some people might have taken him for an Ethiopian. He was tall beyond the ordinary and his figure was so stalwart and strong as to convey to the minds of all those who viewed him, that he was a veritable giant in strength and courage.

His face was an honest expression and Ahmed instantly set him down in his mind as a man who might help them much.

Mustapha untied the package and found within six European pistols of the latest type, and six yataghans or long Turkish daggers of very excellent steel. Added to this was another, but smaller package containing six small bags of powder and a large bag of bullets.

Attached to one of the pistols was a sheet of parchment containing these words:

"My friends, I promised you I might send you other things than those you find in your room. Do not let the spies or any of the sailors know that you are armed. You can trust the bearer and send your return message by him, if you have any to send. To-morrow night he will come to you with six more pistols and more powder and bullets. As these things should be well-concealed I will tell you what to do. You had each better carry one of the daggers with you, for you never can tell what the spies will do. You may also carry the pistols if you want to, but in case you do not press all over the wall on your left side as you face the door, just above the berths till something yields. This will turn out to be a secret spring and upon vigorous pressing a small door will swing open revealing to you a large cavity in the wall in which you can hide your ammunition and weapons when you want to.

"Beware of Kerrim and his two friends, and that brings me to the point. To-day, when I spoke to you in my cabin I did not tell you their names, but now I will, and will also give you a curious and eccentric reason for my not doing so. The reason may seem to you only an idle superstition of a sea-faring man, but I have never known it to fail.

"The short man's name is Misabic. The tall man's name is Morabec. The reason is: A sailor should not tell everything at once.

"Baber Yataghan."

"I do not understand our friend's reason," said Mustapha. "He seems to speak it in riddles."

"Neither do I," said Harun. "But I will sit down and write a reply to him." The answer to Baber's letter was as follows.

"To you, O Captain of the 'Serpent' I send my salutations.

"I must thank you for your kindness in sending us the weapons.

"I do not understand the reason which you gave, but I am sure there was a secret meaning behind it. I trust that Akmat who among the six of us is most skilled in such matters can unravel it for us.

"We all send to you our united thanks for your kindness.

"Thy Faithful Slave,
"Harun Beg."

"Take this message to thy master," said Harun to the sailor after folding the parchment. The man bowed and withdrew.

"Well, what shall we do now?" asked Mustapha.

"Don't ask me," said Ahmed and relaxed into silence.

Akmat sat on his stool with set brows, staring intently at nothing. He was thinking deeply. Finally he raised his head as one waking from a sleep and said:

"I have it now."

"Have what?" asked Harun.

"The solution to the captain's words: 'A sailor should not tell everything at once.' It is a long story but you must hear it all before you will understand. The words have been a saying of the Turkish sailors for over a hundred years and originated in quite a curious way."

"Well tell the story," was the chorus from all corners and so Akmat began thus:

The Story of Neptune and the Ten Sailors.

"Once upon a time, so long ago that no one remembers the precise date, a ship set sail from Bagdad on a voyage to Cathay and China for the purpose of obtaining silks and spices.

"The ship which was named the 'Asp' had scarcely entered the Persian Gulf when a great storm arose and she was driven far out into the Indian Ocean.

"For many days the crew did not get a moment's sleep and then the storm abated as suddenly as it had begun.

"The ship was quite near a beautiful island, and here the crew landed. A delicious brook shaded with date and cocoanut palms ran into the sea itself, and further into the interior of the isle many beautiful trees were to be seen.

"The greater part of the crew stayed by the brook to eat their breakfast (for it was morning) but ten of the most adventurous set out to explore the place.

"After walking half an hour through gigantic groves where parrots and other tropical birds abounded in the greatest plenty, the ten found themselves at the foot of a hill.

"Up this hill they went and at the top what a magnificent sight met their eyes. Within two hundred yards, and made very distinct by the thinness of the air, was the sea itself. Twenty or thirty feet from the rugged shore rose a great palace from the depths of the briny deep. Its highest minarets were lost in the clouds and throughout it was made of solid gold.

"Now the ten sailors were all poor and what they saw tempted them. They saw nobody near the palace or in it and concluded that it was deserted.

"They ran to the beach and throwing themselves into the water swam to it and entered.

"'What a beautiful place!' said one of the sailors. 'I wonder who the owners can be. Well, now we'll just take a few of these golden chains and things.'

"Just at that moment Neptune, who was the owner of the palace, passed by and heard the man's speech. At the first sentence he would have gone but the second filled him with rage and he entered and said to them:

"'Know he that I am the owner and that I well defend my property. If you had not said that last sentence you would not have attracted my attention. Henceforth let this be one of thy maxims: "A sailor should not tell everything at once."'"

"Did Neptune let them go?" said Ahmed, at the finish of the tale.

"The story does not say," said Akmat. "I have told it to you just as I heard a man telling it in a bazaar at Samarcand, when I went there on a trip when I was not quite fifteen. The tale impressed me so that I have remembered it from that day to this. The story-teller afterwards informed me that it was a very common legend among Turkish sailors. Of course, it didn't happen as the story has it, so I suppose it was started by some strange happening, or originated in the brain of some sailor who wanted to play a joke. For the last two hundred years it has been told among mariners, but nobody can tell how long it will endure. Very probably, however, until its untruth is proved it is a proverb which has now degenerated into a mere fancy, and most Turkish mariners have formed a curious habit of observing it. It is a custom that I trust will soon be lost. I don't believe half our sailors think it to be true, but all the same a habit is hard to throw off."

"Well, so that's the captain's reason?"

"Yes, but is so trifling that we will not speak of it any more."

"Quite right," said Ahmed. "What shall our next topic be?"

"Tell some other tale that you heard in the bazaar's."

"Wouldn't you rather hear the history of the two black diamonds which Abdullah stole from us?"

"Of course, of course!" was the chorus from all sides. Everyone there had heard it except Mustapha, but all the same everyone wanted to hear it again.

"Now this tale may seem extravagant in some ways," said Akmat to Mustapha, "but nevertheless it is true and I have the written statement of the lama who told it to me."

"Well, hurry up," said Ahmed. All drew near to Akmat as he began to speak as follows.

The True History of the Black Diamonds.

"Once upon a time there lived in the city of Amber a beautiful princess Margiana by name.

"So beautiful was she that princes came from the far corners of the earth to win her.

"Every time one proposed she would show him a box containing two magnificent black diamonds, very large, and without a single flaw. Both were absolutely alike.

"'He who would marry me must choose one of these diamonds,' said she. 'One is false and the other genuine. He who picks out the one that is genuine shall be my husband. He who fails forfeits his head, and must die.'

"Many a brave prince tried his luck. Guessing was forbidden, so the hapless fellows each had to confess that he wasn't certain which was the right stone. Eventually he lost his head.

"Finally there came to the palace a handsome young Hindu prince. With him the princess fell in love.

"In his right hand he carried a long, strange looking instrument, hollow, with glass fitted in each end.

"Through this he looked at the diamonds for awhile and then turned to the king and the princess laid his finger on one of the diamonds and said:

"'This is the one.'

"'Young prince, how can I know you are not guessing?' said the king.

"'I am not,' said the prince. 'Look through my glass and see the proof.'

"The king did as desired.

"'By ——' he began but stopped for the expression was an unkingly one.

"What do you suppose he said? Now to a person looking at the diamonds with the naked eye they both looked exactly alike with not the slightest difference in their hue. But when his majesty took a look through the glass a great difference was perceivable.

"One diamond sparkled and glowed like fire but the other remained opaque and unshining.

"'The sparkling one is the genuine diamond,' said the prince.

"'You are right,' said the king. 'You will marry my daughter to-morrow. And now I entreat you to tell us the story of this interesting instrument by means of which you picked out the false stone.'

"'With pleasure,' said the Hindu prince and he began thus:

"'I was born twenty-three years ago in the land of Tartary. My father was the king of that land and had five other sons all older than me.

"'My father the king was not very much attached to me, nor I to him. As I could have no chance for the crown, I quarreled with him and he banished me from the kingdom forever. This, however, was just what I wanted.

"'I entered Hindustan with all my retinue and treasure and was well received by the king who had heard of my story. He had no son, so he told me that I should be his heir at his death.

"'Then, hearing of your beauty, O Margiana of Amber, I came here with this glass to win you.

"'And now for the story of the glass itself. It was neccessary to give you a brief sketch of my own history first.

"'The glass which is known as a telescope was given to me by a lama under the condition that I would bring him a false diamond and a genuine one in payment.

"'Really, it is not a telescope. The name I have heard given for it was very long and awkward to pronounce. I have forgotten it. So we will call it a telescope and nothing more.

"'The lama had made this telescope by dint of hard labor. An occult process had been used in making the glass and that explains why it can tell genuine jewels from false ones. Under its eye the genuine brightens, but the false remains dull and opaque. It can be used upon any kind of jewel. And that O king of Amber, is my tale.'

"'A very strange one,' said the king. 'I presume you want the diamonds to fulfill your promise to the priest. Of what cult is he? Brahmin or Buddhist? A devotee of Vishnu, Siva or the sacred cow? Or is he a fire-worshipper?'

"'He is a good Buddhist, as I am,' said the prince.

"'Do you know why he wishes to possess the diamonds?'

"'I have not the slightest idea. I suppose, though, that he is making a collection and needed these two to finish it.'

"'A reasonable theory. Now, let's eat dinner.'

"The next morning when the king went to awake his guest he found the bed empty. He rushed to look where he kept the diamonds. They were gone. The princess was in her room, sleeping soundly. The king deemed it unneccessary to wake her.

"Horsemen, armed cap-a-pie, were sent to Hindustan without delay. Others were sent to Tartary.

"When they arrived at the palace of the king of Tartary they found everything as usual.

"One of the horsemen told his message to the king and showed him the king's seal, so he would know they were not impostors.

"'I have only three sons!' cried the king in amazement.

"'I haven't banished any of them either. That fellow was probably an impostor.'

"The horsemen returned to the city of Amber and told the king their tale. There was no recource but to believe it.

"The next day the horsemen returned from Hindustan with a similar tale. The king of that land knew of no prince of Tartary who had been visiting at his court. Into the bargain he told them that he had seven sons and seven daughters and offered to prove it. The horsemen had leaped upon their horses at this point and had set out on their return journey satisfied that the king's word was true.

"For reasons known only to himself the king desired to regain the diamonds. For five years he kept up the search for them, sending men to the very corners of the earth and the northern lands of Europe. Even to the northern extremities of Russia they went, and when they returned home they told of a great sea covered with ice.

"Ten years after this the truth of the matter came out. All three of the kings mentioned had died. In place of the king of Hindustan the eldest of his seven sons reigned. The king of Amber's daughter ruled in his place. The eldest son of the king of Tartary reigned on that monarch's throne.

"A messenger came to the king of Hindustan with this story: A lama, his master, and a young man not much over thirty were in possession of the diamonds. The young man was the lama's servant and had heard and seen the two talking of the diamonds and had actually seen the stones themselves.

"The king instantly sent soldiers to the lama's home to demand the diamonds. The lama refused. The soldiers struck him dead. The twang of a bow was heard at that moment and the leader of the soldiers fell dead, with an arrow sticking in his heart.

"Before the soldiers could recover from their surprise another shot was heard and the soldier who had struck down the lama fell to the ground with an arrow in his brain.

"The soldiers instantly ran to the door and out of the house. They were just in time to see the lama's son running down the hillside toward a small river which flowed from the Himalayas. These mountains themselves overlooked the scene being only fifteen miles distant.

"The soldiers pursued him and saw him leap into a boat and row up stream. The shore was so rocky that the soldiers did not try to pursue him. They had no boat. They returned to the palace and told the king their story.

"The house of the lama was searched but the diamonds were never found. It was the general theory that the lama's son had taken them with him when he escaped from the soldiers.

"Where that person had gone, no one could tell, but most thought he had reached the Himalayas in safety, hidden the stones somewhere and then left the country or perished in some avalanche or snow storm, or from hunger or cold.

"From that day to this he has never been heard of, though the peasants of India who live in the shadow of the great mountain range have strange stories of what their ancestors saw. One of these tales is interesting. It is as follows.

"Three years after the disappearance of the lama's son a peasant was passing near one of the mountains. It was night and a violent snow storm was coming on, so he rushed to reach home as soon as possible.

"Suddenly, just as the storm came up, he saw, or thought he saw, a figure surrounded by light rushing on the coming storm down the mountain side.

"The figure was that of a young man hardly over thirty. The peasant was so terrified that he dropped senseless. When he recovered he found some one bending over him. Everything was dark and he could dimly make out the outline of the person. It was a man.

"The peasant struggled to his feet and was about to thank his benefactor, when that person abruptly disappeared not leaving a single trace behind.

"The peasant soon reached home, for the storm had gone down and told his family of what had happened to him.

"The next day the story was all over the neighborhood and other people told of similar experiences.

"It was agreed upon by all that the mountain was haunted by the ghost of the lama's son. Whatever the apparition was no one ever saw it again and before many years had passed all that had happened became a mere tradition.

"From that day to this the diamonds have passed through the hands of many lamas. The Himalaya mountains still keep their secrets, however, and what really became of the lama's son will probably never be known."

Chapter X

"A very curious story indeed," said Mustapha. "But if the lama's son carried the diamonds away with him when he fled to the mountains, how was it that the jewels were gotten by another person and handed down through the generations from man to man? Did some person come to the lama's son on the mountain side and recieve the stones from him?"

"That is what is supposed to have happened," said Akmat. "The real truth is not known."

"Why was it that the priest sent his son to steal the jewels from the king of Amber?"

"Because he wanted them to complete a very curious collection of precious stones he had accumulated, and because he wanted to make certain chemical experiments with them which were needed to prove the truth of a certain discovery he had made."

"Can you explain to me the correct nature of these experiments?"

"Yes, my cousin, I could; but I could do so better still if we were at the very spot where they were to have been made. If ever we get out of this affair alive I will take you there."

"Very well, that is settled. Now perhaps you would not mind telling me why Abdullah Houssain wishes to possess these black diamonds which have caused so many people so much trouble."

"Certainly not, my dear cousin. He has stolen the diamonds because he is the only living descendant of the king of Amber. The tradition of how the stones were filched from this ancestor has been handed down through the family, though his dynasty was superseded by another several hundred years ago. Abdullah probably found out that the jewels were in the possession of my family and also learned that we were coming to Turkey. Finding that the two of us in possession of the stones were coming to Bagdad he watched them carefully and by the aid of a Hypnotist stole one of the diamonds from Cassim, and got the other from Harun by accident."

"Everything is clear to me now," said Mustapha.

"It ought to be," replied Akmat. "It is almost bedtime now. Let's conceal our weapons in the secret recess the captain mentioned."

Scarcely had he risen from his seat when they heard stealthy footsteps in the corridor without. These footsteps seemed to approach the door and all six wondered what it meant. Nearer and nearer the steps came till they were almost athwart the door. Then they suddenly stopped and a silence fell in which those waiting could hear their hearts beat.

"Who is it?" said Akmat breaking the silence and starting for the door, pistol in hand. The weapon was loaded and he had his finger on the lock ready to cock it at the slightest provocation.

For answer a roll of white parchment came flying out of the darkness and struck in his face. It dropped to the floor and he heard the sound of running feet.

His next action was to leap into the corridor and cock the pistol. Looking toward the stairway at the end, he saw a short man running up it in the moonlight. He was a very short man and in an instant Akmat knew who he was.

It was the work of a moment to lift the weapon and pull the trigger. The sound of the discharge echoed and reechoed and through the cloud of smoke he dimly saw the figure reel and stagger, then steady itself, and the next moment it was out of sight.

His first impulse was to pursue but instead he stepped back into the room and was about to tell the others what had happened (they had not risen from their seats, so great was their astonishment), when three or four sailors came running in to demand what was the matter. The shot had awakened them and they had leaped from their beds and run into the corridor.

Akmat was about to explain when the captain entered and dismissed the sailors. He then turned to the ex-sorcerer and asked him to explain what it all meant.

Akmat did so without any seeming excitement. The captain stroked his beard in silence. "You did right," said he at last. "Hello, what's this?"

His eyes had fallen upon the roll of parchment which had been flung in Akmat's face by the short man.

He picked it up and unrolled it. It was of very stiff goatskin finely prepared and when fully unrolled was about a foot in length. One side was entirely covered with fine handwriting in black ink. At the foot were three lines of writing in red ink, more carefully and clearly written than the rest. Below these three lines was the signature of the writer. The whole missal except the words in red ink was in Hindu, but these three lines were in Turkish characters.

Baber was perfectly able to read and write both Hindu and Turkish so he had no trouble in reading the letter, for letter it was. He read out loud and the others listened. The contents were as follows:

"To you Emir Beg and to all your friends I send a greeting of hate and ill-feeling.

"This day you fought with me because I told you to do some trifling errand, and by some fiendish means or other, triumphed over me.

"Baber Yataghan, the captain, took your part, you miserable slave, and compelled me to retire. I suppose he is your friend and if he is, all the sailors will side with him. It makes no matter, however. All the sailors in Turkey and on the seas could not cope for one moment with those powers of the deep that I and my two friends could summon at our will. It is therefore hopeless for you to expect to resist us, so you had better let us have our way. If the captain surrenders all six of you into our keeping without question of what we will do with you we will let him and his crew go unmolested; but if this order is not complied with our revenge will be fearful. You had best speak to him about it as soon as possible.

"It will be well for you if you yield yourselves to us without resistance for it is more than possible that in that case we will spare your lives and let you go free after keeping you in captivity for not over three months. We act with the orders of our patron and master, Abdullah Houssain, and he has authorized us to take whatever measures neccessary in dealing with you.

"Further I have this much to say to you: In Hindustan there exists a powerful secret society to which we belong which is known as the _____. I leave this blank because I do not wish to frighten you. You would probably faint with fear if you knew the name of your enemy. (These were the three lines in red ink)

"I remain

"Your Worst Enemy,

"Kerrim Beg."

"Ah!" said Emir when the captain had finished reading. "Please hand me the parchment. Our friend Kerrim left a blank. It would do no harm and some good if I were to fill it out."

He carried the parchment to the table and seated himself, pen in hand. Then, he wrote a single word in the blank space. The black ink he used shone out with great distinctness amidst the red. The single word was this: "Fire-Worshippers."

Mustapha saw it and gave a cry of astonishment. He knew well that the Fire-Worshippers were to be dreaded. He had heard of the great temple in Hindustan where they were said to conduct their horrible rites.

The captain himself was also astonished. Also he trembled with fear. The mention of that dread word in those days was enough to frighten the most courageous. Dreadful was the revenge of the society upon all those who were its enemies. Let anyone offend a person who was a member of it and before many days had passed the offender disappeared and was never heard of again. It was not recorded that any person who had fallen into the hands of the Fire-Worshippers had emerged alive. Their bodies were never even found or heard of. It was whispered that the victims were sacrificed to the god of fire and were cremated alive in a pit of flame. It was even said that they were in league with the devil.

Who the author of these rumors was nobody knew, but it was thought that he was some member of the Fire-Worshippers who had turned traitor, and had begun to rival its workings, though very cautiously at first, from fear of inciting their vengeance should they learn who their betrayer was. At any rate this secret society was dreaded throughout the Orient at that time.

"Well, a pretty kettle of fish we've stirred up," said Akmat who was sometimes addicted to a kind of slang, which was very expressive at the right time.

"You are right," replied Ahmed who had also seen what his son had written.

"What is it?" asked Harun and Emir who had not yet seen what Akmat had written. The parchment was shown to them.

"Well, now what shall we do?" said they.

"Place these rascally spies under arrest!" yelled the captain.

"By all means," said Mustapha. "They are a menace to the safety of the ship. For all we know they may have gunpowder stored up in the ship which they could set off at any moment when they are threatened with danger."

"Not them!" said Baber with contempt in his voice. "I know them too well to think they'd do that. They would be too careful of their own skins to do such a thing as that. It would be no revenge to them to blow up the ship when they themselves would be blown up at the same time. What satisfaction would that afford them?"

"None," said Mustapha, conquered by the captain's superior reasoning. "But what then is this danger with which they threaten us?"

"Time only will prove," was the reply. "We won't worry about that now. I imagine from what you told me," Baber went on turning to Akmat, "that you wounded the short man. I will summon some sailor to go to their room and find out, if possible, what damage you did."

Drawing a conch shell from his pocket, he blew a shrill blast which brought nearly every sailor on board into the corridor in less than five minutes.

Baber then singled out five of them, the strongest of the lot, and informed them of the mission he entrusted them with. They instantly withdrew and did not return for at least ten minutes. The captain had dismissed all the other sailors and they had returned to their beds and wherever else they had been when they had been called by the captain's blowing of the conch shell.

When the four returned the youngest told Baber that they had found the door of the spies' room locked and that knocking had brought no one to the door.

"Seeing that it was useless we came back to report to you," he ended with.

"You did quite right," said Baber. "Had you done more you would have exceeded my orders.

"Now what will we do?" he added, turning to Mustapha.

"Place them under arrest, as you advised before," replied that person.

"Very well," said the captain. He turned to the sailors and told them what was to be done. They could not well understand Turkish as that was the language Mustapha had spoken in. They were Persians.

"Arm yourselves," said Baber to the four sailors. They retired and he turned to the others and bade them take their pistols and daggers and follow him to his cabin.

Here he presented each with a bright new scimitar, and they returned to the corridor. The four sailors were already there, each being fully armed.

Then he led the way on deck. The men of the watch were there each in his place, motionless figures in the moonlight. Several sailors, not feeling inclined to sleep, were strolling about the decks, but except the light footsteps of them and the heavy tread of the eleven marauders and the washing of the waves against the ship there was no sound. The banks of the river were much further away than they had been at the beginning of the voyage, so Mustapha knew that they must be nearing the Persian Gulf. They would be in the sea by morning, he thought.

The moon was directly overhead and was full that night. Seemingly not far from him gleamed the planet Mars, a bright red color in the moonlight. All the other stars and planets were thrown into oblivion by the brightness of these two. Off to the northwest was the Great Dipper.

All these things were observed by Mustapha, and though he had seen them a thousand times before, he noted them at this time more than at any other time in his life.

It was nearly midnight. All had stopped to look at the water and for a few moments all was silence. Then the silence was broken by the tolling of a bell in some village far away on the land. The sound was borne to them through the still night air with startling distinctness. It did not seem half as far away as it really was.

This was preceded by another brief silence. Then they went on across the deck and soon reached a small hatchway near the bow. Everything was in darkness at its foot, and one of the sailors took from beneath his cloak a taper and lighted it.

By its light they saw the stairway and all that was at the foot. A closed door could be seen and it was the door to the apartment of the three spies.

They descended the stairs and knocked upon the door. There was no response. Through a small crack they could see light within.

"Open!" cried Baber. "I, the captain of this ship command you to do so. Open, or I'll—"

His last words were broken short by the abrupt opening of the door. They were given scarce time to see what was inside when three pistol shots rang out. One of the sailors fell to the floor. Two bullets whistled past Mustapha's head and struck the staircase behind him. A cloud of powder-smoke enveloped them. Akmat drew his pistol from under his cloak and fired into the room. They heard the bullet strike against metal, and suddenly the light went out. A shot from near where his ball had struck, knocked the candle from the sailor's hand and for awhile everything was in darkness. Confusion reigned everywhere.

Mustapha heard the loud report of several pistols close by and judged that his cousins and the captain were shooting. The flash of one of these weapons revealed to him for one brief moment Cassim struggling in the grasp of Kerrim Beg. grasped someone by the throat. The flash of another pistol showed him that he had hold of Morabec, the taller of the three spies.

The giant was struggling for breath and tried to make Mustapha loosen his grip. The young Ottoman held on tenaciously however and Morabec dropped limply to the floor dragging his foe with him.

Over and over they rolled striking against several bodies. The flash and report of pistols showed that the fight was not yet ended.

He saw Misabic crouching in a corner, a cocked pistol in each hand, his face distorted with fear and rage. He saw Kerrim and Emir still struggling, though neither seemed to gain the mastery, and saw at the same time a tiny flame shoot up in one of the corners.

Instantly he released his hold on Morabec and jumped to his feet leaving that astonished person lying on the floor.

It was but the work of a moment to stamp out the flame which had been caused by the upsetting of the lamp.

Then, before Morabec, the spy, could struggle to his feet Mustapha was upon him again like a flash of lightning. Three blows from his fist knocked the fellow unconscious and then Mustapha arose and drew his scimitar.

All was darkness now. The pistols were silent and nothing could be seen except the flash of steel and the dim forms of men writhing to and fro.

Then suddenly the conflict stopped. Steel ceased to clash upon steel. Nothing was now heard except the heavy breathing of men and another sound as of the rustling of rope.

Someone groped for the taper and picked up a fragment of it and lighted it. The light revealed the scene.

Morabec lay motionless on the floor. Emir and Ahmed lay still in the same position. Kerrim lay on his back with two sailors bending over him and tying his hands and legs while another held him down with his arms. The fourth sailor lay still and motionless at the foot of the stairway. Baber and Akmat were binding Misabic with ropes while Cassim sat on his chest and Harun stood leaning on his scimitar surveying the scene and holding the candle fragment in his other hand.

The rest of the taper lay trampled into fragments on the floor. Splinters of wood lay on the floor and corresponding gaps in the walls showed where bullets had struck. The overturned lamp lay in the corner and the oil was flowing all ovewr the room. Three vials of ink stood on the table, which singularly had escaped damage. Near them was a pile of sheets of parchment and a half written sheet under two or three quill pens.

Five or six broken chairs and about a dozen pistols and daggers and three scimitars completed the scene. They were lying upon the floor just as they had been dropped by their owners.

Mustapha walked unsteadily to the table and tried to read the writing on the parchment. He was unable, however, in the bad light, so he rolled it up and put it in his pocket. Then he sheathed his scimitar and walked over to where Emir and Ahmed lay.

The flash and report of pistols showed that the fight was not yet ended.

Following his impulse he leaped in the direction of the struggle and The sailor was similarly wounded, but Emir had been more fortunate. He had only been knocked unconscious by a blow from Kerrim.

Misabic was nearly unconscious from a blow from a pistol butt, so he was hardly able to stand when the sailors forced him to his feet.

Mustapha had received several bruises, but beyond that he was not hurt. He lifted Emir in his arms and carried him on deck. Several of the men of the watch and two or three sailors met him at the head of the stairway with eager questions and bade them go below to the scene of the fight and help bring the wounded man on deck.

A cool breeze was blowing and under the influence of this Emir soon revived. He sat up and asked Mustapha what had happened.

Hardly had Mustapha finished telling him when the captain, the three prisoners and all the rest who had participated in the fight came streaming through the hatchway. The men of the watch and the other sailors were carrying Morabec and Ahmed and the wounded sailor.

Before long all these revived from their swoon and Ahmed was carried below to the captain's room and laid on his bed. Emir was able to stand, so he remained behind. The wounded sailor was taken to the forecastle by his comrades and the three prisoners were tied to the mast and a guard placed over them.

It was now after midnight. The conflict had seemed long to those engaged but in reality only five minutes had been occupied. Mustapha felt very tired. He went below to the little room which he and his cousins had recently occupied and soon fell asleep, forgetting all about the roll of parchment in his pocket which he had intended to read when he got a chance and a good light to read by.

It was by far the contrary with Emir, the captain and the others. Far from being sleepy it would have been literally impossible for them to have gone to sleep.

In the captain's cabin, that night they talked over recent events and deliberated as to what had best be done with the three spies.

"It is well for them that they did not kill anyone," said Baber. "Had they done so they would be dead by morning. To-morrow we'll have a trial and pass sentence upon them. There's a sailor on board who was once a Turkish Cadi, so we'll have him help us and tell us what had best be done with the spies."

All agreed that this was the proper course, so they dropped the subject and turned to Ahmed who was still unconscious.

"Is there a doctor aboard?" asked Emir.

"Yes," said the captain. "I had almost forgotten. I'll go get him and have him fix the wounds."

Baber left the room and soon returned with a grave-faced individual in the garb of a sailor.

He removed Ahmed's cloak and shirt and examined the wounds. The bullets had gone clean through the body, and, happily, had touched no organ.

Two ribs were broken but not shattered. The doctor set the broken ribs and bound the wounds with a great strip of linen and then covered his patient and retired, telling the captain not to allow Ahmed to move for at least a week.

Then they talked on about certain matters, and a little before morning Emir fell asleep and the others followed suit.

When they awoke it was morning and the sun had risen. The captain rushed on deck and saw that the ship was already in the sea. Twenty miles to the north lay the land and the mouth of the river Tigris as it flowed into the sea. The sun was half an hour high, and he could hear the cook below, as he lit the fire and prepared to cook breakfast. The scene was beautiful. The white-capped waves rushed against the ship as she plowed her way through them, and even the prisoners bound to the mast appreciated the beauty of the ocean.

Chapter XI

The next thing the captain did was to walk over to the mast where Kerrim and his companions were tied. They were not looking very comfortable, for the sailors had been in a hurry and had bound the men more tightly than was really neccessary.

"Good morning," said Baber addressing them. "We're having fine weather, aren't we?"

"We would be in a better position to appreciate it if you would untie these ropes a little so we could move," growled Kerrim, looking at Baber with hatred in his eye.

"I'll admit that my sailors were not very gentle, but do you think I'm such a fool as to let myself fall into your hands like that?"

"You've spoken the truth for once," said Morabec, joining the conversation.

"The word 'fool' can apply to more than one person by the simple adding of the letter 's'," replied the captain.

"You can insult us safely when we're bound," said Misabic, "but if we were free, and had swords in our hands you could not do so with immunity."

"I beg a thousand pardons," said Baber. "I meant no offense by my words."

"So you're a liar in the bargain, eh?" said Morabec. "Fool and liar is a nice combination, isn't it? What are you going to add to it next, captain?"

"You can insult me all you want," cried the captain, "and I won't do you any harm just now. But everything you say will count for or against you at your trial to-day."

"Trial?" said Morabec. "What do you intend to try us for?"

"Blackmail and something worse," said the captain.

"You cannot do it legally without a cadi," said Kerrim.

"We have a sailor on board who was once a cadi, but for reasons of his own he retired. However, he did so with the understanding that he could resume his office at any time he wished."

Kerrim's jaw fell. "What is the other thing you are going to try us for?" he questioned.

"Belonging to the dread society, called the Fire-Worshippers," was the reply.

Brave and unscrupulous as he was, Kerrim's face paled under its bronze. He well knew that men who were members of the "Fire-Worshippers" were being prosecuted by the Turkish, Indian and Persian governments, and that the penalty was death by Fire, this being a mockery upon the society. It was said that its victims perished by fire, so its members should also perish in the same manner. So reasoned the rulers of these three governments.

The captain turned and went below. Breakfast was served and when he had eaten he sent for the sailor who had been a cadi. Mustapha and the others were with Baber, and Ahmed still lay in bed, though he was now quite conscious of all that had happened. The wounds did not pain him much, so he dropped asleep a few moments after eating his breakfast. The physician said that he would not be able to stand for at least a week. He also added that it was lucky no bones had been shattered and that it was strange that two bullets fired at such close range should not shatter a rib into a thousand pieces.

He was a good doctor but he did not know what serious damage might have been done. Had he examined the bullets he would have found that his patient would have been dead within twenty-four hours had they remained in the body.

The cadi entered the room escorted by the sailor who had been sent to tell him his services were needed. He was short, stout, and merry-faced and seemed as if he could enjoy a joke under any circumstances. He wore a coat with brass buttons and a turban on his head which had done service many a year. His pantaloons were red and the sandals on his feet were of wood bound with leather. His face was dark and swarthy, showing that he had served several years as a sailor. His hands were large and strong and showed the effects of hard work. The nails were well trimmed and his face clean, showing that he was a man careful of his personal appearance.

In the captain's presence he removed his turban, showing his hair carefully brushed back from his forehead, and bowed. There was an awkward silence for a moment before words came to his tongue.

"What do you wish me to do, sir?" said he, at last.

"My friend, I have heard that you were once a cadi," said Baber, "and that you can resume your position at any time you wish. Thus, you are not retired. You have doubtless heard of what happened last night. I have sent for you to preside at the trial of these men and hear all that is said in accusation or defense, and judge the prisoners accordingly. We will abide by your decision and do what you think best, though there is no doubt that these men are guilty of all that is said of them."

"You honor me, sir," said the cadi.

"Akmat, you go below and bring the letter that was thrown in your face and the half-sheet of parchment which was picked up in the prisoners' room after the fight."

Akmat departed on his errand and soon returned with the desired papers in his hand.

"We will now go on deck," said the captain. He issued some order to several sailors he had previously summoned in a low tone and they ran ahead.

When the party emerged onto the deck they found these sailors putting several benches in position with stools behind them.

At one of them the cadi seated himself. At the others the captain and his friends sat down. One bench was still reserved with three seats behind it.

The sailors went over to the prisoners and unbound them and led them to this bench where they submissively seated themselves. All three looked haggard and worn.

"Bring them food and wine," said Baber to a sailor. The man obeyed. The spies ate and drank eagerly while the others looked on in silence. The scene was very impressive. The sun was not over an hour high.

The sea struck the ship again and again with its waves as she sailed on. Land was almost out of sight. Far away on the horizon they saw black specks which soon turned into ships homeward bound.

Hardly had the prisoners finished eating their meal when one of these passed not more than a mile away. All her sails were up and she was sailing tolerably well though the wind was against her. She could scarcely be a merchantman for she carried many guns, yet she flew the merchant flag of Turkey. Mustapha counted eight guns on each side and two at the bows and two and the stern, making twelve in all.

He could also see her crew watching them. Then he looked toward the spies who had laid down their food and were watching the strange ship very intently. The muscles of their faces were set and they seemed to be expecting something.

Suddenly a cloud of smoke arose at the mouth of the guns in the bow and was followed by two reports. Far off the watchers saw two splashes in the top of a white cap where the balls had struck.

Hardly had these two shots been fired when smoke came from one of the guns at the stern, followed by the usual report. This was followed by a black cloth being hauled up to the masthead where it remained a moment and was then hauled down again. Then up went a huge white pennant with these characters on it in huge black letters which could be discerned from Baber's ship:

$$= \textit{ľ} 9 \textit{ċ} 7-$$

Then down went this flag and the ship proceeded upon her way.

"What can it mean?" said the captain. "Who were they signalling to, for signalling they must have been. I understood none of their signals."

Akmat had taken in the whole significance of the matter and realized that these signals might be connected with the spies.

A pail of tar stood near him. He broke a splinter from the side of his bench and producing a piece of parchment from his pocket, he dipped the splinter in the tar and took down these notes:

"Two shots from bow. One from stern. Black flag hauled up. White pennant hauled up with black characters on it thus: $= \textit{ľ} \ \textit{℈ċ}.7$. Eight guns on each side ship. Two at stern and two and bow. Twelve guns total. Merchant flag."

This he slipped into his pocket and turned to see what was going on. The trial was about to begin. The cadi was clearing his throat to speak. The captain had writing materials and ink at his side to take down what was said and what occurred.

"The prisoners may stand up," said the cadi. Said prisoners promptly obeyed.

"The accusers may stand up and tell me what they charge the prisoners with." Akmat, Emir, Mustapha, Cassim, and Harun stood up.

"Take down what they say," said the cadi to the captain. That person was scribbling away as fast as he knew how. Akmat and the others cleared their throats and said:

"We, Mustapha Dagh, Akmat Beg, Emir Beg, Cassim Beg, and Harun Beg do hereby accuse Morabec Beg, Kerrim Beg and Misabec Beg of blackmail, and of belonging to the secret sect known to the world as the 'Fire-Worshippers.'"

"Prisoners," said the cadi, "you have heard the accusation. Accusers, produce your proof that these men are blackmailers."

Akmat read the piece of parchment which had been thrown in his face and related the circumstances which had attended that incident.

"You were in the wrong to shoot," said the cadi. "What argument do you defend your act with?"

"I thought at the time that the parchment might turn out to be some infernal machine, so I shot at the man I supposed had thrown it."

"You who threw that roll of parchment, be seated," said the cadi to the prisoners. Morabec stood up.

"Show us where you were shot."

Morabec lifted his left arm and showed his shirt red and stiff with blood just under the arm-pit.

"The wound was a slight one," said he, "but it made me reel and stagger for the moment."

"Why did you attempt to resist the captain and his friends when they entered your room?"

"Because we thought they were going to kill us."

"What reason had you for thinking this?"

"The fact that the captain and these men have in some unnacountable way contracted a hatred toward us. Why should Akmat Beg have shot at me if he had not hated me and wished to do me harm?"

"You have just heard his reason."

"How do I know that he is not lying?"

"Indeed we do not. But what proof is there that he is telling a falsehood?"

"None that I can see."

"Then we'll drop that and proceed. Akmat Beg, you may read the other parchment which you have in your hand."

"It is nothing but the first act of a play that I have been writing," said Morabec. "I was doing so when he and his friends broke into our room."

"No matter. Akmat, proceed."

Morabec could scarcely conceal his uneasiness when Akmat unrolled the parchment. He evidently dreaded what would follow. Akmat read it aloud thus:

"To thee, Abdullah Houssain, Grand Commander of the secret illustrious sect of the 'Fire-Worshippers,' I send my humble greeting.

"I wrote a letter to the slaves you told me to keep my eyes on, and myself took it to their door and threw it within. Akmat Beg, the ex-sorcerer, shot me as I ran along the corridor, but did not hurt me seriously. I will not annoy you, my master, by telling you the trivial nature of this wound which does not matter.

"The captain, Baber Yataghan, is very friendly with these men and seems to treat them as his equals. I would advise that you get rid of him as soon as possible.

"This morning, Emir Beg, his brother, quarreled with Kerrim and they fought, Emir gaining the battle by some dishonest trickery. He is a very insolent man, and I advise that he be tortured more than the others before he is thrown into the burning lake.

"Your Servant,

"Morabec Beg."

Down at the foot of the sheet were these words evidently written in a great hurry:

"I hear steps without the door and think that the slaves and Baber the captain are about to take us prisoner. The gods of fire——" The blank was traced out as if the door had been burst open at that moment and their foes had rushed in.

"This shows that you are 'Fire-Worshippers,'" said the cadi, gravely. "There is no doubt that you are guilty. The punishment for blackmail is five years imprisonment, and that for being a 'Fire-Worshipper,' you know. As soon as we reach land you will be burnt alive. Captain Yataphan, I think you had better herd your ship for Persia where this punishment will be executed upon the prisoners. Bring me pen, parchment and ink, and I will write out an order which you can give to the authorities at the nearest town."

The order was written out as follows:

"These three prisoners, Morabec Beg, Kerrim Beg and Misabic Beg, have been convicted of being members of the 'Fire-Worshippers' and of blackmail. I command that you execute upon them the punishment for the first mentioned offise, as it is much more important than the other.

"Your Servant,

"_____ ____

"Cadi."

This order was handed to the captain and then the cadi retired below to his duty and the three prisoners were put in irons.

Akmat put the two pieces of parchment in his pocket and walked over to them.

"What have you to say in your defense?" he asked of them.

"I say," said Morabec, "that the fellow you had for cadi never was a cadi, and that he was in your hire to judge us guilty. Any cadi who ever was a cadi would have never convicted us upon the hare-brained evidence you produced. But beware, you rascal, we are not dead yet."

"You soon will be, though," said Akmat.

"Don't be so sure of that," said Morabec. "You've got to catch your hare before you cook him."

"But we've caught you."

"Yes, but you haven't cooked us yet, have you?"

"No, I admit the truth of your argument."

"Well, then leave us alone awhile."

Akmat walked across the deck and leaned over the bulwarks watching the waves.

As he did so something caught his eye. It was a patch of sooty gray just showing through the water, but of what material he could not discern.

Then, suddenly it disappeared and he saw it no more.

He watched the place where he had seen it in a most curious manner, wondering what it all meant.

Then, as the ship swept past it, he looked in a certain direction and saw a round, tapering point of the same color sticking two feet out of the water. It was a foot and a half in thickness at the base and tapered sharply till it came down to the round point at the top. Then this thing disappeared and though Akmat searched the sea with his eyes he saw it no more.

He must have stood there for hours lost in a reverie. His thoughts went back to the days in Bagdad when he had been re-united with his father and brothers, and when he and Mustapha had met with so many strange adventures concerning the diamond.

He wondered, too, if he would live to solve the mystery and meditated on what might happen to him if the "Fire-Worshippers" laid their hands on him.

He was certain now that Abdullah Houssain was the commander of this sect and wondered if this had any connection with the diamonds.

These thoughts, however, were rudely interrupted by the captain coming on deck, and calling him to dinner.

He went below and related what he had seen in the water to his brothers and the others. Each one had his own theory concerning it, but all forgot this occurrence when they had eaten dinner.

Toward evening they saw land ahead and knew that they were nearing Persia. A town could be discerned and a fleet of ships in the harbor adjoining it.

There were ships of every nationality there—merchant vessels of Turkey, India and Persia, China, France and several nations of Europe.

The sky was cloudless and scarcely any wind was blowing. The ship proceeded at a very slow rate and the captain said they would not reach land for an hour yet.

Mustapha was on the deck when he suddenly heard a deep rumble and saw clouds begin to gather overhead. Then a streak of lightning suddenly shot out of the zenith and a terrific wind arose which drove the ship off to sea.

He made great haste to retire below, but Harun came on deck in spite of the rocking of the ship to see what was the matter. Neither he nor Mustapha or any of the others had ever been at sea in a storm before.

Everything was dark except when the flashes of lightning illuminated the sea, showing great hills and valleys which tumbled and soared and broke and formed again. Sometimes two waves struck against each other and were shattered into a thousand pieces. Salt spray flew in his face, almost blinding him, and when a neat wave rolled over the ship, he was compelled to grasp hold of the bulwarks to save himself from being washed overboard.

He finally concluded that he had better go below, but he found that all the hatches were all barred down and his yelling was drowned in the roar of the storm.

For many hours he remained in this position buffeted and thrown about by the storm, but not washed overboard.

Finally the storm so abated that the waves no longer engulfed the ship. Then, one of the hatches was cautiously opened and a sailor peered out.

Harun staggered across the deck and almost fell into this man's arms. The sailor carried him to the captain's cabin where his brothers were all huddled together with the captain.

As the man laid him upon the floor, he fainted and the captain reached for restoratives. In a few moments he sat up and told them what had happened to him.

"We thought you had been washed overboard," said Emir with tears in his eyes. "If we had opened a hatch the ship would have been filled with water and everyone drowned. Also, the captain thought you might possibly escape the fury of the storm by holding to the bulwarks."

"What time is it?" asked Harun, weakly.

"About midnight, I think," said the captain.

"Where are we at?"

"Somewhere in the Gulf of Persia," said Baber.

"Where will we be in the morning if the storm continues like this?"

"Somewhere in the Indian Ocean if the wind does not shift about and carry us back to Persia or the Tigris or the coast of Arabia."

Harun dropped asleep in a few minutes and they put him in the captain's bed with Ahmed who had not been awakened by the violence of the storm.

All through that night the storm continued, but abated so that Harun was able to go on deck. About four in the morning a rain began to fall and this continued till 8 o'clock.

Then the captain went on deck to see how matters stood. Every movable article there had been washed overboard and little pools of water had gathered in places. Half of one of the masts was gone and all the rigging was more or less damaged. Some had been carried away entirely and many ropes hung over the sides of the ship. Every sail was in tatters and a piece of the bulwarks had been washed away.

After ascertaining how much damage had been done Baber went below and ate breakfast with his friends.

When he went on deck the storm had gone down entirely and he sent for the sailors and gave them orders to repair all the mischief that the storm had done.

Before long new ropes were brought on deck and the sailors tore down the tattered rigging and placed the new ropes in its place. Others brought sails and removed the tatters from the masts and put new sails up.

By now the ship looked as if she had never been harmed by the recent storm. Mustapha and his cousins had watched all these proceedings with interest. They had never seen such things before and were naturally much interested.

"It seems to be very interesting to you," said Baber after watching them awhile.

"Naturally it is," said Akmat. "I don't suppose you take much interest in it except to see that the sailors do their work well?"

"No, I don't. I'm used to such things."

"I agree with you. I suppose that if I had sailed the seas as long as you have I would entertain the same feeling."

"Of course you would. Familiarity breeds contempt, but it also breeds disinterest."

"Would you mind giving us a brief sketch of your life?" said Mustapha.

"Of course not," replied Baber. "I'll tell you the most important parts relating to my life in as short a manner as possible."

"I am thirty years old and was born in 1620 on the 6th of March. My father was a rich merchant of Bagdad named Abon Yataphan. My mother was a Hindu and I was born in Hindustan though I afterward went with my father to Bagdad. She died when I was seven years old.

"When I was twenty my father wished me to be a merchant but I ran away to see on a ship belonging to Abdullah Houssain. My father died a year after that from heart disease leaving me all his possessions.

"When I was twenty-five I became a captain in Abdullah's employ and have kept my position there five years."

Chapter XII

Toward the night, the storm, which had abated in some measure during the day, now abated completely and the wind went down leaving the ship to drift about as she or her crew pleased. No sign of land could be discerned.

All clouds had vanished, and the sun was setting. Half of its fiery sphere was out of sight behind the water when Akmat who happened to be on deck at that time, saw in clear outline against the western horizon, the very ship that had passed them homeward bound, not many miles from the mouth of the river Tigris.

A breeze from the south came up just then and the "Serpent" was turned in her tracks and sailed northward for more than a quarter of a mile.

The strange ship tacked about in the wind and followed suit. No flag could be seen on her. Everything which would betoken her nationality was out of sight.

"Why are they following us?" thought Akmat to himself. After thinking a few moments he let the matter go and went below just as Mustapha and the captain came on deck.

The sun had nearly set. The first thing that caught their eyes was the ship which seemed to be following them.

"That is the strange craft we passed in the Persian Gulf," said the captain. "How is it that they have been brought here by the storm? By all the rules of navigation they should have been safe in the river Tigris or some harbor of Arabia by the time that storm came upon us. How do you account for it, Mustapha?"

"It is either a coincidence or they are following us for some purpose."

"But why should a merchant craft follow another through such seas as we have had? What might be the object in taking such a course?"

"We have prisoners on board," ventured Mustapha.

"Yes, but how could they know it? We arrested these men only yesterday."

"Still, I cannot but think that it has something to do with these men."

"I fervently hope it does not," said the captain.

"I can but hope that too, whatever the outcome may be," replied Mustapha.

At that moment they saw a pigeon alight on the bulwark not far from them. It was of a bluish-white color and attached to one of its legs was a little white roll.

"Let's watch it," said the captain. The bird did not seem to be afraid of them but flew quite close. Finally it alighted on Mustapha's shoulder, and pecked his cheek.

Angry at this, and wishing to know what the white roll was, he put up his hand and grasped the bird. It made no objection.

He next drew his dagger and cut the packet from the pigeon leg and unrolled it. It was a piece of fine parchment written on one side only.

Mustapha could not make anything out of the jumble of words that met his eye. They were Turkish but he could make no sense out of the sentences. The message, if it was one, was as follows: "We if will we attack are the not ship able five to days rescue from you now. Jump if overboard possible you. Have will no be fear picked answer up this by message our by men the. If pigeon we if cannot you attack have we anything will to let say. You ———— know."

"What can such a jumble mean?" said the captain, looking at the message. "Do you understand it?"

"Not at present," replied Mustapha, "but perhaps I may after a while."

"Read it backward," suggested Baber. Mustapha tried it but the combination "know you say let to will," did not sound more promising than the original.

Mustapha finally gave it up in despair and handed it to his companion. Baber could no more understand it than he, so he gave it back to the Turk. That person folded it carefully, slipped it into his pocket and closed the matter with ado.

The captain was about to reopen a conversation on the subject when his attention was attracted by a strange commotion in the water not far from the ship.

Some oblong object gray in color and very shiny was floating about in the sea. A present-day man would have called it cigar-shaped. It was about 15 feet in length and 6 feet at the center, tapering to a sharp point at the end.

Half of this object was above water and the rest was submerged. A dozen sea-birds were flying about it, screaming with rage and terror. The cause of this was soon apparent.

An ugly head appeared on the waterline and some strange creature slowly drew itself out of the sea. It was a gigantic species of crab with the fore part of its body somewhat like a lobster.

In its claws it held a young gull which was vainly trying to escape. This was why the sea-birds had been screaming.

As Mustapha looked on much astonished he saw at once what must have happened.

The crab, or whatever it was, had been running itself on the oblong object when a flock of birds had come flying past and one had swooped down upon the crab, knocking it into the sea. The crab had caught hold of the bird's leg as it went overboard and had not been able to get away. Its screams had brought its companions back, and they were now trying to kill the crab.

Filled with pity for the poor creature Mustapha called for a pistol and one of the sailors brought him one.

He levelled it at the crab's body and then fired. The smoke and the confusion among the birds which followed was astonishing to him. The whole flock with one accord flew away uttering wild cries and were soon out of sight.

The crab had been hit by the bullet and instantly dropped its prey. The bird made a feeble attempt to fly and indeed went quite a distance into the air and then fell, completely exhausted, directly at Mustapha's feet. The crab had disappeared.

Mustapha picked up the gull and glanced at the strange object in the sea. To his astonishment it was far astern, and almost out of sight. Suddenly it shot into the air revealing its full length and then plunged into the sea again point foremost and disappeared from sight.

"What could that have been?" said Mustapha addressing the captain who had been looking on.

"I could never tell you," replied Baber. "It's beyond me."

He glanced in the direction where the merchant craft had been a few moments before. It was still following them, but was at least three miles away.

"What can it mean?" thought Mustapha.

"What are you going to do with that gull?" asked the captain, turning the conversation into another channel.

"The first thing I'm going to do is to bandage its foot."

A sailor who was nearby offered him a strip of cloth. He accomplished the task of bandaging the wound very well, and though the bird was much frightened it seemed to comprehend that he would do it no harm.

"Hello, what's this?" said Mustapha who had been examining its wings. Directly under the left wing he had found a little piece of parchment tied to one of the feathers.

He removed it and then set the bird at liberty. It flew away and was soon out of sight. Then he unrolled the parchment. A number of strange looking characters were on it. He could not understand them. He handed it to Baber. Baber did not understand either.

"What do you suppose it means?" asked Mustapha.

"I could never tell you," was Baber's reply. "It looks to me like Chinese writing, though I don't think it is."

Mustapha took it and glanced over it again. It was as follows:

"Read it backwards," suggested Mustapha after awhile. "We will begin with the right hand end of the first line and see how it is."

He tried it. "Ah! That is the way it runs," said he.

"You are right," said the captain peering over his shoulder. Mustapha read it through to the end and then read it as it would have been had it been written in the usual manner. It was as follows:

"To you, High Priest of the Fire-Worshippers, I send greeting on this day of July 2, of the year 1650.

"Nothing of note has occurred since I last met you in Bagdad the day before you embarked. I have sent the diamonds to their destination where I trust you will soon arrive with the prisoners."

"Thy Faithful Servant,

"_____,"

"Member of the Fire-Worshippers."

"To you, High Priest of the Fire-Worshippers, I send greeting on this day of July 2, of the year 1650.

"Nothing of note has occurred since I last met you in Bagdad the day before you embarked. I have sent the diamonds to their destination where I trust you will soon arrive with the prisoners."

"Thy Faithful Servant,

"_____,"

"Member of the Fire-Worshippers."

"Well done, Mustapha, well done!" said the captain enthusiastically when his companion had finished reading. "I could never have done that myself."

"I fancy I did very well," said Mustapha, "but what are we to gain from this message?"

"I don't know," said Baber.

"I see this much," said Mustapha. "The gull that carried this message is trained to fly to a certain ship—the ship that Abdullah Houssain must have embarked on. We already know that he is the Priest of the Fire-Worshippers, so it is certain that it is intended for him.

"In all probability Abdullah is on board the ship that has been following us. The gull, in its search for this ship, fell in with a number of its kind and journeyed on with them till it fell into the clutches of the crab from which we rescued it. So much is clear. Did you notice which way the bird flew when I released it?"

"It flew toward the strange ship," said Baber. "That much I noticed."

"Ah! Then my statement is true. The proof points that way.

"I also know from the message that the diamonds have been sent to some place, presumably the temple of the Fire-Worshippers where Abdullah is expected with some prisoners. My friends and I are probably the prisoners. That means that this ship will be attacked by the one which has Abdullah on board."

"I cannot but think that you are right," said the captain, with a groan.

"Why not turn the ship about and sail toward them? If they are friends they will not alter their course, but if they are enemies they will sail the other direction."

"Quite right," said Baber, and he shouted an order to the sailors and to the helmsman.

Instantly the ship turned in her tracks and sailed towards the strange vessel. There was little wind and the sun had gone down. Its light, still above the horizon lighted the scene.

Scarcely had the "Serpent" turned when the other ship was seen to do the same.

"Haul every sail into service!" yelled Baber to the sailors. "We'll find out why a strange ship tries to evade us."

Faster and faster went the "Serpent" until the spray she sent flying in sheets of foam flew all over her decks.

The strange ship was making every effort to escape but the other gained steadily for awhile. Then the breeze went down altogether and the "Serpent" drifted idly on the surface of the waters. The sea was calm and not a vestige of land could be seen.

A flock of sea-birds flew overhead in the light of the waning twilight and their mournful cries added materially to the impressiveness of the scene, and made it seem more lonesome and weird.

Five minutes later the darkness began to lower and the watch took their places on deck. The captain went below to eat his evening meal but still Mustapha lingered near the bulwarks watching the stars appear one by one. Then over the waters he saw a strange and silvern light and then something golden-red like a fire on the eastern horizon. Larger and larger this grew until a massive golden ball of spherical shape seemed to lift itself above the ocean, and Mustapha knew that the new moon had risen.

The pale light shone on his dark face as he stood there, and to an observer at a distance he might have seemed the image of Buddha, so silent and motionless was his body.

Then, feeling hungry he stepped from his position and slowly walked to the hatchway, only a few steps away.

He descended down the little stairway and found himself at the open door of the captain's cabin.

The light of a lamp shone upon him and he heard the voices of his friends in merriment as they conversed of various subjects.

"What is the matter with you, Mustapha?" asked his uncle. "You don't seem to be hungry to-night. You've been watching the new moon rise, I suppose?"

"Yes," replied Mustapha. "I stayed on deck for that purpose and was so rapt in my own thoughts that I little thought of eating. I am hungry enough, however, to pay justice to a hearty meal."

"We've just finished supper," said the captain, "but I'll order the cook to send in more food. You are not averse to a bottle or two of good wine, are you?"

"Not at all," said Mustapha. "I am not a habitual or heavy drinker, but I do not mind a little once in awhile."

"What kind do you like best? I am an epicure on the subject of wines and have a good supply of all kinds, both European and Oriental. What kind do you like?"

"White wine of any kind, provided it is not too sour."

"I can give you sweet wine if you wish it?"

"No, not too sweet, nor too sour. A mixture between the two, and white of color is what I like best."

"Very well. I prefer red wine. What is your favorite, Ahmed?" Ahmed had been much shaken about by the storm and this had not done his wound any good. However, he was able to sit up in his bed and talk and eat with the rest. The physician had said he would be able to stand in less than two weeks. As the bullets had not touched any vital organ the wound was not so serious as had been supposed at first.

"White wine, very sour," said Ahmed in reply to Baber's question.

"What kind do you want?" said the captain, turning to Cassim.

"Red wine, sweet," said that person.

"And you?" to Harun.

"White wine, very sour."

"And you?" to Emir.

"The same."

"And you?" to Akmat.

"I do not wish any kind of wine. I will take water."

"So you are an abstainer? I never would have thought it."

"Not always. I drink sometimes, however. I made a vow when I was twenty years of age never to touch any kind of liquor more than twice in the year, and I have kept that vow. This year I have drunk twice, and am not free to drink again till the first day of January, 1651."

"What a strange resolution. I can hardly wonder at it, however, for I have observed that you are of a very eccentric temperament. Pray tell us what other vows you have made?"

"With pleasure. I have vowed never to marry unless I can marry a princess."

"Ha! Ha! Ha! Any more?"

"Yes; several. I pray you not to laugh if I relate them."

"Certainly I won't," replied the captain. "I am master of my laughter. If I were not I wouldn't be fit to be master of anything."

"I notice that you have many several sayings at your tongue's end. Before I relate my vows pray tell us your motto."

"I have many and I know not which is the best. I will send an order for the wine I desire for myself and my friends before we go on with our conversation." Here Baber tapped a bell on the table and an African appeared in the doorway.

"Go to my store of wines and bring a pint bottle of white wine, neither very sour nor sweet, a pint bottle of red wine, sour, a pint bottle of white wine, very sour, a pint bottle of red wine, sweet, two pint bottles of white wine, very sour, and a quart bottle of mineral water from the Himalayas. Each has a label on it so you will have no trouble. Can you remember all that?"

"You have a good memory," remarked Mustapha to the captain, as they waited for the wines.

"Yes, my father had, and I have inherited it. What do you want for your supper, Mustapha?" he went on.

"I don't know exactly what I do want. Fruit and meat are what I like."

"What kind of fruit and what kind of meat?"

"Anything except figs and salt pork. I do not like them."

"Well, here comes the servant with the wines."

The servant entered at that moment with the desired articles on a tray. This he laid upon the table and awaited further orders."

"Go to the cook and tell him that I want him to send in some hot vegetable soup, and half a leg of boiled mutton."

The man went away on his errand and the party helped themselves to the wine which the captain poured out into small glasses. He also passed a tray filled with fruit to Mustapha, who selected what he wanted and ate it with the wine.

Before long the servant returned with the soup and meat and set it on the table.

Mustapha helped himself and as he was very hungry did honor to the simple dish.

There was very little left when he had finished twenty minutes later, and the servant found scarce any food to remove when he came to take the dishes to the cook's gallery.

When the table had been cleared they sat a few minutes longer to finish the wines. When this was done the servant came to take away the empty bottles and the tray.

"Now it is time for you to tell us what other vows you made," said Baber turning to Akmat.

That person instantly complied by saying:

"Certainly I will. I vowed not to eat fish more than ten times a year and not to speak to a Buddist priest until I had met him three times. That is all, I think. Now tell us your motto or mottoes please. Which do you consider the best?"

"'Nothing is impossible' is the one I like best, though I know not whether it really is the best."

"Well, what other one? You said there were several."

"'Don't fight until you know how' is another."

"Very good. Tell us one more and I'll let you go."

"Of course, but you must keep your promise. Here it is: 'Don't die till the sun goes down.'"

"I never heard that before. I know that a snake doesn't die till the setting of the sun."

"Then it ought to apply to any ship called the 'Serpent,' or any other variety of reptile."

"Explain it please?"

"Don't you understand? It means that a man should not give up hope till all chance of success is gone."

"Very good. I like that one the best of all."

"Perhaps it is the best, but I like the first one I mentioned better."

For two hours they talked on, Mustapha and the captain telling of what they had seen and showing both of the strange messages which had so strangely fallen into their hands.

"I cannot imagine," said the captain, "how this storm carried us through the Strait of Ormuz without taking us close to the land. I do not know exactly where we are, but I think we are not far from the Arabian coast. The compass tells me that we are bound eastward, but as I have seen no land all my charts can be of little avail. It is said that there is a difference in the color of the water of different seas and oceans. The water we are on now is green just the same as that of any other salt water I have encountered, so I think we are in the Indian ocean. If we see land I shall consult my charts and maps and learn our exact position."

"Is it not time to retire?" asked Mustapha breaking into the conversation.

"Yes," replied the captain and within five minutes all were in bed, Akmat sleeping with the captain, Mustapha in the apartment of the three spies, and the rest on rugs and couches.

Chapter XIII

Somehow or other Mustapha could not sleep and toward midnight he arose and dressed and went on deck. Hoping that the fresh sea air would prepare him for sleep when he should return to his couch he strolled around the deck and watched the men of the watch.

The moon was high, high overhead and its pale golden light illuminated the ship, and was in the sea, being much distorted, however, by the action of the waves.

Mustapha glanced to the westward and saw in the distance the mysterious ship which had steadfastly followed them on the proceeding day, and which had sailed in the opposite direction when they had turned.

A light breeze had risen and both ships were borne onward rapidly.

Not a cloud was in sight, and the scene could not have been more peaceful.

Nothing but water in sight and the stars and the moon overhead shining in silent majesty.

Mustapha's feelings were strangely affected by such surroundings, but he wondered at such an occurrence. Perhaps it was the loneliness of the scene and perhaps it was something else,—no one knows what,—but he was so fascinated that he remained on deck much longer than he had originally intended.

At any rate the moon was an hour farther from the position he had found it in when he had come on deck, when he descended the staircase and found himself in the little corridor into which the door of the spies' room entered.

Everything was dark within and his first act was to light a small taper which he set in the mouth of the overturned lamp. This lamp was lying on the floor in the exact position it had occupied after the fight. No one had taken the trouble to pick it up or remove it.

Mustapha then undressed and retired. He could not sleep however and his busy thoughts kept him awake till dawn, when he arose and went to the captain's cabin. The sun had not yet risen.

His cousins and the captain had already risen and dressed themselves and were talking of various matters.

Preparations for breakfast were evidently going on in the cook's gallery, and after exchanging greeting with his comrades Mustapha set off for that part of the ship without delay to have a private talk with his friend, Alzim, the cook.

He found Alzim preparing some meat with a man helping him. This man had a very peculiar appearance and was very short and somewhat stout. His face was grave and it seemed as if it had never known a smile. It was of a fiery bronze in hue.

The man's hair was of a deep red color, and his eyes were of a changing color, now dark green and now shining black, whatever way the light happened to strike them. Red hair was very rare among Orientals, so Mustapha was somewhat puzzled. The shape and general contour of the face was Oriental and yet not Oriental. It seemed to shift with the changing color of the eyes.

"Good morning, sir," said the cook.

"The same to you," said Mustapha. "How is your health to-day, my friend?"

"It is in excellent condition. Pray tell me the state of yours."

"It is the same."

"Good. I would like to introduce you to my friend and assistant, Pir Khan, if it is not presuming on your patience."

"Certainly not. I would be delighted to meet your friend, even if he is not of my station in life. I would deem it an injustice not to speak to a man whoever he is unless he was my worst enemy."

"This man, Pir, is Mustapha Dagh, to whom you will remember I am indebted for my life. I told you the story last night," said Alzim.

"Ah! I remember," said the little man. "I am greatly honored, sir, by your deigning to speak to such a worm of the dust as I."

"Not at all, my good friend. I presume you are a Turk?" Mustapha went on. "Pardon my impudence in asking the question, but what nationality do you belong to?"

The little man drew himself up proudly. "I am a Greek," he said.

"Then when did you get the Hindu name, 'Pir Khan'?"

"I assumed it, sir. My real name is Alexis Pontoff. I am a man of considerable wealth and position among my own people, but I left my home a few years ago and set out to see the world. After a year's voyaging I found myself out of funds and being unwilling to send home for more I secured a place as cook's assistance on board this ship at Bagdad not many days ago. That, sir, is a brief sketch of my adventures, sir."

"Well you have certainly had hard luck," observed Mustapha.

"You may call it hard, sir, but to me it is delightful. I take great pleasure in such adventures."

"Perhaps you do, but I have had stranger adventures than that," and here Mustapha told the story of all his adventures, from the time a shabby man sold him a black diamond for a piece of gold up to the present date.

Both Alzim and Alexis Pontoff listened with great attention. Such a story they had never heard before in all their lives. "Marvelous!" ejaculated Alexis when he had finished. "I don't see how you could have survived such perils."

"Well, I must go back to my friends now," said Mustapha and bidding them good-bye he left the room and stepped forth into the corridor and shut the door behind him.

Just as he did so a pigeon flew past him bound he knew not where. It was very large and of a grayish blue color.

Under its right wing he could see a tiny packet almost the same size as the one carried by the bird of the day before. No doubt now remained in his mind that the men on board the strange ship that was following them were trying to communicate with the prisoners.

As soon as this thought entered his mind he set off in pursuit of the bird, which was almost out of sight. At the end of the corridor was an open door through which the bird flew, and through which he followed and found himself in the forecastle of the ship.

The room was very long and wide and had two doors—the one Mustapha had entered by and another at the other end. This one was open.

Against each wall was a row of berths only a few feet above the floor. Several feet above this was another row. These berths were scarcely large enough to contain a man over six feet in length. It was evident that no space had been wasted in their construction.

In many of these beds sailors were slumbering but most had awakened and had dressed themselves. They were standing about in groups talking among themselves or were sitting on stools.

In the center of the forecastle stood a long table about which were ranged stools in regular rows. It was evident that the sailors were waiting for their breakfast.

The pigeon's appearance in the room followed by that of Mustapha was the cause of much astonishment among the mariners. One made an attempt to catch the bird, but failed and it dashed through the open door.

The sailors recognized Mustapha and made room for him to pass as he rushed through their midst and reached the door through which the pigeon had flown but a moment before.

Here he found himself at the top of a short stairway which led into the hold of the ship where the prisoners and other supplies were stowed.

It was dark here and he had nothing to guide him except the flutter of the bird wings. It had disappeared in a mass of huge barrels and boxes, which he could dimly see in the faint light.

Down the stairway he went in two jumps and tripped himself against a cask in the darkness. He fell forward and landed on something very hard. It was a small bag of rock salt. From this unfortunate mixup he recovered himself and rushed on determined to catch that pigeon.

The next thing he knew down he went again. It was a coil of rope in which he had entangled his foot. He was precipitated forward as before and landed against a cask of water, his head being the first portion of his anatomy to collide with this formidable object.

For a brief space of time he saw stars and was even able to count the points on one of them. There were three.

In spite of efforts to curb his rising temper he was rapidly losing it. He struggled to his feet struggling against a threatening tide of profanity and rushed on.

That rope in which he had been entangled was not to lose its victim so soon, though. His foot was thoroughly caught and the rope hung on stubbornly and refused to be kicked off.

A large portion of it straightened out and dragged along behind him. For a short space of time he did not collide with anything and was beginning to think that he was out of the neighborhood of casks, bags and boxes.

Suddenly he received an unexpected check. The end of the dragging rope had caught in some object and Mustapha was thrown violently forward. He put out his hands to break the shock, but where they should have touched the floor, they touched nothing.

His whole body seemed to fall through some opening and the next thing he knew he was hanging by his left ankle, head-downward in some pit.

In a flash he realized that he had fallen through some trap-door in the darkness. What was beneath him he did not know, but he did know that his ankle pained him most acutely. The strain was so great that he feared that the bone was broken. Also, he was in a most dangerous position.

The rope was not thick and might break at any moment. Then, too, the object in which it was caught might release it at any moment. In either case he would come off with a broken neck. He thought very quickly and at last formed a plan of escape. If there was a trap-door there must be a ladder, he said to himself.

At any rate there could be no harm in finding out. The first thing he did was to reach out his hand as far as he could. It touched nothing. Then he reached out the other arm in the opposite direction. His fingers touched and closed upon an iron rung. Then he swung his body around and grasped it with both hands and then shouted for help.

He heard an answering shout and saw a light. Next moment someone was looking down at him and holding a torch.

"Can you hold on if we cut the rope?" said a voice.

"Yes, yes," said he in response.

A few seconds later his ankle was suddenly released and his legs and body came down to a more natural position. The shock was not so bad as he had thought it would be.

He put the injured foot on a rung and and commenced to climb. The next moment he wished that he had not. A spasm of acute pain permeated the injured ankle, and he almost shrieked in agony.

No need to say that he put the other foot in its place without delay. A few rungs and he was pulled up onto the floor of the stateroom and saw the cause of his fall. The light rope had a large knot tied in its end. A huge iron box stood nearby and had been raised from the floor about half an inch by square bars of iron.

The end of one of these was somewhat irregular and the knot in the end of the rope had been caught under a small depression.

A strange coincidence this seemed but the cause was soon to be explained to Mustapha. The large iron box was about five feet high and six feet long, a very extraordinary size. It was not over four feet wide.

The sailor who had rescued Mustapha from his perilous position assisted him to walk up the stairway. He was not able to use the ankle that he had injured but he managed to hop along on one foot assisted by the sailors.

They conducted him through the forecastle, and the corridor past the cook's apartment up the stairway at the end of this, and then on deck. A few steps brought them to the hatchway that led to the captain's room. Down the companion way they went through the short corridor and into the cabin where Baber and his companions were beginning breakfast, being waited upon by a negro boy.

"Well!" began the captain in his astonishment; "what does all this mean?"

Mustapha hobbled to a chair and seated himself while the sailor lingered in the doorway.

"You are lame!" said Akmat coming over to him.

"Yes," said Mustapha, and he told them what had happened to him.

"You are certainly unfortunate," said Baber. "Your ankle is badly sprained. You will not be able to walk again for a week."

"Yes, it ought to be attended to now. Summon the physician, boy." This was Akmat's utterance and the command was addressed to the waiter.

The lad bowed and left the room soon returning with the desired person. He was quickly informed of what had happened and asked to see the wounded ankle. It was badly swollen and he announced it to be only a bad sprain, as Akmat had said. He then bandaged it with a soft cloth saturated with some liquid.

"You will be well in a week or two if you do not attempt to stand. I will come again to-morrow and apply another cloth, and I warn you not to remove the bandage without my order," he said and left the room.

The captain then turned to the sailors and dismissed them, speaking a few words of praise on their conduct in releasing Mustapha.

"You must be hungry," he said turning to that person.

"Of course," was the reply and the Turk drew his chair closer to the table and ate in silence.

His cousins did so also. Ahmed had not yet awakened. Baber ate with the rest. The meal was very silent till near the end, when Mustapha broke the quiet by saying:

"What is that huge iron box, which caught the rope, for?"

"That's where I have confined Kerrim the spy. The other two are locked up in similar receptables at a distance from each other. There are holes in the bottom of these boxes to let in air, but we had to raise them to let the air reach these holes. It was a lucky thing for you that that rope was caught, else you would not have got off so easy as you did. A broken arm would have been the least injury you would have received. The place into which the trap-door opened is the very bottom of the ship where the ballast is."

"Where could the pigeon have gone to and where did it come from?"

"It is probably one of Abdullah's messengers which he has sent to the spies with some message."

Just then a sailor walked into the room with the bird in his hands. He handed it to Mustapha, saying:

"Here's the bird you were chasing, sir. I found it among the casks and boxes in the hold. It had lost its way in the dark and couldn't escape me."

"Thank you," said Mustapha. He put his hand into his pocket as if in search of something and drew out a small silver coin. It had been there ever since the time our story begins.

This he handed to the man.

The sailor thanked him and left the room.

Mustapha lifted the pigeon's wing and saw the roll of parchment. It was tied to the feathers by a thin cord. This cord he cut with his dagger and removed the parchment and handed the pigeon to Akmat.

He unrolled the parchment and saw that the message was written backward just the same as the one carried by the sea-bird. It read when translated, as follows:

"To my friend Kerrim Beg, I send my best greeting.

"I sent a message to you by the pigeon not long ago, but as I received no answer, I think that it must have been intercepted. Whatever the case was I will tell you what the bulk of the contents were: We will attack Baber Yataghan's ship five days from now if possible. If they suspect you jump overboard and our men will rescue you. That was the bulk of the message. We sent it out two days ago so the attack will be made three days from now. There is no possibility that we will not attack on the day mentioned.

"I hope that you and your companions are in good health. I am, at least. I think that a trip on the sea does me good. I feel much better now than I did when I left Bagdad. The guns on our ship are all in readiness, the sailors are spoiling for a fight, and in short everything is ready for the coming battle.

"Your Friend,
"Abdullah Houssain."

"So they're going to attack us, are they? Abdullah Houssain is my master no more! Under the flag of Turkey at my masthead I fly his merchant flag. I will have it torn down instantly."

He called a sailor and gave an order. The man ran on deck and pulled a rope. Down came the offending flag. It was of white silk and no other color, and was in the shape of a pennant.

He brought it to the captain who thanked him and dismissed him from the room.

"Bring me pen and ink," said Baber. Harun handed him the required articles. The captain wrote upon the white silk a few minutes though it was much weather-beaten. Then he read what he had written to his friends. It was in Turkish and was as follows:

"To you, Abdullah Houssain, I send a greeting of hate.

"I have had your message to the three spies intercepted and read. My friend, Mustapha Dagh, translated it to us. Of the spies I will say nothing. You can attack us in five days if you wish, but I will not fight you under your own banner. I am sending it to you with this message written upon it by the pigeon. I am no longer your servant. I consider that this ship belongs to me more than to you.

"Your Enemy,
"Baber Yataghan."

"That will not please him," said Mustapha.
"Indeed it will not," replied the captain.
"What will he do?" inquired Cassim.

"Will he hasten the attack?" interrogated Harun.

"Will he believe what you have written?" asked Akmat.

"I don't know what he will do," said the captain in reply to the first question. "I do not know whether he will hasten the attack or not, but I think it probable that he will. He will believe my words or I am much mistaken."

"What will you do do in case of an attempted attack?"

"Try to escape. We can give his ship a long chase before she catches us," said Baber.

"I hope that my foot will be well by the time that event occurs," said Mustapha.

"If I am not much mistaken your ankle will be entirely cured by that time. At least I can but I hope with you that it will."

Here the captain rolled up the pennant and tied it under the pigeon's wing. He then took the bird on deck and released it.

As soon as it found itself free it flew away in the direction of Abdullah's ship which was still three miles away. He watched it until it disappeared and then rejoined his companions.

"The pigeon has returned to its master," he said. "I marvel at the number of creatures he employs to do his work and run his errands. Altogether, he has about 100 servants in his employ at Bagdad, and he owns at least a dozen ships. His wealth is said to be illimitable. Why he has taken it into his head to steal a couple of diamonds from you I do not know, but he has some reason, good or evil.

"It is also evident that he fears you and wishes to get rid of you. He gives you to me as slaves with an order to dump you overboard someplace in the Chinese seas, but I will not do such a thing. I do not tell him so, but take you with me with the intention of putting you ashore someplace.

"Somehow or other Abdullah changes his mind during the night and sets off on board another of his ships.

"He turns backward in the Persian gulf just before the storm. He raises some sort of a signal to the spies whom we are trying for blackmail and belonging to the 'Fire-Worshippers.'

"During the storm he manages to keep track of us and is now following us.

"He will probably attack by to-morrow. Such is the case." Here the captain stopped speaking for a sailor had entered the room and was asking for permission to speak.

"Well, what is it?" said Baber. The sailor replied in a very excited tone:

"Sir, the strange ship is putting on all sail to catch up with us. Shall we wait for her?"

Chapter XIV

"Put on all sail to escape her!" said Baber in a whirl of excitement. "Don't let her catch us! I'll go with you and tell the men what to do."

"Yes, sir," said the sailor and rushed on deck followed by the excited captain.

Akmat, who was anxious to see what was happening, followed him without delay.

He found Baber in the act of issuing an order to hoist every sail. A slight breeze was blowing. Not more than two miles away to the west was the strange ship which the captain and his friends had good reason to believe, contained Abdullah Houssain.

This ship was evidently trying very hard to overhaul them. Every sail she could muster was in the wind and she came flying along with great speed.

In a few minutes every available bit of canvas on the "Serpent" was in use and, she, too, went flying rapidly along.

For half an hour it seemed as if she would escape, but the pursuing ship rapidly gained after that and the fugitive soon saw that she would be up with them within an hour if the wind did not increase.

Unfortunately, the unobliging wind did no such thing. On the contrary it degenerated into the faintest motion worthy of the name of "breeze," and this greatly retarded the speed of the "Serpent."

But, naturally, it had much the same effect on the pursuing vessel. "It's an ill wind that blows nobody good" had its application in this case. For, though slight as this good was, it gave the crew of the fugitive ship time to prepare for the seemingly inevitable battle.

Baber, aided by Akmat, assisted the sailors in bringing ammunition on deck and in other matters. Muskets from the hold were brought up and placed in stacks with bags of powder, bullets and slugs near at hand.

By the time everything was ready the strange ship was within half a mile of the "Serpent."

It was evident that preparations for a battle had been taking place on board her too, for all her cannons were ready and the men on her deck were armed.

Akmat went below and informed his brothers and Mustapha of what had happened. Mustapha drew his scimitar and saw that it was ready for service. Even if he could not walk he could strike a blow or two if it came to the worst.

He also examined his pistols and loaded both with an extra-heavy charge. Then he calmly seated himself and watched his cousins go through a similar performance.

By the time each had finished with his weapon, they heard the roar of a cannon, followed by a volley of musketry. The battle had begun.

Akmat and all the others except Mustapha and Ahmed went on deck. Mustapha was half-sitting, half-standing, with a pistol in each hand when they left him. Ahmed had been given a pistol, and was sitting up in bed with his motionless eyes fixed on the open door of the cabin.

Akmat and his brothers found that Abdullah's vessel was only a hundred yards distant. The cannon-shot had been fired by her crew, but the volley of musketry had been the answer from the "Serpent."

A strong breeze had just risen and both ships were carried along at a lively pace, though the distance between them gradually lessened.

A period of silence proceeded the shots and was broken by the strange vessel with a double volley of musketry.

Few of the balls struck the "Serpent" but the remainder struck the water not thirty feet from her side.

"Those muskets were not heavily loaded," observed Baber. "Next time the bullets will do some damage."

There was no answering shot from the "Serpent" and the strange ship came on till she was within fifty yards of her antagonist.

Then Baber gave the order to fire and a simultaneous roar from seven cannon broke the silence. Five or six of the balls took effect and the bulwarks of Abdullah's ship were badly splintered. Some of the rigging was also destroyed.

Baber walked to the stern of the ship. Here he ordered planks to be placed. He then gave an order to the gunner and then one to the helmsman. The ship suddenly swung around and her stern was pointed directly toward the center of the strange ship.

"Now is the time!" whispered the captain to the gunner. "Quick! aim at her main-mast. Now fire!" he roared.

Instantly there was an answering roar from the gun and the next moment the main-mast of the enemy's ship tottered in the wind and then fell, taking everything with it—rigging, sailors, bulwarks and many other things.

The wreckage hung over the side of the ship and retarded her motion greatly, besides keeping one side down in the water while the other was high in air.

Baber and his friends saw a dozen sailors armed with axes spring forward to clear away the wreckage, but he did not wait for further results but straighway issued an order to the sailors to turn the ship about and make away from the scene as fast as possible.

This course was north-east, as the captain deemed that the quickest direction to reach land. Akmat then went below and informed Mustapha that there was no present danger. He assisted him on deck and showed him what had happened to the pursuers' ship.

"It will be many hours before they will be ready to follow us in the state their ship is in now and by that time the captain hopes to reach land," he said.

"I fervently hope that it will be so," said Mustapha. "I hope at least that they will not catch us before my ankle is well."

By this time they were about a mile from the strange ship. Before long they were another mile away and by noon they were completely out of sight.

All were now seated at dinner talking over the events of the forenoon. Mustapha was eating a piece of bread and the Captain was drinking wine.

Suddenly there came a great shock as if some heavy body had collided with the ship. The room seemed topsy-turvy for a moment and when the whole party had partially recovered from their surprise and were about to ask each other: "What's the matter?", a frightened sailor burst into the room with the information that a great hole had been broken in the bottom of the ship, and she was filling rapidly.

"What shall we do?" said Baber wringing his hands in despair.

"Meet death like men," replied Mustapha, seemingly unmoved.

"It's all we can do," said the captain. "We had better go on deck and see what the chances of escaping are. If there are any signs of land we'll launch the boats and trust to luck to reach it safely."

Mustapha forgot his sprained ankle in the excitement of the moment and rushed after them. Ahmed leaped out of the bed and followed, buoyed up by the false strength of excitement.

Baber was the first one on deck and rushed for the bulwark shouting to the others that he saw land. Akmat was next and the rest in order. The first thing that met their gaze was the deck of the ship, then the sea and the sky and then something dark on the north-eastern horizon. The captain also observed that the bulwarks were not far from the water and that they had better lose no time.

There were four boats on board and three of these were found sufficient to hold the entire crew which consisted of forty men altogether while the remaining boat was quite sufficient to hold the captain and his party. Each sailor took with him, by the captain's order, a loaf of bread and a large cask of water and a large box of salt beef was placed in each boat, the captain's included. Every man had a loaded musket, two pistols, a scimitar, a dagger, a plentiful supply of ammunition, and half the crew had axes. In the captain's boat was an extra supply of ammunition and a chest of tools and other articles besides a good supply of food.

"Now pull for the land," ordered the captain. "It cannot be more than fifteen miles away. We ought to be safe by night."

In a very short space of time the boats had left the side of the "Serpent" and were being rowed toward the distant land on the horizon.

A quarter of a mile from the ship they looked back and were just in time to catch a last glimpse of her as she sank beneath the waters, her stern being the last part to disappear.

"We will never see the three spies again in this world," remarked the captain when he saw that the ship had sunk.

"No, not in this world," said Mustapha.

"Nor in the next, either," said his uncle.

"It was a horrible thing to do," said the captain, "but I think that if we had brought them with us they would have tried to betray us into the hands of our enemies."

"And probably have succeeded," replied Mustapha.

"But at the cost of their own lives," retorted Baber.

"Then it is just as well that they are dead now. If we had received them they would have betrayed us. They have only met death a few days sooner, perhaps only a few hours. They have met a much more merciful death than the law would have given them if such a storm had not come upon us in the Persian Gulf."

"Quite right, Mustapha; you would make a good philosopher," said Emir joining the conversation.

"It is not often that you pay me compliments, Emir," replied Mustapha, "and I cannot say that you would make a good professional flatterer. Your flattery is so blunt and outspoken that your victim knows in an instant what you are trying to do."

"Yet it is not the less honest and sincere," retorted Emir, feeling a little piqued at the sally though he did not show it, being too much of a gentleman.

"I did not say that it was not, did I?" said Mustapha.

"No, but I thought you did," returned his cousin. "My imagination makes me believe things that were not said."

"Naturally. It is a sign that the Hindus have strong imaginations. People have said so, but I never had much experience regarding the matter before."

"So you have entered the profession of flatterers, have you?" said Emir seeing through the ill-disguised compliment.

"Yes, it pays well," said Mustapha impudently.

"Who told you so?"

"You did."

"When?"

"About a minute ago."

"I did not know it."

"You were not thinking about it at the time."

"Explain the enigma you have set me."

"Why should I?"

"Because I cannot solve it."

"At least you can try."

"I can't think of any solution."

"Fall back upon your imagination."

"Why?"

"Because it is a good resource in such emergencies."

"I suppose I must."

"Of course. Hurry up."

"Well, give me time."

"Vivid imaginations like yours should not require much time to solve such a simple problem."

"I fear I do not quite understand you."

"Stupid! I suppose I must explain my puzzle after all," said Mustapha in disgust.

"Yes. You had better."

"I mean that you could imagine something very quickly if you wanted to."

"So that's what you were trying to make me understand."

"Of course. You should have seen it in an instant."

"I saw that, but I thought the real meaning might be underneath."

"Then I must apologize for calling you 'Stupid.'"

"I accept your apology."

"Now solve the original puzzle I set you."

"I cannot. It is impossible."

"Then fall back upon our imagination."

"Very well. I imagine that you meant that the pay you would hope to receive would be the amusement you could have in flattering people."

"Of course. That is exactly what I meant."

"Very well. We'll drop the subject now. It is somewhat tiresome."

The foregoing is a brief specimen of the dialogue carried on by Mustapha and Akmat while they were being rowed to the land.

Emir and the captain, and Harun and Cassim rowed the boat while Mustapha and Ahmed rested.

"Let me take your place awhile," said Mustapha to Emir when they were several miles from the place where the ship had sunk.

"Very well," said Emir with a sigh of relief as he handed the oars to Mustapha. The unaccustomed exercise had taxed his strength greatly. He was a strong man but this was the first time he had rowed a boat for at least fifteen years.

Mustapha, on the contrary, was used to the exercise for he had rowed upon the river Tigris many a time.

He soon fell into his place with ease, and Emir watched him in amazement.

"I did not know that you could row a boat so well," he remarked.

"Well, it is nothing new to me," replied Mustapha. "I have rowed often just for pleasure. It is fortunate that I am used to it."

"I used to row on the rivers of my native land when I was a boy, but now I am out of practice," said Emir with a sigh.

"I would advise you to get in practice as soon as possible," said Mustapha. "It is one of the best exercises I know of."

"Then I will. You had better let me row again when we have gone a few miles more.

"I shall. Don't worry about it, however, till the time comes."

The sun was almost out of sight when they came within a hundred yards of the land they had seen from the ship. It was a small island very thickly covered with large trees and thick shrubs and bushes with hills all along the shore.

"Now we are safe," said the captain, and a few minutes later they stepped ashore and found themselves on dry land for the first time in many days.

"Haul the boats into this little cove," said Baber to the sailors. "Conceal them behind that clump of bushes, remove the provisions and other articles and follow me."

In five minutes all this was done and the sailors loaded with every movable article followed Baber up the hillside among the giant trees and bushes.

Fifteen minutes of walking brought them to the summit of the hill. Here they had a fine view of the island and were able to determine its extent.

In the center of the island stood a great hill completely surrounded by a narrow valley. The side of the hill they stood upon sloped steeply into this little valley, which was not more than a quarter of a mile in width at the bottom.

Half a mile distant, as the crow flies, was the top of the great hill which was higher than the one where our heroes were now standing. Its steep sides were clothed with great trees and bushes and several brooks thundered down them and flowed more smoothly in the valley, and then flowed into the sea through breaks in the chain of hills.

These hills surrounded the entire center of the island in regular order with regular breaks or valleys between each. If seen in a certain manner the whole island would have reminded you of a king's crown with a great mass of gold in the center towering above the points which surrounded it.

On the very top of this large hill was an open space in which stood the massive ruins of a castle. This added to the loneliness and impressiveness of the scene.

"Well, that old castle is our destination for tonight," said Baber. "In the morning we'll go to the other side of the island and see if there is any land in sight. If there is we'll row to it, and if there isn't we'll have to stay here till a ship comes along."

Then, without more ado the whole party set off to reach the castle. Down the steep hillside they went holding onto bushes and roots so as to avoid slipping. Then they went across the narrow valley fording two brooks and having much trouble in the marshy spots.

Mustapha did not have much trouble in walking for the captain and Emir assisted him one on each side.

Once across the valley their real troubles began. The steep hill was much steeper than the one they had just descended and was covered with very slippery rocks and grass on the treeless spots.

It was growing dark and the trunks of the trees could be dimly seen. More than one sailor collided with one, and let loose a flood of profanity, which cause Baber to rebuke him.

Suddenly Emir collided with a rock and went down. He had hold of Mustapha's arm, and the fall was so sudden that he had no time to let go so Mustapha went down too. Baber had hold of Mustapha's other arm and tried to prevent him from falling. In doing this he slipped on a small pebble which happened to be very loose. This suddenly caused him to fall on top of Mustapha and the party was complete.

When the sailor coming up assisted them to their feet Mustapha's ankle was worse than before and Emir's shins were very sore. Baber had received no harm but the incident made him feel somewhat angry and upset his temper.

Therefore he did not talk much the rest of the way. When they reached the ruined castle everyone was breathing hard and the whole party stopped to get their breaths before entering.

Then Baber gave the order to enter and they passed through a ruined gateway into a courtyard choked with small bushes and grass.

At the end of the courtyard was the great door of the castle wide open as it had been for many centuries. Through this they went and found themselves in a ruined hall gigantic and dark. Through this bats and vampires flitted and the cry of some small animal echoed through the vast corridor sounding loud in the almost unbroken silence.

Then Baber's voice joined and those of the sailors and the rest of the party. Then came silence again when they stopped speaking. The vampires startled and frightened by voices that had never echoed there for many years stopped flying and their gleaming eyes shone through the darkness like twinkling stars as their owners seated on cornice, crack or protruding stone or corner, viewed the intruders in astonishment and alarm.

Then the footsteps of the invaders broke the silence as they walked around in the darkness like the tread of an army. Soon they reached a doorway and the captain took a taper from his bosom and lighted it with powder and flint and steel.

The tiny light revealed a vast chamber before them with a gigantic fireplace at the end. Around this were rude stone benches and in the centre of the room was a great table of mahogany which showed no sign of decay. It was almost the same as it had been centuries ago when the owners of the castle had left, except that it was covered with dust.

Two or three small windows in the side of the room let in the twilight and this and the candle enabled the intruders to see very well, though the shadows in the corners were undisturbed.

Great benches of the same material surrounded the table, but they had no backs.

"Some of you go without," said Baber to the sailors, "and bring in wood to make a fire. The cold and musty appearance of the room is not at all cheerfull. Hurry for the sooner you do so the sooner you will get your supper."

Chapter XV

A dozen sailors armed with axes sprang to execute the order. They left the room and returned in ten minutes, laden with faggots and logs.

A fire was then built on the hearth and supper was cooked and eaten before another hour had gone by. Most of the sailors went to sleep on the stone floor, but the captain and his friends did not retire so soon.

On the contrary they sat up till midnight talking of their adventures and watching the dying embers of the fire and their flickering shadows on the wall. They heard the loud snoring of the sailors and saw their dim forms lying on the floor in the semi-darkness.

"Now," said Baber, "we will explore this ancient castle and learn our exact position."

"I am too tired to accompany you," said Ahmed.

"I will stay with you, then," said Mustapha. "I myself am tired and my ankle throbs painfully. I shall be asleep before you return. I will do my exploring in the morning when I am not so fatigued."

"Very well, then," said Baber. "Your cousins and I will do our exploring now, that is, if they will go with me."

"You may be sure that we would not lose such an opportunity, my dear friend," said Akmat. "I would not miss going with you for the world."

"I heartily agree with you, my brother," said Emir.

"So do I," said Harun.

"And I," said Cassim.

"Then our party is complete, except Mustapha and Ahmed," replied the captain.

Herewith he produced several small tapers, and reserving one for himself, he distributed the others among the brothers there being just enough to go around.

"Do not light them yet," said the captain, and followed by his companions he picked his way between the bodies of the crew. Finally they reached the opposite side of the room from the door of the hall by which they had entered.

Here there was a small door through which they went and found themselves in utter darkness. Baber lighted his taper and the others followed suit.

The light revealed to them a small room with couches and draperies, the draperies embroidered with beautiful designs concealing the bareness and roughness of the wall, and the couches made of mahogany and covered with beautiful silken robes, standing nearby, and close to the sides of the room. The silk of the draperies was musty and old and rotten, yet they still preserved reminders of their ancient splendor.

The floor was covered with woolen carpets from Persia beautifully made, yet they, too, like the draperies, and the cushions of the couches, had succumbed to the ravages of time.

They were torn in many spots and were covered with dust and filth and were almost rotten. The droppings of birds and the remains of swallow's nests littered them and did not improve their beauty by any means.

"It cannot have been fifty years since this castle was last inhabited by man," said Baber. "When I saw the exterior and the hall and the room the sailors are now sleeping in I thought that it must have been hundreds of years since it was last the home of human beings. But now I see my mistake. These carpets are of a recent date, for I recollect having seen similar specimens when I was a boy. A traveler, selling Persian carpets, came to our home and showed us his entire stock. He had several large rugs of the same pattern as these which he said had been woven in the year of 1600. The draperies and cushions, too, are of the same date. So, you see, this castle cannot have been vacated as long as we first supposed."

"You must be right," said Emir. "I am not much versed in carpet-lore, but I will accept your word. Had we not better be moving? It is past midnight now."

"Yes, we will go on now," said Baber and leading the way he entered another room similarly furnished. A staircase was at the end of this and up it they went.

At the top they came full against a closed door of dark-hued mahogany.

"This door is wonderfully preserved," remarked Baber.

"Yes, but that is not the real problem," replied Cassim. "The real one is to open this door if it is barred."

Here he gave it a vigorous push. There was no yielding and Cassim stepped back. "The inmates evidently bolted it when they vacated the premises. They must have been in a great hurry."

"All of us must put our shoulders to it and give one great push," said Baber.

Everyone in the party did as desired and the captain gave the word. Simultaneously five strong bodies, the captain included, gave one great push, and the door cracked.

"Again," said the captain. Once more they pushed and the door gave way a few inches.

"Again," was the order, and this time the door collapsed suddenly and all five followed it in a heap. The tapers which had been set upon the highest step of the stairway flickered in the slight breeze caused by such a commotion. The crash of the falling door awoke the sleeping sailors, who crowded into the room almost before Baber and his companions had scrambled to their feet.

"You had better go back to sleep," said the captain. "We are all right now, but you did quite right in coming to see what was happening."

The sailors instantly disappeared, talking among themselves, and the captain re-entered the room into which they had broken so rudely and unexpectedly.

The room was similar to that below except that it had windows. Through these the room could be seen shining. Far away was the sea, glimmering in the light of our nocturnal planet.

Coming toward the shore was a ship. But a ship is not such an extraordinary thing. But this was out of the commonplace because her mainmast had been broken off near the deck, and because Baber and his friends recognized in her the ship of Abdullah Houssain.

Akmat was frozen with astonishment and fear.

"They are going to land on this island," he exclaimed. "They will probably find our boats and will know that there are people here. They will come to this old castle and find us here. Allah only can help us then."

It was soon evident that the occupants of the ship were going to land. Just before they came under the hills of the seashore, where they could not be seen, a boat filled with men, was launched. The ship then cast anchor and the boat went on alone.

"There are at least fifteen men in that boat," said Baber. "If they come here we will take them prisoner and hold them as hostages. I hope that our dear friend Abdullah is among them. I would like to have the rascal in my hands."

"You may be sure that I entertain the same sentiments," said Akmat. "We will go down and inform the sailors of what is about to happen and get them ready for a possible fight."

Baber led the way and taking the tapers with them they went down the staircase and entered the great room.

Not a sailor had closed his eyes yet and the captain's excited face showed them that something of importance was about to take place.

"Well, what has happened?" said Mustapha, as they came up to him. Ahmed had fallen into a deep sleep. "I heard the crash of the door where you broke it down," he went on, "and I was about to come to see what was the matter but I was too slow and the sailors preceded me. They returned before I reached the door and told me of what had happened. I came back to my seat and when Ahmed heard my story he fell asleep."

Akmat gave a brief narration of what had happened. Mustapha heard him to the end with evident astonishment.

"Well, if there is liable to be a fight I won't allow my ankle to trouble me," he said, cheerfully.

"I have no doubt of that, Mustapha," said Cassim, "but it will do us no good if they come in great numbers. I think that we had better make a dash for the boats and carry them across the island and set off for the mainland. It will be a risky undertaking, though, and perhaps we had better not try it. At least we can hold out here for a week. There is, however, a chance that they will not find the boats. If not, I think we can consider ourselves safe, unless they have some object in coming here."

"Well, I will tell the sailors what to expect," said the captain. This was done and the sailors armed themselves and prepared for a fight.

Alzim came to Mustapha during the confusion.

"I have a strange foreboding of evil," he said. "I think that this will be my last night on earth. I have had forebodings of good and evil throughout my life, but never such a strong one as this. You may think me foolish or superstitious but I tell you that every foreboding has come true. I think that you, my friend, had better be on the alert."

Then he slipped away and was gone.

Mustapha was startled by such a strange warning and turned it over and over in his mind.

He did not allow himself to be frightened, however, yet he was strangely excited and agitated. He said nothing of what Alzim had said to his companions, but stood leaning against the table with one hand on the hilt of his scimitar while the other clutched a loaded pistol.

An hour of anxiety passed by—an hour which seemed an age to Baber and his friends. Suddenly a sailor made some noise by slipping on a stone and Mustapha turned to see what was the matter. Now he had been facing the door of the hall but when he turned he was facing the door at the other end of the room.

The fire in the fireplace had been stirred up and more wood piled on, and the cheerful blaze illuminated the doorway at which Mustapha gazed, frozen to the spot with astonishment and horror, for there stood Abdullah Houssain with a fiendish smile upon his face. A breastplate encircled his body and on his head was a metal cap with an eagle in brass on the top.

But his face was unguarded by any protection and neither were his legs. A richly jeweled scabbard hung by his side but it was empty, for his right hand held the sharp and curved scimitar which had recently occupied it. In his left hand was a cocked pistol and on his face was the fiendish smile before mentioned.

He was leaning against the wall in an easy manner and seemed to be regarding the armed men in the room with some amusement. Apparently he was alone.

Suddenly his gaze, which had been roving all over the room, fell upon Mustapha's face, and the fiendish smile deepened.

At that moment Akmat saw him and he communicated his intelligence to the others. In a very short time every sailor in the room knew the fact, but Abdullah still stood there and his body did not stir an inch though his eyes still roved about.

An ominous silence fell upon the room like a funeral pall and the occupants scarcely breathed. The only sound was the crackling of the fire and this was more distinct than ever.

Suddenly Mustapha's voice broke the silence. He raised his scimitar high in the air and then lowered it slowly till the point was pointing at Abdullah.

"Seize that man," he said quietly and without a tremor in his voice. With a roar of anger the mass of sailors sprang toward Abdullah. A sharp pistol shot rang out and Alzim leaped high in air rushed backward from the crowd and fell dead at Mustapha's feet. His foreboding had come true!

Then there came a roar as of many voices and the patter of running feet which rose far above the tumult in the doorway.

The sailors were scattered like chaff before a wind and a hundred mailed figures rushed into the room. The great scimitars in their hands mowed down the crew right and left. Alexis Pontoff, the Greek, burst out of the confusion and ran to Mustapha's side.

Before he could speak a word a shot rang out and Alexis sank to the floor beside Alzim. He was dead.

Then, before Mustapha's astonished eyes three forms whom he recognized came at him.

"Have the dead come to life?" he said as he recognized Morabec, Kerrim and Misabic.

He had scarcely strength enough to raise his pistol and discharge it almost in Kerrim's face. Kerrim fell across the bodies of the two cooks and lay quite still. Misabic and Morabec hesitated a moment and then came across with drawn swords.

Mustapha's sword cleft Misabic's head and that person fell across his brother's body. Before Mustapha could draw it out, Morabec was upon him with uplifted scimitar. Mustapha sank to his knees under the force of the rush and because his ankle had failed him. He thought that he had seen his last moment when a pistol shot rang out in the tumult nearby and Morabec's weapon slipped from his nerveless hand. Mustapha fell forward on his hands and knees and rose to his feet in time to see Morabec collapse across his brother's body.

Baber stood close by with a smoking pistol in his hand. It was he who had fired the shot.

"You saved my life," gasped Mustapha.

"Yes, yes," replied Baber, "but say nothing more of it. Here they come! Look out for yourself!"

As he spoke a mass of mailed figures rushed upon them. Mustapha rose to his fullest height, upon one foot, and lifted his sword high in air. It sank upon the head of the foremost man with terrific force and that person staggered but regained his feet again. The blow had scarcely pierced his helmet, and had only stunned him for the moment.

The next instant Mustapha found himself on his back with the man he had struck atop of him and binding him hand and foot with rope.

Then he was lifted in the man's arms and borne out of the tumult. Dimly he saw on either side of him rushing figures and turning his head saw Baber go down with a man atop of him. But this man did not stir. Baber struggled to his feet sword in hand but was thrown down by a great giant of a fellow who bound him hand and foot. At the same moment four pistol shots rang out in the corner near the fireplace where a confused struggled seemed to be taking place.

Then he caught sight of Cassim for one brief moment and then of Emir and Harun. Then he saw a figure, sword in hand, burst through the line of mailed figures and rush at Abdullah, who was still standing in the doorway. It was Akmat!

Behind him raced a group of men and ten feet from his object he was tripped by a man and fell forward only a few feet from Abdullah. His sword, striking the stones, turned a complete somersault in air and came down point foremost on Abdullah's left foot. The sharp point pierced through his shoe and far into his foot and the hilt of the weapon struck him on the thigh. An expression of pain came upon his face for one moment and then it changed to anger.

He took the scimitar in his hand and took a step forward to where Akmat lay and waited till the man had bound him and had then lifted him to his feet.

Then with that fiendish smile on his face once more, Abdullah lifted the weapon as if to strike Akmat down.

Suddenly the expression on his face changed and he lowered the weapon and giving Akmat a look of contempt dropped the scimitar and turned on his head and walked away, limping.

Then Mustapha saw the mass in the corner part again and three men emerged each carrying a man in his arms bound hand and foot. Needless to say, Cassim, Harun and Emir were these men. But three mailed men lay on the floor where they had fallen, apart from the bodies of the sailors. These men with their prisoners all assembled in a group and followed Abdullah, who had almost disappeared. Others followed with the bodies of the three spies and the three mailed men who had been wounded during the fight. One, the one that had been struck by Baber, was dead.

Through many rooms they went and finally seemed to have reached the cellar of the castle. Here everything was dark and several men carrying torches pressed to the front and led the way.

At the end of the cellar was an open doorway. Upon going through this they found themselves at the head of a stairway cut out in the solid stone.

There was scarce room for one man on this stairway, so the party proceeded in single file.

The tallest men had to stoop in places to avoid collision with the stone roof.

"What a contrast to the one under Abdullah's house in Bagdad," thought Mustapha.

Far down they went and Mustapha began to wonder how fresh air was admitted to such a place.

After what the young Turk thought to be a mile the steps ceased and they stepped out onto a smooth floor cut in solid granite. Fresh air seemed to come through a small passage in the wall of the chamber, but this was so dark that Mustapha could see nothing in it.

The room, or grotto, as it was, was cut in the solid rock and was about fifty feet in length by twenty in width. At the end was a door which seemed to lead into another cavern. The roof was fifteen feet above their heads.

"If you will promise not to attempt to escape, I will liberate all of you and allow you to walk," said Abdullah.

"Anything, you fiend," said Mustapha, "only let us stand upon our own legs once more."

"Then you promise to make no attempt to escape if I give you the freedom of the place," said Abdullah.

"Yes, if you will tell us where we are."

"I will. You are in the antechamber to the Temple of the Fire-Worshippers."

"I thought so," groaned Akmat to himself.

"Cut their bonds," said Abdullah to the mailed men.

Next thing Mustapha and his comrades knew they were standing free, with the ropes lying on the ground. Their captors had disappeared and they were alone with Abdullah.

Ahmed was standing and Abdullah saw that he had been wounded.

"You are hurt," said he.

"Yes," said Ahmed, faintly. "Your men gave me a slight slash on my shoulder, but that is only the wound you see. The real wound is the one your spies gave me in the fight on board the ship. Tell me, if you are fiend incarnate, or only a human being, how did they escape from the sinking ship."

"I will tell you the story some other time," said Abdullah. "Come with me and I will cure your wound and the one that Akmat gave me in my foot."

"I have a sore ankle," said Mustapha.

"Then come, too, and it will be cured. There is no hurt except that which is mortal or of what you Mohammedans call the 'spirit' that I cannot cure with my fluid of Life!"

Mustapha and Ahmed had little faith in his promise, but they went with him leaving the others in the chamber of stone.

Akmat thought it strange that he should so trust their word, but an afterthought told him that they were watched by unseen eyes.

Abdullah and his two companions went through many chambers carved out in the solid stone and at last entered one smaller than any of the others. Everything seemed to be hot in this place and the wall, on which Mustapha placed his hand, was steaming. The air was almost suffocating and a smell as of something burning floated to his nostrils.

Chapter XVI

At the side was a small door thru which Abdullah went. His two companions followed and found themselves in a small grotto. At one end of it was a basin-shaped cavity in the stone.

From this a blue flame leaped constantly, yet there was no visible fuel to keep it burning. It leaped and capered all over the basin, and then leaped upward in the form of a spiral.

"Hold your foot near the hole from which the flame comes," said Abdullah to Mustapha.

Mustapha did so and instantly the pain left his ankle. He placed the foot on the ground and found that he could walk better than ever before in his life. A feeling of strength seemed to pervade his whole being and the shock caused by the excitement of the fight and the resultant fatigue dropped from him like a false mask which its owner throws off, revealing his true personality.

Abdullah then motioned Ahmed to draw near the flame. Ahmed did so and instantly both his wounds were cured and the strength of his youth was his once more.

Then Abdullah presented his wounded foot near to the blue flame and the hurt was cured.

"What think you of such things?" he asked, turning to Mustapha.

"You are evidently the master of a strange force," said Mustapha in reply. "You have done marvelous things, yet I am sure that they are within the realm of nature."

"You mean that this strange liquid fire has done marvelous things. I did not do them."

"Yet you must be the master of such a force," said Mustapha. "If not, how could you make it cure us?"

"I will explain nothing whatever about this. Be grateful that it has cured you and say no more," replied Abdullah with dignity.

"Tell us what our fate is to be," said Mustapha to Abdullah as they walked back to the grotto in which they had left Cassim and his brothers.

"Death," replied Abdullah, and Mustapha was not surprised. Neither was Ahmed. He had known what their fate would be if they fell into Abdullah's hands since the time he was wounded by the three spies.

"Chain us with chains," said Mustapha bitterly, "but absolve us from our promise not to attempt escape."

"I shall not," was the firm answer. "You may have the freedom of this whole building if you wish. No, indeed, I will not absolve you from the promise you made me. Yet you will meet death all the same and before a week has passed. Tell your comrades to prepare for the same fate."

"What will be the nature of our death?"

"You will be burnt in a lake of fire."

"A lake of fire?"

"Yes."

"There must be a deposit of natural oil in this island," said Mustapha.

"There is."

"By what name do you call this lake?"

"We call it the 'Lake of Holy Fire.'"

"How old is it?"

"Then you insist on hearing the story?"

"If there is one."

"There is. I shall tell it to you and your cousin." By this time they had reached the antechamber when they found Akmat and the others waiting for them.

Abdullah seated himself on the hard stone floor and told the story thus:

"Five hundred years ago the 'God of Fire', whom we worship, came to this island with a hundred followers from the four corners of the earth.

"Their first temple was the great castle on the hill, but the God was not satisfied with this, but told his followers to dig down into the island from the cellar of the castle. This was done and the stairway and the grotto you have seen were the result.

"Then, in a small chamber he put the 'Fire of Life' and placed it in their care, telling them that it would cure all their wounds and give them renewed strength.

"Then he had his followers hollow out a great hollow pit in the largest grotto and in the center of this, he built a great pedestal of stone upon which he set his own image in blue flame of the same origin as that which was placed in the little grotto.

"Then he bade us dig tunnels into the stone at the bottom of the great hollow and from these oil spouted up in torrents and soon made a lake. This he set on fire and then left his followers telling them that the petroleum was eternal and that the supply would never give out.

"He bade them stay there and watch the fire and live in peace and pray to him.

"When the death of one of these men seemed near another person from the great world was converted and joined the society, for after two hundred years it became a society of mutual protection.

"There are at this day only a hundred members of the society and I am at their head.

"The purpose of its existence is plain to you. As I said, it is a society for mutual protection. When a member is in danger all he has to do is to ask his brothers to protect him. If he seeks revenge they aid him."

"A good institution," said Mustapha, with sarcasm in his voice. "I daresay it does its work very well."

"It does," said Abdullah. "Come with me, all of you, and behold the lake which is to end your days."

All followed him through several grottoes and at last they entered the large one in which the lake was situated. No language can adequately describe it. The chamber was at least half a mile wide and in its center was this lake of fire.

They were standing on the very edge of the lake and could look into it. The waves of fire lapped high and curled in fantastic shapes. The heat and the suffocating smoke and the knowledge that he was to be in such a place caused Mustapha to feel very sick. He could scarce muster courage enough to face the lake.

Far out in the center stood a great black pedestal upon which stood the Statue of the God of Fire. It was of blue flame and in its hand was a great scimitar of the same material.

The weird lake, the still more weird statue and the surrounding weird scene could have but one effect upon people not used to such sights. The knowledge that they would be thrown into such a place acted upon Mustapha and his relations in just such a way. Everyone swooned except Baber who stood erect and pale with not a change of expression in his face.

"Is this the worst you can do?" asked he.

"Yes," said Abdullah, angrily. "Is it not bad enough?"

"No," said Baber with sarcasm in his tone.

"Then what did you expect?"

"That is none of your affairs."

"Tell me and I will see if it is practicable."

"I will not. Find it our for yourself."

"I cannot."

"It is of no use to ask me to tell you."

"Then I will drop the matter at once."

"Do so. It is odious to me."

"So it is to me. The fate you are to meet is bad enough, you traitor!"

"Do you dare call me traitor, you hound of him whom the Christians name 'Satan'?"

"I do. It is the only name by which you should be called, the only name which you have earned, and consequently, the only one of which you are worthy."

"I did not know that before."

"You would not know anything, traitor."

"I am no traitor."

"I tell you that you are. Why did you not, if you are no traitor, kill the wretches I consigned to your care?"

"Because I could not be so cruel. They were men innocent of any crime, so I had not the heart to kill them. I befriended them and by doing so I earned your displeasure."

"You did, traitor."

*Far out in the center stood a great black pedestal
upon which stood the Statue of the God of Fire.*

"I would call you traitor a million times if I wished, traitor."

"Then take that as a reward, you friend of Eblis." Baber had struck Abdullah in the face with his fist.

Abdullah went down, and at the same moment a dozen men sprang upon the captain and bore him to the ground. They bound him with chains and carried him out of the room. They also found Mustapha and the others and took these along, too. Abdullah followed, looking very sullen and angry, as he deserved to be.

They went up a flight of eighty-six steps, and came to an iron door which was barred and bolted. This was unfastened and the prisoners carried in and thrown down upon the floor. They were in an immense grotto just over the lake of fire.

The floor was warm from the fire below, so its inmates were not cold.

"This is to be your prison until the day of your death," said Abdullah. "There is no other entrance to it besides the one you were brought in at."

With this he left the place and the armed men followed.

"Well, we'll have to make the best of it," said Mustapha when his enemy had gone.

"This act of his in locking us up absolves us from the promises you made him," said Baber.

Then he told them of what had happened after they had swooned.

"I struck Abdullah, partly because I was angry and partly because I wished to make him absolve us from that foolish promise," he said at the end of the narrative.

"No one can blame you for that, Baber, though I don't really think that there is any possible way of escape," said Mustapha.

Here Akmat broke into the conversation.

"I will find a way of escape," said he, "if there is any."

"Then we had better explore our prison and see if what Abdullah told us is true."

"Very well," and Akmat and the others started out on a search. Mustapha and Ahmed had already related what had happened to them when Abdullah had taken them to the "Fire of Life," and the tale had been deemed a wondrous one by all except Akmat, who had had his own thoughts and had not spoken them.

In the center of the grotto Emir espied a hole in the floor and shouted out the discovery to his friends. They immediately came trooping to his side and peered into the hole.

It was about three feet in diameter and a man could have been lowered into it easily.

It seemed to slant downward gradually and the end could not be seen.

"If we had a rope I would lower myself into it," said Mustapha.

"We can make one out of our coats," suggested Baber.

The plan was thought to be a good one and was carried out. The coats made a very good rope about twenty feet in length. Mustapha's dagger had not been taken away from him and it was used in cutting the garments into proper shape. Then the strips were tied together and the rope, such as it was, was finished.

It was quite strong enough to support a man's weight. After the signal for hauling up was agreed upon, Mustapha tied the rope around his waist, clutched the dagger in his hand and stepped into the hole and gave the order to lower.

He slid gradually downward for about ten feet and then the passage made an abrupt turn. He closed his eyes a moment and realized that he was hanging over some great pit, swinging in the air.

Suffocating odors reached his nostrils, and he opened his eyes and saw that he was hanging over the great lake of fire. Two feet above his head was the mouth of the small passage through which he had descended.

The heat and the smoke from the burning oil caused him to give the signal to haul up in a great hurry. As his head reached the mouth of the passage he discerned something hanging there. It was a small iron box hanging on an iron hook fastened in the stone by another iron hook.

Mustapha quickly unhooked it and when he was pulled out into the grotto he handed it to Akmat. It was not locked, and so Akmat lifted the lid, not knowing what he would find inside. The others, including Mustapha, who had released himself from the rope, crowded around him. Wuthin the box, on a bed of soft cotton, lay the two black diamonds.

If a thunderbolt had struck them they could not have been more astounded. Emir was the first to regain his senses and eventually his tongue.

"Abdullah evidently thought that a good hiding-place for his plunder," he remarked.

"But it was not," replied Mustapha, and he related his experience. The others listened patiently, and at the end Ahmed said:

"I see now the purpose of this hole. Abdullah will use it as a method of killing us. It is worthy of such a fiendish ingenuity as his. He will cause his men to throw us into it and we will slide downward and at the end shout out into the air, to land in the lake a hundred yards below. Ah! I see a way of defeating his purpose!"

"What is it?" said Mustapha. "Perhaps he does not mean to do such a thing to us."

"Well, it will do no harm to carry out my plan," said Ahmed. "This is what I suggest: Only three coats were used up in the manufacture of the rope. The rope is strong enough to hold at least two men. There are yet three more coats. Make these into another rope. Then we have rope enough to support four men. Our sashes and turbans ought to supply another rope capable of supporting two more men. Each rope is twenty feet in length and can support two men. There are six of us altogether. The three ropes would thus be sufficient to support us all. You say that there was a great iron hook on which this box hung, Mustapha.

"Well, we can tie these ropes to this hook you speak of. They will thus hang over the great lake of burning oil in which we go to meet our death. They could not be discerned from the edge of the lake when Abdullah will be wanting to see us fly out of the passage and down, down into the 'Lake of Holy Fire.' Only one of us can slide through the hole at a time. The first of us that does so catches one of these ropes as he flies out and slides down to its end, where there is a loop through which he can put his arms. He can hang there a long time. The next person will hang in another loop above him. So on till each of us is hanging on these ropes.

"As soon as these men have done their duty they will go away and probably leave the door open. Abdullah will see us hanging in air up there, but will not see the ropes.

"He will set off to get his men and come up to see what is the matter. In the meanwhile we will climb up through the passage and escape by the open door. We will be able to fight our way out and reach the boats. We will then row to the mainland and thus get away, safe and sound, and come back with soldiers to destroy this place forever. There is much risk in the undertaking, but it is the only practicable one under the circumstances."

"It is a good plan!" cried Mustapha excitedly when Akmat had finished speaking. "What an imagination you have! I almost envy you, Akmat."

"Yes, I suppose it is a good plan, but now we must get ready to put it into execution."

By morning this was done and the three ropes hung from the hook over the great 'Lake of Holy Fire.' Akmat had put the diamonds into his pocket and had let the box slide through the passage and into the lake where it doubtless is to this day.

The grotto was lighted by quite a number of torches and these illuminated the place very well. They were held in steel brackets on the walls not far from the floor, six on each side of the room and two at each end.

Mustapha watched them and a plan flashed into his mind.

"Why not set the door afire with these torches?" said he.

"A good plan!" said Akmat enthusiastically. He went to one of the pine torches and tried to pull it from its socket. He could not. Then he tried to break it by the middle. This attempt proved unsuccessful.

The wood was too stout and hard for his strength.

"Give me your dagger, Mustapha," said he.

Mustapha handed him the weapon and Akmat set to work to cut the torch in two. After fifteen minutes hard work, he succeeded and triumphantly carried his fiery weapon to the mahogany door.

In a very short time the door caught fire and burned quickly. The wood was old and brittle and took fire easily. In five minutes the remnant of the door collapsed and the whole party walked out.

There were six strong iron bars that had held the great door, and each took one of these. They were massive and heavy and of just the right weight to crush a man's skull.

"Be quiet," whispered Mustapha, who led the party. They crept down the stone steps with stealthy feet and went through many other apartments. Finally they reached the one where Abdullah had released them.

Within, Abdullah and his men were standing, holding carousal among themselves.

Mustapha saw this before he entered and drew back and held whispered conference with his cousins and the captain.

"Make a rush and fight our way through," said Baber. "It is the only way."

They agreed upon this and rushed into the room with uplifted maces and charged upon the group near the stairway. This group saw what was about to take place and drew their swords.

Mustapha knew better than to rush upon these swords, so he changed his course and made for the cave-like opening at the end of the grotto. Where this would lead him to, he had no idea, but he preferred uncertainty to certain death or recapture ending in death.

As he entered the cave he shouted to the others to follow him and went on. After running quite a distance in the darkness he stopped and waited for them. He heard footsteps coming but they sounded only like one or two men, not half a dozen.

Then he heard voices not ten feet away. These were not those of his friends so he started off again, realizing that he was pursued.

Finally he saw a tiny spark of light ahead and soon emerged on the sea-shore, not ten yards from where the boat had been hidden.

He rushed to this place and hauled the lightest of the boats from its concealment and into the cove just as three men emerged from the mouth of the cavern.

They did not see him till he was in the sea. Then they set up a great shout and ran to the shore. They were fully armed and carried pistols in their belts.

These they fired at him, missing the boat, and then jumped into the sea and swam after him.

He had a hundred feet the start of them, however, and they did not gain on him. Half a mile from the shore they swam back and he saw them enter the passage. The ship of Abdullah Houssain was not to be seen. The sun was an hour high and Mustapha realized that he was hungry.

Two miles from the island he saw three large boats put off from its shore and come toward him. He was evidently pursued, for the boats were full of men.

Mustapha did his best to outdistance them but they gained rapidly and he saw that they could easily prevent him from making a circuit toward the mainland as he had intended to do. So the only thing he could do was to strike out to sea and trust to luck to escape his adversaries.

Suddenly he discerned a ship far off on the horizon. She was coming toward him, so he continued on his course. Nearer and nearer came the ship and nearer and nearer came his pursuers. They were not half a mile distant when the crew of the strange ship espied him and put on all sail. When the pursuers saw this they turned about and made all speed for the island.

Five minutes later Mustapha's boat was along-side the ship and a rope was lowered to him by the sailors. He caught it and was hauled on deck. Then the boat was hauled up and Mustapha was conducted to the captain to whom he told his story. The captain was bound for Bagdad so he promised the young Turk a free passage home.

Chapter XVII

It was night in Bagdad, the night of July 18th when a young man passed before the door of the home of another man, named Balbec Khan. It was at this house, you will remember, that Abdullah entrapped Mustapha and his cousins on the night that Ahmed's house was burned by the servants of that same victorious villain.

The young man just mentioned had passed and you might have had a good look at him had you been there. It was about ten o'clock and the full moon would have revealed him to passersby, if passersby there had been on that street at such an unholy and unheard of hour as ten at night.

He was tall and strong, his face was handsome, but his bold black eyes were his most distinguishing features. They were piercing and bright and seemed to look you through and through. At times they had an angry glitter which betokened that their owner had a temper, which, though apparently under control, might break out under provocation.

This young man appeared to be about twenty-two to twenty-three years of age and was the possessor of fierce black mustachios which curled in a threatening manner and added to the effect the glitter of his eyes would have had if you had seen him at that particular time.

He wore a long seaman's cloak and a battered turban of faded silk with a silver crescent fastened to it. His Turkish pantaloons were of faded cloth and had once been of a bright scarlet hue, though they resembled a dark pink or purple more than any other color at the present date of their lives.

By his side was a large but battered scabbard which contained a scimitar. The sash he wore was bright red and was the only new article of apparel he seemed to possess, except his yellow and blue alternately striped jacket, and his shoes, made of yellow Persian leather.

This man, you will have probably guessed by this time, was Mustapha Dagh, our old acquaintance whom we last met on board a ship found for Bagdad.

The details of his voyage were not of any importance, so I will only give you a brief sketch of it. After the captain had promised him a free passage to his native town, Mustapha had told him that he would pay him at the first opportunity.

The captain had then made him a present of a scimitar, and its scabbard, an old turban and all the other articles mentioned except the pantaloons and Mustapha's shirt, which hung beneath his jacket and, not being visible, I did not mention in my brief description.

The voyage had been uneventful and the captain had put his unexpected passenger ashore in safety. Before landing Mustapha had made him promise not to tell of his information regarding the island upon that public nuisance the "Fire Worshippers" had their temple. Mustapha gave various good reasons why he should not tell and in the end the captain was won over and gave his promise.

Upon landing, that evening, Mustapha had bidden his friend, the captain, farewell and had set off for the house of Balbec Khan, thinking that the best place he could go to under the present situation and state of affairs.

Now it was the unholy hour of ten, and he was standing before the door of this man's house, hesitating to knock. In an instant he banished his timid and undescribable fears and walking up to the door rapped upon it with his fist. There was no immediate response, so he drew his scimitar and struck the door a blow or two with the heavy hilt.

The response was both surprising and instantaneous. A window, twenty feet above the Turk's head, was thrown violently open and a loud voice bellowed and a head was stuck out to see what was the matter and what in the world what such an unearthly racket could mean.

Mustapha had scarcely time to sheathe his sword before the eyes of the man at the window fell upon him.

"What on earth and the other world do you mean by knocking down a peaceful man's door at such an unholy hour as this?"

"I mean that I want shelter," replied Mustapha.

"Do you know my master?" replied the man in the window, somewhat reassured by the knocker's reply.

"Yes, I am an old friend of his, Mustapha Dagh," replied Mustapha.

"You are? Well, I'll call my master before you'll have time to walk in. You'll find the door unlocked, sir. Just push it and come in and make yourself at home. If I'd known who you were, sir, I wouldn't have been so rude. A thousand pardons, sir."

With that the head was withdrawn and Mustapha opened the door and walked into the corridor, closing the door behind him. The corridor was dark and he had some trouble in finding the door at the other end.

He then entered the room where he and his relations had stayed in that memorable night mentioned at the beginning of the chapter.

Everything was dead here and he had to grope for a chair. At last he found one and seated himself and lit a candle. He always carried little wax tapers in his pockets with flint, steel and powder to light them with if necessary.

By the light this one gave him he was able to see quite well. The room was little different from the condition it had been in the last time he had seen it.

Hardly had he been seated ten minutes when steps were heard in the corridor and Balbec entered, fully, though hurriedly dressed, not quite awake, and accompanied by a servant carrying a tray on which Mustapha espied a large bottle of wine, a loaf of bread and various other articles of food.

"How are you, my good friend?" said Balbec smiling, and motioning the servant to put the tray on the table and go out. "It has been a long time since I last met you."

"I am in the best of health, and will acknowledge that a great many days passed since we last met. I must ask how you are."

"I am quite well," said Balbec. "What has happened to you since the night you and some relations of yours came here? I was not awakened by my servants and heard nothing of it till the next morning. There have been strange tales afloat and an investigation has been made into the case and the servants of your uncle have circulated strange stories. The mystery seems to hedge about a couple of black diamonds and it appears, from these accounts, that a well-known citizen and rich merchant of Bagdad, with whom I am acquainted, Abdullah Houssain, is mixed up in the affair.

"He was last seen on the night you came here and was with you and from what my servants said not on good terms with you. It seemed that he was your prisoner and that your house had been set fire to by his servants, from what you said, which he was a prisoner in it.

"There are many other tales and the mystery is inexplicable to me. Perhaps you may be able to tell me of it when you have eaten. Eat first, however, and afterwards you may tell your story. Your mysterious disappearance and the disappearance of your relations is very puzzling. It is thought that Abdullah Houssain set sail for the far east on some mercantile expedition, and his servants appear to know nothing, except that he told them that they might not see him again for many months. Then he disappeared and two of his ships disappeared with him. These ships were the 'Serpent' and the 'Eagle' by name. The 'Eagle' was the largest of the two and carried the most guns, though both carried more guns than the average merchantman. It is known that the 'Serpent' was on a voyage to China, but no one knows why the 'Eagle' is missing. It is thought that both of them might have perished in the great storm in the gulf of Persia."

"I can answer all of that," said Mustapha, helping himself to the wine. "I was aboard the 'Serpent' and I can answer that neither she nor the 'Eagle' perished in the storm you speak of. When I get through eating I will tell you everything. Abdullah is one of the blackest villains that ever lived, and is High-Chief, or something, of that society they call the 'Fire-Worshippers' that have been ravaging the Orient with their deviltries. Just wait till I'm through with this food and you'll hear all that I know. I am lucky to be alive at safe at this moment. If it hadn't have been for Abdullah's carelessness you would never have heard of me again."

"The Fire-Worshippers!" cried Balbec in amazement.

"Yes, the Fire-Worshippers," said Mustapha, very deliberately, and very slowly. Then he went on eating and when he had finished told his story from beginning to end. It was midnight by the time he had finished.

Balbec listened with amazement to the recital and when Mustapha had finished he said:

"Well, what are you going to do now?"

"Avenge the death of my cousins by exterminating the Fire-Worshippers," replied Mustapha with a gleam in his eye.

"What will you do to do that?" asked Balbec.

"I am going to the pasha of Bagdad to-morrow, and I shall lay the whole case before him and ask him if he will let me take the law into my own hands and have a private revenge."

"Good! It is just what you should do. I am sure he will agree to your petition."

"Then I will want ships and men to accomplish my object. I know the position of the island so well that I could not miss it. I shall ask the pasha to let me have two or three war-ships and plenty of men. I also want this to be private, for I do not want everybody in Bagdad to know that I have returned. Therefore you must lend me a disguise in the morning, for I am too well-known to avoid recognition, and have too many friends. There would be much talk if my return becomes known, and you know that people are altogether too inquisitive when they think that a person can explain a mystery to them."

"I shall keep the matter secret as long as you wish, Mustapha, and shall order my servants to do the same. I am sure that the pasha will lend you all the ships and men you want in such a cause."

"I shall hope that he will, at any rate, Balbec. But if he does not let me do all the fighting myself, I will take my own ships and men and be ahead of him."

"Yes, he may want to manage the matter himself. If he does, I would advise you to forestall him. You could get your ships ready for the voyage before he could. He would be in no hurry."

"Perhaps you are right, but I think it my duty to inform him of all that I know and get his permission to act in the matter."

"Permission would hardly be neccessary, Mustapha, but you had best do as you like about it."

"I certainly shall. Have you heard whose hands my property is in? I have been gone nearly two months."

"Nothing has been done about the matter so far. Your house has been rebuilt, I know, by order of Emir Beg's wife, who would have been the only heir, as you have no relations beside your cousins and both they and you had disappeared. If none of you returned or were heard of in three years she would inherit both your property and that of Ahmed Beg. At present she or her representatives are in charge of the property. Ahmed's house has been rebuilt also. I will send a messenger to your house in the morning for them to prepare for your coming."

"Are my ships all returned from their voyages? All but two were off on a voyage to China before I disappeared."

"Three have returned, richly laden with silks and a great profit has been made. Your entire fortune now amounts to fifty thousand pieces of gold. Five more ships are expected to-morrow, or sometime during the week. Your entire fleet consists of eleven only and so only three are yet to be expected. They left only three days before the time you disappeared. It will be a month at least before they will be back. You will probably have a gain of twenty thousand pieces of gold for the whole year of 1650."

Chapter XVIII

Mustapha knew the way to the pasha's palace, so he had no trouble in getting there. No one recognized him as he went along the streets though he met many people with whom he was acquainted.

Some greeted him with the Turkish equivalent of the "good morning," but most ignored him if they saw him, and if they did not, of course, did neither.

Finally he reached the palace and going up to the servant at the door told him that he wished to have an audience with the pasha. The man replied that his master was very busy and had no time to give an audience today. Then he inquired what Mustapha's business might be. Mustapha replied that he could give the pasha information as to the whereabouts of the temple of the "Fire-Worshippers" and various other things relating to the same.

The servant was convinced by this and told Mustapha to enter. Mustapha went in, and found himself in a large corridor at the end of which was a door.

"Wait here till I return," said the servant.

"Hurry," said Mustapha as the man vanished through the doorway. In five minutes the man was back and told Mustapha that the pasha would grant him an audience.

Mustapha followed the man through several rooms and at last entered one in which the pasha was sitting.

This room was about twenty feet long by fifteen in width, and the ceiling was low. There were three doors. The place was filled with tables covered with books, writing materials and various other articles. The pasha was seated in a large, well-cushioned mahogany chair. He was fifty years of age, or at least somewhere near that, and his hair had already turned gray. His long beard reached to his waist and showed signs of snowy white.

The old man's eyes were black and bright, but somewhat small and sunken. His face was of the hue of old bronze and his nose was slightly ac-quiline and red at the end showing a tendency for alcoholic liquors.

Slatin Baabbec, which was his name, wore long red pantaloons and shoes which showed signs of long wear. His black and white cloak was new however, and the turban which lay on the table was new also.

Before him lay a number of letters which he had been reading, and a plentiful supply of parchment, pens, and black ink.

"Well, what do you want?" asked Slatin, gazing at the young man who had so rudely broken in on his work.

"Didn't that servant tell you, O pasha of Bagdad?"

"Yes. But I have gotten into such a habit of asking that question that I could not help it. It is clearly a case of habit, absent-mindedness and careless-ness. I hope that you have no such things, young man."

"I have a habit of not rising till I awake, pasha," was Mustapha's grave reply.

"Is that intended for a joke? If it is it is lost upon me entirely."

"No, it is not intended for a joke. You asked me if I had any habits and I merely answered your question by citing one, O pasha."

"Well, state your business and be done with it," in a very gruff and impatient tone.

"There he goes again," thought Mustapha to himself. Aloud he said: "I have come to you, O pasha, to give some information regarding the society of the 'Fire-Worshippers.'"

"Your voice sounds familiar, yet your face is not. Who are you anyway?"

"Mustapha Dagh, a young merchant of the city, who mysteriously disappeared several months ago." Mustapha was so excited that he forgot the customary "O pasha." The pasha himself was so astonished that he too forgot all about it; so no harm was done, though at any other time it might have been regarded as a bad breach of etiquette and a bad specimen of disrespect.

"The ———! Do you really mean it?" was all that the pasha could say. I have left out the word that came after "the" as it is not to be used in polite society.

"Yes, O pasha, I mean what I say."

"Well, sit down and tell me all about it." Mustapha accepted the invitation by seating himself, cross-legged, on a rug in front of the pasha in true Turkish style. A few families in Bagdad had adopted the European custom of sitting in chairs, but all of them still retained the custom of sitting cross-legged on the floor.

"Well hurry up," said Slatin, impatiently, when his visitor was comfortably seated. "I haven't much time to give you, for I am very busy."

"Pardon, O Slatin Baabbec," said Mustapha. "Had I known that you were in such a hurry I should have waited another day before encroaching upon your kingly patience."

"I don't call that hurrying up," thought Slatin to himself. "It seems to me that the fellow is too much of what I call a 'honey-tongued falterer.'" Aloud he added, "I accept your apology. Go on."

"First, tell me how much time you will give me to tell my story in," said Mustapha. "I would like to know so as to be able to accommodate the facts and details of my story into the space of time in which I am to relate them."

"I will give you an hour," said Slatin. "I didn't think he had so much forethought and consideration of others," he added, to himself.

"Now, O pasha, I am quite ready to relate to you my tale," said Mustapha. He cleared his throat, shifted his position on the rug so that he would be more comfortable, folded his arms, lifted his gaze, till it rested upon the pasha's face, which looked back at him with an expression of rapt attention and interest, though not betraying the inward astonishment which the owner felt, and then began his tale gaining more expression as he told it, till his voice was like the mellifluous sound of a trumpet.

The expression of interest on the pasha's face deepened into one of astonishment, and he did not note the time passed. It was double the time he had alloted Mustapha in which to recount his adventures when that person finished his recital and rose to his feet and unceremoniously stretched his tired limbs, and yawned.

"It was only part of my purpose in coming to you to tell you of what I have experienced, O pasha," said he. "The other part is to request you to allow me to take the law into my own hands and punish this Abdullah Houssain and his fiendish confederates in my own individual way and manner. As you already know, I have a personal grudge against the fellow, and I also wish to earn the glory resulting from such an exploit. I do not know whether my own fleet of ships and all my crews will be sufficient to punish the fiend, so I ask you to lend me several of your own ships to aid in the plan."

The pasha thought for several minutes before answering.

"No, I will not lend you any of my own ships," he then said. "I do not think that it would be quite fair. However, I will allow you to 'take the law into your own hands,' as you say. I have no heir to take my place as pasha when I die, so the Turkish sultan will have to select a man to rule then. If you succeed in exterminating these 'Fire-Worshippers,' I will exert all my influence with him to select you as my successor. Naturally, if you do Turkey such a great service as you intend to do, he will be greatly pleased and may go as far as that in the favors he will confer upon you. As I have promised, if you are successful, I will hint the matter with him, and if that does not succeed, send him a written appeal, if he does not forestall my actions and act for himself in the matter, by appointing you my successor without my having time to speak.

"If such is the case, I shall give you my blessing. That blessing is yours, Mustapha, even if you fail in your quest and if you die, still you shall retain, that same blessing, though it be only that of an old man. Go."

"I thank you from the bottom and inmost chamber of my heart, O pasha," said Mustapha, at the door. "I must bid you farewell for a time, but Allah grant that I return safe and sound, my lord."

"Farewell, Mustapha," said the pasha, turning to his abandoned task. "Allah grant your wish. I can but hope that he will, but his will is our will; we must accept what he ordains. Once more, I order you to go. I wish you success in your quest, and hope that you will be my successor and rule the people wisely."

Then Mustapha stepped forth from the room, and turning at the door, saw, or thought he saw, a tear from Slatin's eye fall upon a sheet of parchment. The aged shoulders of the pasha bent closer to the writing-materials, and for a moment all that the watcher heard was the scratching of the pen and the beating of his own heart.

The next moment he had shut the door quietly so as to not disturb Slatin, and was tip-toeing across the room.

Three minutes later he was out in the narrow, dirty street, now filled to overflowing with people of all classes on their way to market.

Mustapha had removed his disguise while telling his story to the pasha, so that that person might see that he was no impostor. Slatin had seen him before and had recognized him, professing himself satisfied. Then Mustapha had donned it again, and now, in the street, he was just as immune to recognition by his friends as he had been before. He had also asked the pasha not to tell of his return to anybody and the request had been granted. Slatin was a man who had never been known to break his word.

In a few minutes Mustapha was in the center of the crowd and was on the way to his old home, though he was sadly hindered by the people, who jostled him rudely about. He dared not retaliate from fear of causing a fight and subsequent arrest, so he meekly allowed them to do as they pleased.

A tall Arabian, dressed like Mustapha, struck him with his fist, and strained his temper to the breaking point. Had the man done it again there would have been trouble, but Mustapha turned around and glared at him ferociously. The Arabian made great haste to absent himself and the next moment he was lost to sight in the motley crowd.

Then Mustapha went on and soon reached a small by-street or alley which seemed to be entirely deserted. This he entered and came out upon another street after walking a hundred yards.

This one was not so crowded as the other, and the young Turk had little trouble in reaching the southern wall of the city near the river Tigris. The great gate was open and through it came a caravan, returning from the deserts of Arabia. The camels were laden with great bundles and the swarthy Bedouins who accompanied them looked worn out, and footsore.

Behind the caravan came a number of horsemen gaily dressed, and their horses richly caparisoned. They were ambassadors from Persia, on their way to the pasha of Bagdad, doubtless laden with some important message or mission.

Mustapha slipped through the gateway just in time to escape meeting another caravan and beheld the gardens of the river Tigris among which his own home was situated. Just down the great white roadway in front of him he saw the gardens surrounding the place where his house had been before it was burnt, and in its place, a sumptuous edifice of stone, two stories in height.

He reached the gateway and went in, walking up to the door, at which he knocked. It seemed such a strange and novel experience to knock at one's own door that he would have refrained from doing it, had it not been that he wore a disguise. If he walked boldly in, in his present condition, the servants would take him for a burglar and either arrest him or drive him out. It was for these reasons that he went through the ceremony of knocking.

Scarcely had he done so, when the door in question flew open in his face and a dapper little negro slave stood before him, bowing with all his might. "Please enter, sir," he said. "I will inform my mistress that you wished to see her without delay."

"Very well, but hurry," said Mustapha, entering the room and seating himself on a small divan near the door. Scarcely had he entered when the servant ran out of the room and the next moment was out of sight.

First thing Mustapha did when he had seated himslef was to divest himself of his turban, false beard and wig. Then he laid upon the divan and then threw off the long Arabian cloak and most of the other articles of Arabic clothing that he wore. These he laid beside the turban.

Then he rubbed the dye from his face with the end of his sash and stood up, himself once more, as a veiled woman entered the room.

"You—Mustapha Dagh?" she cried, in amazement, taken completely aback by what she saw.

"Yes, I am Mustapha Dagh, the rightful owner of this house," he replied with dignity.

"Then I shall have to hand over the reign of government to you," replied the wife of Emir Beg with true Turkish calmness and resignation.

"It seems that such is the truth," he replied. "However, of course, I shall not be so unkind as to deprive you of all income. The house and servants of Ahmed Beg your father-in-law I give to you and all his trade, ships and other articles, to be controlled for you by your representatives."

"I thank you," she said, simply. "I scarcely hoped that if you returned you would be so kind to me. Can you tell me anything of my husband?" she added with a tremor in her voice.

"I hate to tell you the truth," was the young Turk's answer, "but I suppose that it is best for both of us that you know the worst. He was alive when I last saw him, but he is doubtless dead by this time. Be assured that if such is the case it will not pass unrevenged for long. Shall I tell you the whole tale of my adventures?"

"Yes, if you will be so good." The voice almost broke this time and the owner hid her face in her hands.

Mustapha reseated himself upon the divan and beckoned her to do the same.

Then, once more he told his tale of privation, hardship and wrongs and a most sympathetic and attentive listener till the end. It was noon by the time he had finished, and she informed him that dinner would soon be ready.

Mustapha immediately left the room, just as he was, without disguise, and the first person he met was an old servant of his, with whom he was somewhat intimately acquainted. The fellow was an Arabian and was not a slave, being among the few servants in that house who were paid wages. Most were slaves from Nubia and Africa for whom Mustapha had paid a large price.

The fellow uttered a cry of astonishment and dropped the plate that he was carrying. The dish dropped at Mustapha's feet and he had to take a long step to overstep it.

"What do you mean by dropping things like that?" demanded Mustapha, pointing somewhat angrily to the broken plate and the baked fish among its ruins.

"I—I did not mean it, master," stammered the servant. "I was so astounded at seeing you that I could not help it." The look of astonishment had not left his face and Mustapha decided to pardon him. At any rate, the offense was a slight one, demanding a severe reprimand as punishment at the most.

"Well, you can go this time," said Mustapha, sternly carrying out his determination to the letter. "But don't do it again. See here, wait a minute," he added, as the servant walked past him. "Don't tell anyone that I have returned. I'll do that myself."

"Well, you need not fear that I will tell without your orders," promised the servant, picking up the fragments of the plate and the baked fish.

Mustapha passed on and soon reached the kitchen where dinner was almost ready, the finishing touches being put on now.

The servants turned as he entered and stared at him in open-mouthed astonishment.

"Don't let out the news that I have returned leave this house," he cautioned and entered the dining room, giving the servants there the same orders.

Then he calmly seated himself and waited for Emir's wife. A few minutes later she entered with the veil still upon her face and seated herself.

Dinner was eaten in silence and after it was finished she made the preparations for her departure and was soon gone, accompanied by several servants.

Then Mustapha called all the servants together and issued to them the same order that he had given to those in the kitchen and dining room. When this was done he dispersed them and seated himself upon a divan to await the coming of Baabbec.

In his hand he held the keys of the vaults which contained the money. They were peculiarly shaped and made entirely of silver.

Punctually, at two o'clock that afternoon, as he had promised, Baabbec entered the room, panting with exertion. He had run part of the way. He was accompanied by three servants carrying a large box to hold the money.

"Come," said Mustapha and led the way to the vaults. He unlocked the door of one and entered. Within, heaps of money were strewn upon the cold iron floor.

Mustapha took the box and counted the ten thousand pieces of gold into it and then bade the three servants take it. Then they all went out and Mustapha locked the door. Baabbec promptly left the house accompanied by his men with the iron chest, saying that he had very important business to attend to, or he would stay longer. Mustapha bade him farewell and then went to his own room and sat down to write several letters. This room he had selected as his own because of the number of books that it contained. Of course, he had another room as his bed-room, but this he wanted for a library and writing room.

He wrote four or five letters, sealed them, laid them aside and then picked up a book of poetry by a Persian poet. He read for awhile then tossed it aside and picked up the first book that came to hand.

It was a large, leather-bound German lexicon, which had been printed by Gutenburg. How it had gotten there Mustapha did not know, but he could not read it so after looking at the strange characters for awhile he laid it aside and picked up an Arabian book of philosophy.

This occupied his attention for half an hour, and then he threw it down and arose from his chair, feeling stiff. He walked around the room several times to start his sluggish blood to circulation and then went downstairs and roamed about the house.

It was four o'clock when he re-entered the library again and he was feeling tired and sleepy.

He flung himself down upon the divan and straightway dropped asleep, only to be visited by troublesome and horrible dreams. In them, black diamonds, Abdullah Houssain, the "Fire-Worshippers," and ships and turbulent seas were all mingled together in the wildest of confusion.

Then he suddenly awoke to the present state of affairs, and found that a lamp was burning in the room. A man had just entered and was looking around with curious eyes. He stood half-revealed in the doorway and in his half-waking state Mustapha did not at first recognize him. He rose upon his elbow, rubbed his eyes, cleared his brain and then glanced at the stranger once more. He gave a cry of astonishment as their glances met and sprang from the divan. The man was Baber Yataghan, the sea-captain who had so befriended him.

Baber leaped forward to meet him, a smile upon his face and for one brief moment they regarded each other closely in silence. Then Mustapha noticed that Baber was breathing hard, as if from running.

Chapter XIX

"Well, where did you come from?" said Mustapha in astonishment.

"Quick—no time to talk now," said Baber, still breathing hard. "I'll tell you afterwards. Quick—lead me to the vaults under your house. You come also—no time to lose. I'm pursued—by Abdullah Houssain. Hurry—they are at the door now—I'll explain it all afterwards."

"Where is my uncle—where are my cousins?" said Mustapha all in one sentence.

"Dead by this time, I fear," replied the captain. "Hurry, Mustapha, or they'll capture us both. Abdullah will stop at nothing to accomplish his object. Hear them—they are breaking down the door. There are twenty of them—all fully armed. Quick—if you wish to save your own life and mine—lead the way to the vaults—they are the only safe places. Do not fear that your servants will be harmed. Abdullah is after you and me—not them."

Naturally, Mustapha's first impulse was to rally his servants and make a brave defense. But on second thought he determined to accept Baber's advice. The sound of footsteps was in the room below and they were heavy—like those of armed men and regular like the tramp of soldiers.

"Is the house surrounded?" he asked.

"Yes," replied Baber. "There are men on all sides. There is no escape by the windows, and if we attempt to hold the place they will set it on fire. Of course, help will soon arrive but they could end us before that. But if we flee to the vaults we will be safe,—for a time at least, and in that time succor would arrive."

Mustapha hesitated no longer. He saw the reason of his friend's argument and taking the keys in his hand he led the way to the vaults under his house, carefully avoiding all rooms in which there were any of the enemy.

Scarcely had he locked the trap-door behind him when he heard the foot-steps of Abdullah's men and heard a well known voice say:

"They're in there—burst the door open." It was the voice of Abdullah Houssain.

"Do it if you can, you robber," shouted Mustapha through the heavy steel door. "If you do you'll have to burst seven strong bars of iron and a strong lock."

"Oh, it's you, is it, you white-livered cur. In five days from now you'll be at the bottom of the Lake of Holy Fire with your cousins. I'll give you a respite of ten days if you'll open that door. Is Baber Yataghan, the traitor, with you?"

"A sea-captain who was once in your employ, known by the name you mention, is with me," replied Mustapha with dignity. "He was kind enough to cap all his kindly services to me by warning me of your coming."

"I said a traitor by the name of Baber Yataghan," replied Abdullah. "I said nothing whatever of a sea-captain by that name."

"Then the man who is with me must be some other Baber," was Musta-pha's reply. "I know of no traitor by that name."

"Stop your fooling," said Abdullah, somewhat angrily. "Open that door or I shall be obliged to knock it down with my fist."

"What is the use of your command? You know very well that this door will not be opened at your mere threat or command, or by your puny fist. Strong steel yields not to the naked hand."

Abdullah bellowed with rage.

"You'll regret your rash words when you are in my hands," he said. "I'll make you swallow them. However, if you'll kindly open the door and surrender yourself and your companion, I'll pardon you and do just as I originally intended. Come now. Hurry up. I've no time to waste, for my ship is in the harbor."

"Abdullah Houssain," came the deliberate and slowly spoken reply, "you know very well that I will not comply with your insolent demands. I warn you that it will take you at least an hour to batter down the door. Long ere that time is passed, help will come and you will be captured. Try to get me, if you can. That is my answer to your terms. Think well before you decide what to do next."

Mustapha knew well that twenty minutes would suffice for ten or fifteen men to break down that door, but he hoped to fool Abdullah into giving up the task. Abdullah, however, knew what he was about and replied thus:

"Mustapha Dagh, do you think that you can fool me by such a lie? Do you think for one moment that I do not know as much about doors as you do, or more?"

"I think that you are a black villain," replied Mustapha, not deigning to ar-gue with his enemy.

"Suppose that I am, are you any better?"

"What do you mean?"

"I mean that you are a coward."

"Explain your most puzzling enigma."

"I should not think that an explanation would be necessary."

"Certainly it would. Go on."

"I have no more time to waste in arguing with such an insolent young man as you are. Bring the battering-ram forward," added the speaker to his men.

Mustapha lit a candle and revealed to his comrade what kind of a place they were in. It was a long low room, stored with boxes and bags, some filled with coins, others with bars of gold and silver and the rest with some valuable silks which Mustapha did not wish to sell. At the other end was another steel door similar to the first. The entire vault was made of steel and was high enough for a tall man to stand upright in.

Mustapha set the candle in a small hole in the side of a box and turned about to listen to what was going on outside. Baber, who had not spoken a word since they had entered the vault, did the same. Curious sounds met their ears.

These sounds were not at all like those made by a battering-ram. They resembled the pouring of dust or sand from a box onto the floor, and the striking of something soft against it. Then there was a short silence proceeded by a series of sharp blows, as if from the stave of a barrel onto the sand.

Then there came a spitting sound and the quick tramp of running feet, retreating. It was evident that their enemies had left the room. Mustapha feared a trap and would not open the door, so he unlocked the door at the other end of the vault and walked through into the next one, followed by Baber, just as a terrific explosion rent the air.

The door, outside of which the sounds had come, was burst into a hundred pieces which flew in all directions, and a cloud of smoke filled the apartment, making it impossible to see anything.

Mustapha leaped backward, and Baber did the same. He had scarcely time enough to close the door and lock it when the noise of the explosion ceased and he heard the tramp of many feet.

After blowing down the door, the besiegers had evidently returned expecting to have no trouble in capturing the besieged. Great was their rage and consternation on seeing another door before them, through which their intended victims had evidently escaped.

"I wonder how many vaults there are here," said Abdullah's voice.

"At least half-a-dozen," replied someone.

"I didn't think that there were more than two or three in this house," said Abdullah. "Indeed, I thought nothing about it until this moment. Well, all that we can do is to blow down this door."

Mustapha heard all that was said and opened the next door into another vault. Baber came with him and he closed the door and locked and barred it securely. Thus they went through five successive vaults and in the fifth one there was no door.

Mustapha hunted around upon the floor for a few moments with his candle and then seemed to have found what he wanted. He pressed his fingers on a certain spot, and a trap-door swung open. The candle revealed a flight of stairs and down this they went. At the foot Mustapha pressed a knob and the trap-door closed quickly and silently behind them.

"Well, what next?" said Baber, somewhat astounded by the intricate set of vaults he had passed through.

"This, at present," replied Mustapha, waving his hand around him at the cellar-like place they had entered.

"In three minutes we will be safe," he said.

Just at that moment a distant and muffled explosion reached their ears, and they knew that the door of the second vault had been blown to pieces.

Mustapha indicated a ladder of rope at the end of the cellar that seemed to run through the ceiling above by a small opening large enough to admit the body of a man.

He walked to this, candle in hand, and began to climb, followed by Baber. Up they went, through the narrow passage, until it seemed to the captain that the ladder would never end.

Suddenly, looking upward, he saw that Mustapha had reached the top and had stepped off into some floor. A moment later he had done the same and was standing beside his comrade in a small, vault-like room.

Here a curious looking piece of machinery was situated which resembled a windlass. Mustapha gave a crank a turn and this thing began to revolve very swiftly, winding up the rope ladder till it was all wound.

"That rope-ladder and passage-way was made by my father's order when the house was first built," said Mustapha, "for the same purpose as we have used it. That is, to escape by. You must know that he had quite a number of enemies, so such a precaution was necessary. I remember that he used it but once, when a band of robbers entered the place."

"But how was it re-made when your house was burned?" said Baber.

"Several of the servants knew of its existence," was the reply, "and when the house was re-built they had the passage, the rope and the machinery duplicated and placed in exactly the same position."

Mustapha took a key in his hand, stepped across the room and unlocked a small door letting in a flood of light. He blew out the candle, placed it in his pocket and stepped out into a large and well furnished room with several open windows. Baber crossed to one of these windows and looking out, beheld the gardens beneath.

"We are safe now," said Mustapha. "I think that we had better get the servants together and trap Abdullah and his men like they attempted to trap us." He crossed the room to the staircase and went down into the dining-room. Several servants were crouched under the table and at the sound of their master's voice they came out and falling at his feet implored him to save them.

"Listen," said Mustapha, "if you will follow my orders we can entrap these men. Do not fear. Help will be here soon but in the meantime we had better be busy. There are seven of you. Go and get eight of your fellows and then return to this room. By that time I will have all my plans made."

The servants did as he told them and soon returned with eight of their fellow slaves. Mustapha and Baber led the way to the trap-door of the room next to the first vault and went through (Abdullah's men having left it open). Then they stood in the room where Abdullah and his hirelings had been when the conversation between him and Mustapha concerning whether Baber was a sea-captain or a traitor had taken place.

The door of the vault had been torn into fragments by the explosion and lay scattered all over the floor. At the other end of the vault its door lay in pieces. At that moment another explosion announced that Abdullah had blown up the door of the third vault.

"We must follow in their tracks," said Mustapha, "and when they have entered the cellar under the last vault we must pile casks and boxes over the opening. Abdullah will doubtless discover the secret spring in the floor, and indeed his men cannot help stepping on it, there are so many of them. They will all rush in to the cellar and we will close the trap-door over them and put things atop it."

"But will they not blow it to pieces with their powder?" inquired Baber.

"Not likely," said Mustapha. "We will fool them into believing that there are many of us, so many, indeed that such a proceeding would endanger their lives. Even if they do not believe us we can shoot them as they come out, as a last resource."

"I would like the pleasure of shooting Abdullah Houssain," said Baber bitterly. "If I get the chance you can wage your last piece of silver that I will. I do not believe in granting mercy to such a wretch as he."

"I can scarcely blame you, Baber," said Mustapha. "I think that I would do the same. They're going to blow up the next vault. Listen!"

At that moment another explosion reached their ears. It was a little further off than its predecessor.

"I would not wonder if their powder would give out by the time they reach the cellar," said Mustapha. "They cannot have very much with them."

"I hope it does," was Baber's only comment. "It will help us greatly."

"Well, come on," replied Mustapha, entering the next vault. The servants, hesitating and fearful, followed him, huddling together and ready to run at the first moment danger showed itself in their path.

"I fear that your slaves will desert us at the crucial moment," whispered Baber in his friend's ear. "They are exceedingly timid at this very moment. I wouldn't trust a Nubian or an African for anything when it comes to personal bravery. Give me a Turk, a Hindu, a Persian or a Greek, and I will feel much safer."

"I think that I agree with you," said Mustapha, "and the very next time that I have to buy slaves, I will see that I get only those known for fearlessness and personal bravery."

Just then they heard another explosion.

"They are in the vault over the cellar," said Mustapha. "In a few minutes we will have them in our trap."

He rushed into the next vault, with Baber at his side. The servants followed, somewhat encouraged by their master's example. It was well that this was so, for had it been otherwise the two friends would not have been able to succeed in their object.

At the very moment that this occured a cry of triumph rent the air and they knew that the trap-door had been discovered.

Mustapha and Baber ran forward with the Nubians at their heels and entered the fifth vault just in time to see the last of Abdullah's men disappear through the trap-door, leaving it open.

Baber seized the covering in an instant and slammed it in the face of the astonished man, who turned on the stairway to see what all the trouble was about. Then Baber sat down on it and Mustapha and the slaves ran for casks and boxes to place in his stead.

Baber rose from his seat as they returned and Mustapha deposited a heavy box on the door. Each of the fifteen servants did the same and in a few minutes the floor was entirely covered. Each box and barrel weighed at least a hundred pounds, so the entrapped men would have to lift 1600 pounds off the trap-door before they could gain their freedom.

"Even if they have got powder, they will have a hard time in sending all that into the air," said Mustapha. "I fancy that they will not attempt the task."

Just then twenty or thirty of the neighbors entered the vault fully armed.

"Mustapha Dagh!" said the foremost, in astonishment, as he gazed upon the smiling face of that person.

The others all had some profession of astonishment to make and everyone had to ask a thousand questions which Mustapha did not think it best to attempt to answer under the circumstances. Therefore he said:

"Silence, all of you. I will tell you everything afterwards. At present we have too much to do. I must ask you to help me to capture the villains who have entered my house, and who, at the present moment, are entrapped in the cellar beneath our feet." He dismissed the servants, there being scarcely room enough for them and the other men at the same time.

"Now keep silent," said Mustapha to his neighbors. They did so and everything became as still as the grass but for their heavy breathing and the noise made by the twenty-five men in the cellar. These were cursing and raging and above the tumult of their voices rose a shriller voice as if from someone answering a question.

"Master, we have no more powder," it said.

Abdullah's voice then rose above the general pandemonium.

"Why isn't there more powder?" he roared.

"Because we used it all up blowing those doors to pieces," replied the shrill voice, becoming still shriller.

"Why didn't you tell me of this before?" roared Abdullah louder than ever.

"Because we didn't know it ourselves," replied the voice.

"It is your business to know," said Abdullah in the same tone as before.

"I forgot," replied the man.

"Should you have forgotten?" asked Abdullah. "A moment ago you told me that you did not know that our stack of powder was exhausted. Now you tell me that you forgot that it was all gone. You are a double-dyed liar. If you had known that we had no more powder you would not have very likely forgotten the fact. I think that you knew but did not want to tell me. I also think that you are in league with my enemies."

"I deny your false charge," said the man hotly. "When I stated that I forgot I meant that I had forgotten that it was my business to know whether our stack of powder was exhausted or not."

"By these words of yours," said Abdullah, "you plainly intimate that you think me a liar. Men, what is the fate of a man who calls his master a liar to his face?"

"Death," said a chorus of voices, with one accord.

"Then Death it shall be," said Abdullah. "You shall die before our enemies starve us to death." There was a clank of steel as if a sword had been drawn. Mustapha knew at once that Abdullah was about to kill the man who had been arguing with him.

"Abdullah Houssain," he shouted, "if you kill that man I will double the torture you will receive when you are captured."

"I am my own master," said Abdullah with dignity.

"Surrender," said Mustapha in reply, drawing his scimitar and rapping upon the floor.

"Not at your command," said Abdullah, furiously.

"You had better."

"Had I?"

"Yes."

"Why?"

"You will know afterwards. I will have my men make a small hole in the floor through which you and your retainers are to pass all the weapons. Then I will open the door and you are to emerge one at a time and suffer yourselves to be bound hand and foot. You are to come first."

There was a short discussion between Abdullah and his men in a low tone at the end of which Abdullah said:

"We agree to your terms. It will not be necessary for you to make a hole in the floor for we will pass our weapons to you as we emerge. I promise you that we will not do otherwise. There will be no treachery on our part."

"I have your word for it then?"

"Yes; my word of honor. May I die in burning oil if I break my promise."

"Very well, then."

The boxes and casks were removed from the door and it was lifted. The head of Abdullah appeared. He passed his pistols, his dagger, his scimitar and his musket to those waiting and then stepped upon the floor of the vault and suffered his hands and legs to be bound severely with ropes.

Twenty-five other men did the same and in ten minutes the whole of the party was captured. They were led forth by the neighbors and Mustapha. At the door Mustapha ran full against Slatin Baabbec, the pasha of Bagdad, and ten soldiers, armed cap-a-pie in full armor.

"You have them, I see," said he with a sigh of satisfaction. "I had informed several of my officers of your return, they promising not to reveal the secret, and the story of your adventures. One of these officers happened to pass your house, on his way to the river and saw Abdullah Houssain and twenty or more of his men making for your home.

"The officers immediately came to me and told me what was happening. I brought the soldiers with me, and here I am. You may hand the prisoners over to me and I will see that they are lodged securely in prison for the night. In the morning you may come to my house where a trial will be held, with a cadi to officiate. I think that at present you had better get your supper."

Before Mustapha could murmur his thanks the pasha, his ten men and the prisoners were away, and he turned to Baber and his friends and said to them:

"Stay with me, and after supper I will relate to you all my adventures."

Chapter XX

"And I will tell you my tale," added Baber.

"I had quite forgotten about that," said Mustapha. "During the excitement of the last half hour I forgot your promise, and suppose you did the same."

"I did," said Baber.

"Well, come on and eat your supper. You can talk about it afterwards."

By the time they had reached the dining-room, supper was ready. The cooks had not forgotten their duties in the excitement of the moment.

After supper was over they all assembled in Mustapha's room and he told his tale to them, from the time of his disappearance up to the time they had entered the vault on that day to help him catch Abdullah and his men. They had seen these men enter Mustapha's residence and fifteen minutes later had heard the first of the explosives.

They had then formed themselves into an armed band and when all was ready had entered Mustapha's house.

"Now you can tell your story," said Mustapha to Baber.

Baber composed himself, and after a few preliminaries began the story where he had left Mustapha's tale, up to the time he had entered Mustapha's house to warn him. The narrative was as follows:

"When the 'Fire-Worshippers' captured us in the chamber I saw Mustapha make for the little tunnel, directing to us to follow. This was impossible, for our captors had bound us securely.

"I shouted to Mustapha to escape and he went on. Some of Abdullah's men followed him, but I do not know how many. I think there were six or seven. I did not think they would catch him, for he was a good runner and I knew that he would escape if he did not sprain his ankle, or harm himself otherwise, or give out, or the tunnel end in a trap. I hoped that it would bring him to the seashore where he might find a boat and stand some chance of being picked up by a passing vessel if his enemies did not catch him.

"Well, our captors held us in that cave for a long time, evidently waiting for the return of those who had pursued Mustapha. In about an hour they skulked in, looking like whipped dogs.

"'Did you get him?' asked Abdullah.

"'No,' replied one of the skulkers. 'He escaped and was picked up by a passing vessel.'

"'Why did you allow him to escape?' asked Abdullah, furiously.

"'We could not help it,' answered another skulker in a whining tone.

"'Why couldn't you help it?' asked Abdullah in a nasty tone. I knew at once that there would be trouble for the skulkers.

"'You have purposely let a prisoner escape,' said Abdullah, with menace in his voice, 'and you have denied my charges, thus plainly saying that you think me a liar.'

"'We did not mean that!' said the skulkers in a chorus.

"'I don't care whether you mean it or not,' said Abdullah. 'You shall each receive a hundred lashes and be confined in prison for a month and be given fifty lashes each day of that month. Lead them away,' he added, addressing some of his hirelings.

"Well, those skulkers cried and sobbed and whined and protested against their treatment, but it was of no use. Abdullah was as stubborn as a mule and determined to have his way. I almost pitied the poor fellows.

"'Now take these men back to their prison,' said Abdullah to his men, meaning the cousins, their father and I.

"'We might have escaped,' I yelled back at him, as the captors led us out of the room.

"'Yes, you might, but you didn't,' he replied and turned his back upon us as if we did not exist.

"It was useless to say more, so I refrained. The men led us back to our own prison where they locked us up again, and piled things against the old door so that we could not escape. Then they went away and left us there, as unhappy a lot as you would wish to see. We sat down in silence and cursed our luck and vowed to revenge ourselves on Abdullah if we got the chance.

"Ten minutes later a man entered the room bearing a large European clock. He did not seem to fear us in the least, and set the clock up against the wall as unconcernedly as if we had not been there.

"'Now,' said he, 'you can watch the clock and know how many hours you have to live. At four to-morrow morning, Baber Yataghan, the sea-captain, is to die, by means of the chute in this floor. It will send him into the lake below.'

"'That is me,' said I.

"'Well, I can hardly help pitying you,' said the man.

"'When shall we die?' asked Ahmed.

"'Two hours afterwards,' said the man, with a grim smile playing upon his lips. 'However, you will be removed from the prison some time to-night, for you are not to die by the chute. Abdullah will tend to your fate, never fear.'

"'No, I am not afraid that he will forget us,' said Ahmed. 'But I fear that he has some terrible fate in store for us, some fate of which we know nothing.

I am not a coward, but I shall have to admit that the uncertainty does not reassure me in the least. Abdullah is a man of resource and it is not likely that his inventive powers will fail him.'

"'I shall tell him of your compliment,' said the man, with a grin. 'I wager you that he'll be pleased.'

"'I have nothing to wager,' said Ahmed, sadly.

"'Well, that's so, but haven't you your life?'

"'Yes, but that will soon be mine no more.'

"'Well, you are in a tight fix. If I thought that I could help you in the least, I would. But I'm afraid that all my efforts would be in vain. I am heartily sick of this society of the "Fire-Worshippers" and wish that I had never joined it.'

"'Your sentiments are kindly,' said I, 'but would be more so if you would carry them out. That, however, as you plainly say, is next to impossible, though I, myself, do not think that there is any such thing as impossible. However, you may think different. Let us part, thinking that we have done each other no wrong.'

"'I heartily agree with you in your statement that nothing is impossible,' said the man, 'but at present I do not care to run the risk.'

"And with that remark as his farewell, he passed out of the room, and left us to our own meditations. I have seen nothing of him since. If all his observations were true, he was an honest man, and if such be the case I can give him my blessing with an easy conscience and the assurance that it is bestowed on one worthy of it.

"Well, we passed the night slowly, and watched the clock's hand move silently, imperceptibly on. The dim torches shed an unearthly light within that room, and left many corners in darkness. Except for the sway of the pendulum all was as silent as the grave.

"About midnight ten or twelve men entered and took away Akmat and his four sons. That was my last sight of them, and is likely to remain so." Here Baber paused in his tale for a moment to wipe away a stray tear that was trickling down his cheek. As soon as this performance was through, he went on again as follows:

"They all bade me farewell, and then the men took them away. Akmat was the last to pass through the door and he looked at me and pointed to the chute on the floor.

"I understood, and happening to look at the clock, I hit upon a plan for my deliverance. The man had told me that I would die at seven the next morning. Abdullah would be upon the edge of the lake, probably five minutes before that time, to see me shoot out into empty air and then drop to the fiery lake below.

"The men who were to see that I was started on my journey to death would probably be in my room about half an hour before seven. As soon as they had performed their duty they would leave the room and probably leave the door open or else not fasten it.

"I went to the clock and grasping the hour hand with my hand, I turned it back twenty-five minutes and then resumed my seat and waited patiently for doom. My plan is probably plain to you, but I will explain it more plainly.

"If Abdullah's men entered the room half an hour before time, they would see that it was time for the execution and would therefore carry it out. I would hang over the pit by means of the ropes until they were gone and then climb up again and escape if the door were left open. The possibility that from force of habit they might lock it was all that troubled me. However, I could see no way out of the matter and determined to take the risk.

"As I had conjectured, these men entered the room, that morning long before time. They looked at the clock and I did so also. It said three minutes to seven. One of the men murmured an ejaculation of astonishment.

"Turning to his comrades he remarked:

"'We must be awfully slow.'

"They then took me and tied my legs and hands together. I had not anticipated this and began to think that my last hour had come.

"However, they did not tie the ropes very tightly, so I saw that, with good luck, I might yet escape.

"While they were conducting me to the chute I was doing my bit to loosen the bonds upon my wrists.

"I succeeded fairly well and saw that it would be an easy matter to slip the ropes off while I was descending.

"Right on the hour they lowered me into the chute, gave me a push with their hands and I was off.

"I went with frightful rapidity for the first ten feet, and then I managed to get those infernal ropes off my wrists and pushed against the sides of the chute with my hands. By doing this I steadied myself so that I did not go very fast, and when a few moments later I shot out into the air I was able to easily stop my descent when I grasped the strongest of the ropes.

"I let myself slide down to the loop at the end and when there, I took a rest and surveyed the scene a little more calmly. The first thing to be done was to get the ropes off my ankles, and this I soon accomplished. Then I took another rest, and gave a last look at the lake of fire, and then extricated myself from the loop and began to climb. At the second loop I rested a little and then went on and finally found myself in the mouth of the chute. I put my hands and legs against the side and began to climb.

"I heartily assure you that it was no child's work, and when I had reached the brink I felt as if I wanted to stop.

"This, however, would not do, so I went on, though my arms and legs ached with the exertion, and at last pulled myself out at the top, completely exhausted and out of breath.

"For the space of perhaps five minutes I lay there on the floor, unable to rise. When I had regained my breath I rose to my feet and made for the door, which, to my great joy, had been left open.

"I went down the staircase silently and met no one on the way. After passing through a number of rooms, I at last found myself in the antechamber. There was nobody there, so I entered the tunnel and went on. I finally reached the end, coming out near the sea. The ship of Abdullah Houssain was not in sight, so I concluded that it was either off on a voyage or on the other side of the island. The latter surmise was the correct one as I afterward discovered, to my peril.

"Off in the distance I perceived a ship, and casting myself into the sea I swam toward her. The crew observed me when I came within a quarter of a mile of them and a boat was lowered which picked me up soon afterward.

"I was taken on board the ship, which I found to be a Turkish vessel with a Turkish crew and captain bound for Bagdad. I told my tale to the captain and he was so interested in me that he offered me a free passage home. This offer I readily accepted, but promised him that he would not remain unrewarded.

"He was somewhat incredulous when I first told him the story, but I offered to prove it to him as soon as we reached Bagdad. He was convinced by this and said that he did not wish any further proof than my word.

"After we were out of sight of the island I began to think that we would not be pursued, but the illusion was soon dispelled by the sight of Abdullah's vessel far off on the western horizon. I readily recognized it and told the captain of my discovery.

"Every sail was raised and we flew along at a lively rate, but still the other ship gained though almost imperceptibly. In two days we were in the strait of Ormuz and the enemy was not three miles away. When we reached the mouth of the Tigris a day later she had gained a mile.

"Four days afterwards, when we reached Bagdad, she was only a hundred yards behind and I had scarcely landed when a boat was lowered from her side, filled with armed men. I made at my fast pace for your house and arrived about five minutes ahead of them, as you already know. That, my friends, is the end of my eventful tale. You may believe it or not believe it, but it is true, and you have my word of honor for it."

Baber leaned back on the divan where he was lying and drew a long breath.

"I am sure that we do not doubt your veracity," said Mustapha.

"Well, then, we will say no more about it. I am sure that that will be quite satisfactory to all parties concerned. It will be to me, at least."

"I heartily agree with you. Who will start up a conversation?"

No one appeared to be able to think of anything worthy of discussion, so he himself started up an argument as to the different merits of trade by ships and trade by caravans, he himself taking the former. Baber sided with him, citing reasons why ships were better than caravans, but most of the others took the opposite. The argument waxed warmer and warmer, and at last ended with the victory of the side of those who had said that ships were the best. By this time it was almost midnight, so the neighbors bade Mustapha farewell and went home.

Next morning when Mustapha awoke, he found that his tale was common property all over the city. Fruit vendors talked about it in the bazaars and it was the chief subject of conversation everywhere.

Mustapha ate his breakfast early and then started for the pasha's house. He arrived there an hour after his start and was immediately admitted to the presence of Slatin Baabbec.

He found the room almost full. Abdullah and his comrades stood in a row with chains upon their legs and arms and to each was attached a heavy iron ball, fastened to the chain at the ankle by another chain. Besides these men, ten soldiers with muskets in their hands and scimitars loose in their scabbards were there, standing behind the captives.

A venerable looking cadi was sitting cross-legged on a large rug in front of them and by his side the pasha was sitting.

Another man was sitting at a table just back of these two with parchment, ink and pens at hand to keep record of the trial.

Slatin motioned Mustapha to his side and told him to be seated. He did so, sitting down on another rug nearby. All eyes were turned upon him and he grew excited and perhaps a little nervous. The heated air of the room made him feel sick, and his face grew red.

The cadi cleared his throat and said:

"I hope that all present are ready for the trial. It is merely a matter of form, but to let the prisoners have justice and an opportunity of making any statements in their own defence that they wish, it must be given their will.

"Mustapha Dagh, you may stand up and give your father's name, and your position in life, and your personal history up to the time you became complicated in this affair."

"My father's name is Cogia Dagh," said Mustapha, "and he was a prosperous merchant of this city. He died at the age of seventy when I was eighteen years of age. At the present time I am twenty-three years of age. I will be twenty-four next January. When he died, he left me a large fortune and a thriving business. I had quite a number of ships which I sent on voyages to foreign countries for the purpose of trading with the inhabitants.

"As far as I know my father had few enemies, but the worst of these foes is Abdullah Houssain, the head-villain of the prisoners whom you see before you. Just what the cause of the enmity between them was I do not know, but I suspect that it was some old love-affair." At this statement Abdullah flushed angrily and a frown settled upon his face and threatened to stay there. Mustapha went on as follows:

"At any rate he attempted to ruin my father's trade with foreign lands by prejudicing the people against him and various other tricks which I shall not be malicious enough to name.

"These tricks failed and I believe that then Abdullah tried to vent his anger upon me. I think that he attempted to have me assassinated, but I do not know for certain. Whatever happened was kept a close secret.

"I lived a very quiet, uneventful life, up to the time that I became complicated in this affair. I am studious and of somewhat athletic habits and am unmarried. I have many friends with some of whom I am very intimate and few enemies that I know of. That, O cadi, is my answer."

"Secretary, have you recorded all this?" said the cadi, turning to the man at the table who had been industriously scribbling ever since Mustapha had opened his mouth. He wrote a few moments after the cadi had addressed him and then raised his head and said, "Yes."

"Let the trial proceed," said the cadi. He then addressed Abdullah in much the same words as he had used in speaking to Mustapha.

Abdullah told his story, and the scribe at the table scribbled industriously. It was as follows:

"My name is Abdullah Houssain, and I am fifty years of age to-day. I was born August tenth, 1600, in the city of Constantinople. I am not ashamed to state that he was a corsair and earned a living by robbing the Genovese ships and other European vessels in the Mediterranean sea. He made a great deal of money and brought me up in the midst of wealth and luxury. His name was Constantine Houssain, and his father was a Turk of Damascus and his mother a Turkish lady of Constantinople. My mother died on the day that I was born.

"When I reached the age of twenty-one my father died and left me sole heir to his great estate. I immediately came to Bagdad with all my wealth where I have married several ladies of rank. They are at Antioch at the present time with a distant relation of mine. They left the city a month ago. I have no children. I leave the city many times on private business and sometimes do not return for many months. I have always lived a quiet and peaceful life. That, O cadi, is my answer."

Abdullah ceased speaking and watched the scribe till he had finished. Then that person raised his head and the cadi went on with the trial.

He picked up a piece of parchment at his side and read from it the following:

"Accusation.

"You, Abdullah Houssain, are accused of being a member of the secret society of the 'Fire-Worshippers,' which is a crime punishable by death. If you can prove your innocence you will be let free, but if you cannot you will die.

> "Signed,
> "Slatin Baabbec,
> "Pasha of Bagdad,
> "_____ _____, Cadi."

"That is the accusation," said the cadi. "You may defend yourself as well as you can. Scribe, take care that you make no mistakes. Abdullah, you must speak slowly and distinctly and everyone must keep silent."

Abdullah straightened himself and cleared his throat to speak. His face wore an expression of anxiety and worry, and he appeared to be desperate. His face grew white as he began to speak. What he said was as follows:

"I, Abdullah Houssain, do disclose that the accusation is false and that I can prove myself innocent. I am sure that all my friends who were arrested with me will prove it also. I have papers in my pocket which prove that I was the real son of Cogia Dagh and that this Mustapha is an impostor!"

"Let me see this," said the cadi, trembling with astonishment. His brain was in a whirl and he did not think that the prisoner was chained. All eyes were riveted upon Abdullah is astonishment and everyone seemed frozen to the spot. Mustapha almost fainted and knew not what to do.

"Unbind him," said the cadi to the soldiers, scarcely knowing what he said.

"Yes, unbind him and let him bring the paper to us," said the pasha, not knowing what might happen.

The soldiers did mechanically as they were ordered and the long chains fell at Abdullah's feet and left him free.

He quickly drew from his pocket a heavy packet and quickly unbound it and walking up to the cadi, threw it in his lap. The cadi unrolled it slowly and everyone's gaze was riveted on it; no one saw anything else, nor thought of any other thing, least of all Abdullah. They did not notice him at all and when the cadi looked up from the roll of parchment to speak to him, he was gone!

During the excitement which had followed his handing the packet to the cadi he had left the room and escaped.

Instantly an uproar arose and everyone except Mustapha and the cadi left the place in hot pursuit. The soldiers and the pasha led their prisoners away and within a few moments all was silent in that room.

"Come here," said the cadi to Mustapha. Mustapha mechanically obeyed, and rising to his feet walked to the old man's side and knelt down and gazed at the parchment held up for his inspection. He thought rather than saw the one row of capital letters on it, and then rolled over on his back and hid his face in his hands, not knowing whether to laugh or weep. The words were:

"What fools ye be! My psychology is superior to all your reasoning!"

Chapter XXI

Let us traverse the space of time, and go back to the year 1595.

It was spring in the southern lands and along the coast of the Mediterranean. At Constantinople on the Bosporus all was bustle and noisiness. Vessels of many descriptions were in and about the harbor. Among these were two very large Turkish vessels carrying many guns. They were just about to sail for the open sea on a long voyage. They were a pair of noted corsairs and the cpatains were more dreaded by all the merchant ships of other lands.

A young man of thirty or thereabouts, named Cogia Dagh, was the captain of the largest. The other captain was a man named Constantine Houssain, and he was the most dreaded of the two, though his ship was the smaller.

However, both these ships worked in unison, and their commanders were very good friends, though frequent quarrels marred their intimacy, each having a very quick and violent temper.

In those days it was not thought wrong for the ships of one country to attack and rob the ships of another, so the calling of the corsair was one of which the participants were not ashamed. Constantine and his brother-captain had often made rich presents to the Sultan of Turkey, so they had eventually earned his good will; in fact he had become greatly interested in their undertakings and had helped them by giving them money and frequently supplying them with weapons.

The two captains were now standing upon the deck of the largest vessel, called the "Eagle," discussing their plans together.

Constantine was the younger of the two, being about twenty-five. He wore silk pantaloons and soft leather shoes and a turban of cloth-of-gold. His short jacket was of a gay red color and was richly embroidered in many hues.

His face was very dark and swarthy and was a cruel expression, tho sometimes relaxing into a smile. His nose resembled a very small, short scimitar, curved the wrong way, being very acquiline and suggestively Jewish. However, not a drop of Jewish blood ran in his veins, for he was a pure-blooded Turk. His hair was long and very black, and his ears prominent. They suggested the wings of a butterfly, somewhat minimized and more in proportion to bulk and size.

His companion was not at all like him, except in his being similarly dressed. His features were regular and his nose was in proportion to the rest of his face. His ears were close to his head and his hair was cut off short. An expression of firmness was always on his face, but there was none of the cruelness that characterized that of his friend.

"You have all our plans arranged," said Constantine, half in interrogation and half in assurance.

"Yes," replied Cogia. "We will sail into the Mediterranean and make as near the Northern coast as possible. I have received news that a ship from Spain, laden with treasure, is bound for the city of Rome. We will attempt to capture this first, if we do not meet with some other prize. However, there are others in the race besides us." By the last sentence he meant that other pirate ships would be after the treasure ship. "But I think we stand as good a chance as anyone," he added, confidently.

"Yes, I suppose we do," said Cogia. "All precaution must be taken, however, and I would not scruple at putting one of our boats out of business, if it should be absolutely necessary to our success, by battle or some trick."

"Neither would I," said the other, his features relaxing from a dark frown into a grim, cruel smile.

"Bring up the anchor," he shouted to his men and the order was obeyed. The crew of the other ship did the same. Cogia intended to stay on his friend's vessel during the first part of the voyage, and had appointed a man to take his place as captain.

Past the vessels in the harbor they swept, at a rate of four miles an hour, and aided by a strong breeze, they were in the open sea presently, and upon their long voyage. The two friends then resumed their conversation and went on discussing what they should do.

"Now," said Constantine after an hours talk, "Now we had best go below and consult our charts and find when we are most liable to encounter this Spanish treasure ship, and arrange our maneuvers accordingly."

"Then we had better hurry if we hope to be through by dinner-time," said his companion. "We are out of the harbor and into the sea and it will soon be time for me to return to my ship."

"What you speak is true," said the other, stepping toward the hatchway. A few moments later they were in Constantine's little cabin, which was literally filled with books, manuscripts and other articles of the same class. A small table beside a cushioned divan was covered with writing materials and charts and maps.

Constantine seated himself at this table, pen in hand, and Cogia began to rummage among the maps until he found what he wanted. It was a very large one, rolled on a stick. He unrolled it and laid it on the divan beside his friend. Then he deposited weights on each of its four corners and began to look at it. It was a large map of the Mediterranean sea and the shores of all the lands bordering on it, from the Strait of Gibralter at one end to the island of Cyprus and the coasts of Greece and Turkey at the other, with Morroco, Algiers and the rest of the Barbary States on the southern shore, and Spain, France, Italy and other lands to the north.

Though not as accurate as our modern maps, it was as accurate as any then manufactured and had been drawn by a famous Italian Geographer who had made a careful study of all the lands he mapped before attempting to map them. His name was at the bottom, but neither of the pirate captains regarded it in the least.

"The treasure ship will start from Cadiz to-morrow," said Constantine, "and will be very heavily laden. She will travel at the rate of about four miles an hour if she has the kinds of winds that I anticipate. Marseilles in France is her destination. We have over twice as far to sail as they, but we go two or three miles faster than their ship. We will probably catch them on their return voyage, somewhere near the strait of Gibralter, but we must not lose any time. In less than fifteen days from now the treasure will be ours if nothing happens to prevent our expedition."

"Good," said Cogia. "We have them surely. Now draw up your plan of battle and by that time dinner will be ready."

Constantine bent to his work with one eye on the map and the other on his parchment. In half an hour he looked up and announced that he was through. He handed the plan to Cogia who read it and approved of it. Then he handed it back to his friend and seated himself on the divan. A Negro slave soon entered, and cleared the table. A few minutes later two more slaves entered bringing with them a hot dinner on trays. These they placed upon the little table and then withdrew to one side while the corsairs ate.

When this was done they removed the dishes and went out. Cogia sat sipping his wine and watched his friend, who was a total astainer, take up a large, leather-bound volume which he opened. The leaves were of parchment and covered with tiny handwriting in Turkish and Arabic. He sat long, poring over this, and then motioned Cogia to his side and had him read what was written in a certain place, indicating the place with his forefinger.

Cogia read it and then said:

"It is some magical spell, is it not?"

"Yes," said the other; "do you wish me to try its powers?"

"Very well," said Cogia jestingly, not believing that his friend could do any such thing.

"You are not superstitious," said Constantine, with an evil smile, "but I warrant you that your nerves will be shaken when I am through with you."

He walked to the little window of the cabin and pressed a spring. Instantly a large piece of wood was over it, excluding all light in that direction. The room was now very dark. Constantine lit a lamp and then shut the door, telling a man in the corridor without that he was not to be disturbed by anyone until he himself opened the door.

Then he took a copper brazier and filled it with burning coals which he happened to have on hand. Then he blew out the lamp and the room was in utter darkness except for the feeble glow from the brazier's contents.

This scarcely illuminated the cabin and all except the center was in darker gloom. Constantine, with the open book in his hand, stood beside the brazier and his comrade sat on the divan in the darkness and watched him.

He began to read from the book the very paragraph that he had shown to Cogia. The weird light shone on his face as he read, and made it seem more cruel than before, and when he raised his hand as if to punctuate and give emphasis to some part, he seemed, for the moment, transfigured into a fiend of the pit, cursing all mankind with words of evil.

The spell, or magical conjuration, did not awaken Cogia's interest. It was like any ordinary spell, and he had seen many magicians perform their tricks with the aid, or supposed aid, of like ones.

What would be the outcome of his friend's fooling, he did not know but he suspected some prearranged trick and was prepared for one.

In a few moments Constantine laid aside the book of magic and waved his arms in the air over the brazier and in its full light.

"O mighty one, oracle of the sufferings of mankind, I conjure you to speak to my friend and me and reveal to us our fate, whether it be good or evil. In the name of the Evil One, I conjure you to speak."

He stopped with his arms still in air, and Cogia bent forward with a grin of anticipation and amusement on his face, expecting some trick.

A few moments of strained silence passed by and was then broken by a deep, sinister voice, which seemed not of this earth, and which said:

"I speak, and will answer thy question. Not long hence you and thy friend shall become estranged on a woman's account and never be friends again. I speak the truth, though ye may not believe me. I speak words of wisdom, and if ye value thy future happiness, harken to them."

The voice ceased and Cogia said with a smile:

"Very good, Constantine, I see that you have not forgotten the lessons in ventriloquism that were given to us by the Hindu traveler. I fear that I have forgotten mine, but see that you have not followed my bad example."

"Ventriloquism?" said Constantine. "But you speak the truth. It is ventriloquism. And now I think that you would do well to light the lamp."

Cogia did as required and then opened the door and the window. Then he extinguished the light and his friend called a servant and bade him remove the burning coals.

"I thought that I would startle you," he said with a sigh, "but you had too good a memory." Little did he think that the prediction he had given, as the oracle, in play, would come true, and within such a short space of time. But that goddess whom men call Fate has strange whims and sometimes causes things, which are in themselves not spoken in earnest, to come true. And such was to happen to these two good friends, and break their happiness and friendship to bits, never to be mended for the rest of their lives. It is lamented that such things be, yet they be, and what exists cannot be nothing. That something which is called love, though it in itself causes happiness, may break up that same happiness, by allowing Jealousy to share in the ruling of its Kingdom.

The voyage went on, with few events of importance and fifteen days had passed away. On the morning of the sixteenth, Cogia, on board his ship, beheld another ship not far away and in all respects resembling the treasure-ship.

She was going at a slow rate and was evidently heavy laden, being very low in the water. The crew could be seen on the decks, watching the pirate-ship.

A gentle breeze was blowing and Constantine and his friend gave an order to his men. Great sails which had until now been idle were pressed into service and the "Eagle" and her sister ship leaped forward at a redoubled rate.

Foam and spray flew before them and they left a white wake behind. The waters hissed and the masts groaned, but the ship went onward like some bird in its flight.

The treasure-ship did its best to escape but after half an hour's race was caught by the swift corsair. A few moments later the "Eagle" was alongside and her crew was swarming over the bulwarks upon the half-frightened Spaniards.

A minute after that Cogia's ship was on the other side and he and his men, eager for their share of the plunder, sprang over the bulwarks.

In ten minutes the fight was over and such of the Spaniards as had not been killed were bound with ropes and then tied to the masts.

Then the dead bodies were thrown overboard and the Turks made for the hold, where they found an ample reward.

Chest upon chest and bag upon bag of gold were piled there, and these the maurauders dragged upon deck and placed on their own vessels. The plunder was shared equally among the men and the captains, one third going to the latter and the remainder being divided among the crews. But there was enough to keep each for a lifetime, and all professed themselves satisfied.

A young French woman among the prisoners struck Constantine's fancy and he had her brought on board his ship and gave her his cabin.

The rest of the crew he left on board their own vessel and then he and his friend turned their vessels homeward.

Few of the Turks had been wounded during the combat and only one had been killed. However, the death of the man was not much lamented but he was buried with all honors, as befitting a true Moslem.

Constantine had fallen in love with the French lady and was determined to make her his wife. She refused all his offers and he became angry.

"If you do not marry me I will kill you," he said at last. But the interpreter who was a man who did not like Constantine very well, translated his words as follows: "I will give you three hours to consider my offer in and if at the end of that time you refuse, I will sell you as a slave."

"You dare not!" The woman's eyes flashed fire as she said the words and the man translated them literally.

"Why do I not dare?" said Constantine.

"Because the good God would punish you."

"Because I will slap your face," translated the interpreter.

"Then I will make your death more cruel."

"I will kiss you," was the translation.

"And then sell me into slavery?"

"Yes."

"I thought that Turks did not kiss slaves."

"If the slaves are pretty."

"I am not pretty."

"Yes you are. A Persian poet would go raving mad over the color of your hair and your face."

"Yes?"

"It is so. Will you marry me?"

"For the hundredth time I must refuse."

"Why?"

"Because I do not love you."

"Then whom do you love?"

"That is none of your business."

"Why?"

"Because it is so."

"Your answer is an enigma."

"I should hope that it would be."

"Why should you?"

"Because you deserve nothing better."

"You are impertinent."

"I despise you."

"Perhaps you do. But does that prevent me from loving you?"

"I do not suppose that it does."

"Then what do you suppose?"

"That you are a very cruel man."

"Why?"

"Because you are cruel to me."

"I cannot see that I am."

"But you do not see yourself as others see you."

"Perhaps I do not."

"Then will you give me a respite of a few days in which to think over your offer of marriage?"

"Of course. But I thought that you had had enough time already. However, you shall have your wish."

The French lady, who was not lacking in strategy, left him in high glee. His threat to sell her as a slave, as it had been translated, did not frighten her. She intended, when she reached Constantinople, to throw herself upon the mercy of the Sultan, and felt certain that she would meet with success.

A description of her is probably necessary to satisfy the curiosity of the reader, and as it is the custom of authors to gratify this curiosity I will not make myself an expection of the general rule. She was the daughter of a French merchant of Marseilles and had gone on board the trasure-ship as a passenger to Cadiz to visit some relatives in that city. Her name was Marie Cardouy. She was of medium height and well-formed. Her hair fell to her waist in a shower of molten gold and seemed to wrap her head in a halo worthy of a saint. Her small, delicate nose was as straight as that of a Greek and much more beautiful. Her eyes were of a deep blue, being in keeping with her hair. Marie wore the clothing of the time which befitted her well and set off her beauty. And the silk and velvet of the garments showed that she came of a rich family. She was shrewd to a great degree and capable of concealing her feelings, as you have already seen, but the rest of her characteristics will be afterwards shown.

Now the captain of the "Eagle" was very deeply in love with this lady, so deeply as to blunt his usual capacity for cold-blooded reasoning. He did not see that her request to think the matter over was only a ruse to gain time but believed that she was in earnest. Therefore he had granted it, though if he had not been in love he would not have done so.

Next day he sent an invitation to Cogia, who had not yet noticed the young French woman, to dine on board his ship. Cogia accepted the invitation and was instantly captivated by her beauty. During the meal he kept his eyes fixed on her and did not utter a word except when Constantine asked him some direct question.

Constantine himself noticed this and plainly intimated that he was displeased.

Cogia did not notice his angry signals and kept on looking at the lady. To make the matter worse, she smiled at him and he was instantly lifted to the seventh heaven of bliss.

Marie saw then that the poor fellow was in love with her and instantly determined to use him as an instrument to escape from Constantine's clutches.

Therefore she smiled at him again. Cogia thought that she loved him and only desired that Constantine should leave the apartment. The unobliging Constantine, however, did not gratify this desire. On the contrary he kept as close to the two as if they had been a pair of prisoners that he feared would escape.

He was beginning to get jealous, too. A few more of those smiles at Cogia would have caused something to happen, and Marie had sense enough to know that. So she refrained, and poor Cogia sat there waiting until she should be pleased to look in his direction again.

Suddenly there was a commotion on board the ship and all the sounds of a combat reached their ears.

"A couple of the men are fighting," said Constantine, leaping to his feet and rushing out of the room.

Hardly had he disappeared, when Cogia threw himself at the feet of the French lady and told her, in all the language of a Persian poet, that he loved her.

"I love you," she said, simply, when he had finished his recital. Oh! but it was well-feigned! Cogia, poor fellow, was deceived by the hypocrite and thought that she meant what she said. Those three words were to be the ruin of both him and Constantine, his old friend.

After it was all over and Marie had calmed him down a little so that he would listen to what she said, she spoke as follows:

"Cogia, your friend Constantine loves me and wishes to marry me. He had threatened to sell me as a slave if I do not marry him, but I begged of him to give me time to think over his offer and he assented." Here Cogia wanted to rush on deck and kill Constantine. Marie managed to calm him and went on thus:

"You have a ship that belongs to you, so why cannot you get me on board during the brawl that is occurring on the ship and get away before Constantine and the crew recover their senses?"

Cogia was about to recite some string of gibberish when Constantine entered the room.

Chapter XXII

He paused for a moment on the threshold, anger on his face. Then, by a superhuman effort he controlled himself and walked on. He stepped up to Cogia, who had risen to his feet in alarm at his comrade's entrance, and put his hands on his shoulders and drew him out of the room into the corridor, Cogia being too astounded to resist or speak.

"What does this mean?" said Constantine, letting his anger get the best of him and showing it by the menace in his voice.

"I—I don't know," said Cogia, not knowing what to say.

"Yes you do," retorted the other, shaking him. "You do know."

"Well—what if I do?" said the other, beginning to recover his senses.

"You must explain to me," hissed Constantine.

"I will not," said the other, now in full possession of his thinking faculty and being conscious of his position.

"You shall," said Constantine, shaking him again.

"What should I explain?" said the other, trying to gain time to think what he should say.

Constantine's answer came quickly.

"You must explain why you were making love to the woman who is to marry me."

"I will if that is all."

"Then do so and hurry."

"Not at your command."

"Then at my request." Constantine's tone was angrier than ever as he said this and it seemed as if he intended to swallow his friend, or he who had once been a friend to him.

"You are very kind to request me," said Cogia, with a sneer. "Perhaps you will let me think before I answer."

"Not I. You do not deserve it, you scoundrel."

"You are one yourself. However, I'll bandy no more words with you. Draw your sword and we'll fight now."

"Give me an explanation of your conduct first," said Constantine. "I'll give you a chance to defend yourself with words before you have to do so with cold steel."

"You are very kind."

"Why am I?"

"Because you graciously give me permission to explain my conduct before resorting to swords," said Cogia, with another sneer.

This was too much for Constantine to stand.

"I won't give you a chance to do anything," he roared. "If you don't leave this ship within three minutes I'll have my sailors throw you overboard where you belong."

"I'd like to see them do it."

At this Constantine drew his sword and Cogia did the same. They were about to attack each other when Marie came on deck and rushed between them imploring them not to fight. In spite of Constantine's threats and her own hypocrisy toward Cogia, her conscience had rebelled at the thought that the men, even though they were Turks and pirates, should fight about her. Her self-respect asserted itself, and she thought that she should be ashamed at being the cause of a brawl.

"If you will promise to marry me I will not fight this man," said Constantine, "and if he will apologize I will forgive his conduct in making love to you."

"Apologize to you?" said Cogia, "after the way you have treated me? Why, the thought is preposterous; and the lady says that she loves me!"

"Did you tell him that?" said Constantine, turning to Marie in scorn.

"No," said that person, somewhat frightened by his demeanor. If she had been a little braver, and not frightened, she would never have told him a lie, but she feared for herself and prudence told her that the safest course out of the matter was to tell a falsehood. After all, what did it matter if the lie was told to a mere Turk, who followed the unchristian profession of pirate, and was a heathen into the bargain?

"I would rather believe you than Cogia," said Constantine, though doubtfully as if he had thought that she might be telling a lie, but at last his love got the best of him and he believed her.

"You are a liar," said Cogia to Marie, his face flushing at her denial, "and a base hypocrite into the bargain. Constantine, I pity you, and warn you that she is a vile serpent. She told me, not five minutes ago, in your apartment, that she loved me, and now she denies it to my face."

"You are the liar," said Constantine, hotly.

"Well, good-bye," said Cogia, with a sneer, and he stepped to the side of the ship and swung himself into the boat awaiting him, by means of a rope.

"Row me to my ship," said he to the sailors.

They instantly complied and five minutes afterwards he was on board his own vessel.

He went below to his cabin and flung himself upon the divan to collect his scattered thoughts and decide upon a course of action.

If what he thought could have been put into words it would have been somewhat as follows:

"She said that she loved me and then denied it to my face before Constantine. Thus she is a liar and a hypocrite. I hope that Constantine accepts my warning. Love has blinded both him and me and we have been fooled by this French maid, who fell into our hands. All that she wishes to do is to gain time to escape. She suggested to me that I run away with her in my ship, right under Constantine's nose, and fool that I am, I promised her to do so. However, I deem it no crime to break that promise. If she would come to me now and swear by all her saints that she loved me I would still scorn her. She is a base hypocrite, who seeks only to deceive men. She is a trickster and has a gift of fatal fascination, which is her beauty, by which she acts her deceptions and captivates men into loving her. I was a fool to think that she thought anything of me, and I should have seen that she only sought to delude me. Never again will I be led astray by a foreign woman, and I shall make an oath that this shall be my last voyage. I have enough money to settle down and marry happily." Here he stopped thinking of the matter for awhile, or at least tried to, but it was very hard work.

At last he picked up a book, but could not concentrate his attention on it, his mind instantly reverting to the recent scenes that he had witnessed and been an actor in.

A great anger burned within him, the object of which was Marie Cordouy, the woman who had denied her love for him, ten minutes after she had said that she did love him. The anger overwhelmed all his love for her, but did not extinguish it beyond hope of resurrection.

After the anger had in some measure abated he was able to reason more coherently and level-headedly, and began to think that after all she was not so much to blame. He thought to himself that any woman would have done the same under the circumstances, and began to think that he might forgive her. When his train of reflections began to turn, he did not try to stop them, and after an hour had passed was entirely contented with forgiving her offense. His love now began to come back and in a little while all his anger was extinguished, and love reigned in its place.

Then he began to meditate upon what he should do next day and at this he began to grow angry at Constantine and the hatred which he had felt before now returned, and with it came Jealousy, the green-eyed monster which has ruined so many lives.

The venom of its poisonous darts was in his brain and he paced up and down the little room in a fever, meditating many mad means of getting rid of his once friend. Constantine himself was undergoing similar feelings at that time and was working himself into a terrible rage, which Cogia was also doing.

By night Cogia was ready to do anything and so was Constantine. Brooding over the events of the day which had so disturbed them both mentally and physically they had gotten themselves into that rage already mentioned.

Now Constantine was the more angry of the two, and his furious rage and jealousy made him think of murdering Cogia. He still retained some of his old friendly feeling and this and his conscience, which he could not entirely smother, rebelled at the thought. But the more he meditated on the matter the more acceptable the horrible idea became. The more he tried to conquer it the stronger it became until it entirely overwhelmed that remaining friendly feeling and the qualms of conscience.

But how he was to murder Cogia he had not yet thought. When the terrible idea of murder had won its mental battle, he began to think of that problem. Pictures of poisoning came into his brain, and that seemed the easiest way out of the matter. So he determined to try it and at once.

He arose from the divan where he had been reclining, the very picture of a fiend. His eyes blazed furiously and his features were contracted into a terrible expression which was intensified by the cruel look which was his by nature.

Crossing to a small recess in the wall he drew forth a small bottle out of which he poured a whitish liquid into a bottle of white wine. There was not more than a teaspoonful of it, but it was a very powerful poison. Then he laid the bottle aside where it would not be seen.

Then he called to him a little negro boy and gave him a gold piece first telling him that it was to be his for a certain service.

The lad's eyes fairly glistened with avarice but when he heard the errand that he was to be sent on he did not appear to be so cheerful.

Of course, Constantine did not tell him of the intended murder but merely told him that he was to take a bottle of wine and manage to smuggle it into Cogia's cabin on that person's ship.

The two ships were now very far apart, so it was not possible for the boy to swim the distance, so he sat down and wrote a note to Cogia about some unimportant thing and gave it to the lad telling him to deliver it to Cogia, and while that person was reading it, to place the bottle on the table or any other place where it would soon be noticed.

A boat and two sailors were ready to take him to Cogia's ship which stopped as soon as the sailors saw the boat coming toward them.

Twenty minutes after this it was alongside the vessel and the boy went on deck and then to Cogia's chamber. He delivered the note to him and while he was reading it took the bottle from his bosom where it had been concealed and laid it on the table in plain slight, trusting that Cogia would not notice it immediately.

Cogia did not see him place it there, but when he had finished reading the note he deemed that it required some answer and going to the table to write one he noticed the bottle.

"How did this come here?" he asked, turning to the boy.

"I'm sure I don't know, sir," said the lad, innocently, with a look of bewilderment on his face.

"Yes you do," said Cogia looking him squarely in the face. "When you entered there was no bottle on this table and now there is. No one has entered since you entered. How, then, did the bottle get here unless you put it there?"

"I don't know, sir," said the negro boy, trying to look innocent.

"Who told you to place it here?" said Cogia, beginning to get very suspicious.

"I don't know, sir," said the lad.

"Yes you do," said Cogia, tartly, "and if you don't tell me pretty quick I'll have you bastinadoed within an inch of your life for lying."

The boy trembled with fear. Still, he did not want to tell for he knew that if he did so he would get another whipping from Constantine.

"I don't know," he said again, shaking his head, seemingly in surprise.

"What? Do you argue with me?" said Cogia. "I never heard of such a thing before in my life. I'll give you one more chance and if you don't answer me then I'll give you that bastinadoing doubled. Do you hear me, you little black dummy?"

"I hear you, sir," said the boy, "but I don't quite understand what you mean."

"Yes you do," said Cogia. "You understand just as well as I do. Answer me quick or I will call a man to whip you. Your back will be sore when you go back to your rascally master, or I'm no true Turk."

"I am telling you the truth, sir," said the lad, trying to look very quiet and innocent.

"That's about the same song that you were singing before," said Cogia, "but you'll have a new tune to sing if you don't tell me the truth before I have to speak to you again."

"I think that I have told you everything, sir," said the boy.

"You little black imp! Here, Abdoul, here is someone for you to try your new whip on," he shouted. In response to his call a big Turkish sailor entered the room.

"Did you call me, captain?" he said.

"Yes, Abdoul. Go bring your whip."

The man went out and soon returned with a heavy stick in his hand to the end of which was attached a number of thongs of leather about three feet in length. At the end of each thong was a round piece of leather much thicker than that to which it was attached.

"Take off your coat," said Cogia to the negro boy. He obeyed and the sailor raised the whip high in air and brought it down upon his back time and time again. The negro bellowed with pain at each strike, and at last Cogia took pity on him and ordered the sailor to stop.

The man did so and the negro pitched forward at Cogia's feet and implored him not to have him whipped any more.

"Will you tell me why you brought this bottle here?" said Cogia.

"I did not bring it, sir," said the boy.

"Well, you have had enough punishment. Take it back to your rascally master."

The boy was only too glad to obey, and if Cogia had threatened him with another beating he would have told the truth. It was a wonder that he had borne the beating he had received without doing so, but somehow or other he had held his tongue.

A few moments later he was in the boat and was rowed back to his master's vessel, with the wine bottle in his bosom.

Constantine's first question was as to how he had succeeded. The boy produced the bottle and told the whole story. Constantine did not believe him and told him so.

"You were afraid to do it, you little imp," he exclaimed. "I'll give you a severe beating myself if you don't confess the truth."

The boy persevered in his statement, and in consequence earned the promised beating. However, he kept the gold coin, and considered that a sufficient recompense for all that he had undergone. Being a very truthful lad except when he was told to lie, he deserved better than he got, but people, whether they be good or bad, do not always receive their just due in this hard world.

Constantine put the bottle away in a small recess and began to think of some other way of getting rid of Cogia. His jealous rage had not abated and he was still determined to commit murder. But the way to do it was what puzzled him.

Finally he settled upon stabbing as the next best method and determined to carry it into effect that same night. It was now dark and he had lighted his lamp. He then began to examine his dagger and while doing so another idea entered his head which he deemed more practicable.

A sailor on board the ship possessed a pet cobra of the Egyptian kind, which was very small.

This Constantine purchased from its owner, who was only too willing to part with it at a reasonable price, for it had become very vicious of late and had several times tried to bite him.

Constantine took it to his cabin, still in the basket, and called to him another negro boy and gave him a note to Cogia, and also the basket containing the snake, bidding him liberate the reptile in Cogia's cabin.

Away went the boy and was rowed over to Cogia's ship and went on board telling the sailors that he had a message for the captain.

He went to Cogia's cabin, and entering, found Cogia reading a book. Before Cogia looked up from this book to see who had intruded upon him, the lad had unfastened the lid of the box, though not removing it, and had set the whole quietly on the floor behind an iron box containing books and manuscripts.

Then he went forward and presented the note to Cogia who read it, wrote an answer, and giving it to the boy, bade him begone, at the same time turning to his book again.

The lad returned to his master's ship and reported his success. Constantine gave him three pieces of gold for his conduct and praised him, telling him that he was a fair lad even if he was only a slave.

Then he laid himself down on the divan, first eating his supper, and tried to go to sleep. This was utterly impossible because of the tumult his mind was in, so he sat up and tried to read a book, and proving more successful at this, went on for several hours, though with some difficulty, his mind persisting in wandering.

In the meanwhile we had best see what Cogia is doing.

After eating his supper he had returned to rest, undisturbed by such thoughts as were agitating Constantine, and his jealousy and rage having somewhat exhausted themselves left him still more exhausted. He soon fell asleep and was visited by the most harrowing and horrible dreams.

Suddenly, about midnight, he was awakened by the sound of something hissing not far from his couch. He was lying on the divan, covered with a long rug. In the pale moonlight which streamed through the open window he saw something which caused his heart to stand still for the moment.

On the iron box lay a coiled snake, which he recognized as an Egyptian asp. Ever and anon it raised his hooded head, showed its deadly fangs, and hissed. Cogia was so frozen with fear that he was afraid to cry out, thinking that the reptile would become angry and sting him before help should arrive.

His tongue was frozen to the roof of his mouth and every portion of his body was rigid with fear. His hair stood on end and he clutched the edge of the rug which covered him with fingers that could not loosen their grip. Of all things that he hated a reptile was that thing. He was a brave man and would have died any death bravely, but to be helplessly stung to death by a snake, a degraded creeping thing, was more than he could bear.

The very thought of it froze the blood in his veins and made a miserable coward of him. The atmosphere of the room seemed to grow colder and he thought that he should die of fright.

For many minutes he sat there mute and rigid and the snake kept its original position. It was the same that the negro had left than by Constantine's order.

Then the horrible creature began to move, and to his great terror it came toward him. It crawled across the floor, slowly at first and then faster, and the moonlight glittered on its scales turning them to seeming scales of silver.

It raised its hooded head on the edge of the divan and looked at Cogia, with its small, beady eyes, aflame with fire. Cogia shrank back imperceptibly and his hair stretched itself to its greatest height across his head and there remained. Every hair was standing straight and tall, rigid with fright. His eyes seemed to start from their sockets and his lips whitened till no blood remained in them. His brown face paled, too, under its dark hue, and gave him a most ghostly pallor.

The snake now began to sway to and fro and its hood swelled and swelled until it was many times as big around as the reptile itself.

Then it crawled upon the divan, at Cogia's feet, and then stood on end and glared at him, still swaying, and showed its deadly fangs.

Gradually Cogia's senses came back to him and he began to think what had best be done. His fear was in no wise abated, and he shuddered with repugnance at the thought of a hand-to-hand struggle with the asp. But evidently this was the only thing to be done and it would have to be done quickly for the reptile was now swaying further and in a few moments it would spring.

By a superhuman effort Cogia called his rigid limbs into service and suddenly lifting the rug that covered him, he threw it as hard as he could at the swaying form of the hooded cobra.

The effect was very encouraging for the snake went over with a parting hiss and the rug kept it from springing at him.

Cogia sprang from the divan, and snatched a loaded pistol from the table and drew his sword, shouting for help at the same time, as loudly as he could.

He walked up to the rug, under which could be heard the hissing of the reptile and fired at the part where he thought it to be. Then, rushing up to it, he dealt it several blows with the sword, and removing the rug which was almost cut to pieces saw under it the writhing portions of the asp.

He took another pistol and fired a bullet into the head just as several sailors entered the apartment in their night-clothes, armed with all variety of weapons.

"What is the matter, captain?" said one of the men. "We heard you scream for help and came as fast as we could. We heard a pistol shot and feared that some harm might have befallen you."

For answer Cogia pointed to the remains of the snake on the divan and then sank upon the floor, from the shock of what had happened to him.

In a few moments he recovered and went on deck assisted by two sailors while the other removed what was left of the cobra and washed the blood from off the divan. Cogia stayed on deck all night and when morning came went back to his cabin and lying down went to sleep and slept several hours. When he awoke he ate his breakfast and felt much better, though the effects of his experience had not yet left him.

Chapter XXIII

When Cogia recovered from the shock of his fight with the snake he began to think about the matter and finally arrived at the conclusion that Constantine was trying to murder him. He recollected the incident of the wine-bottle and found the cage which had contained the reptile behind the box where the negro had dropped it.

Then he questioned some of his sailors and they told him that they had seen the negro who had come with the second message with this same cage in his hand, but had not known what it contained.

By this time Cogia was sure that Constantine was trying to get rid of him and determined to take measures accordingly. He armed himself well and then getting into a boat told his men to row him to Constantine's ship. His intention was to defy the would-be murderer in his own den and then escape before the fellow could retaliate. That there might be fighting he argued to himself, so he had armed himself and had his men arm themselves also.

Then he was rowed to Constantine's vessel, which waited for them to come up and went on board. All of his sailors but one accompanied him, for he thought it best to be prudent and the man excepted remained on guard in the boat.

Accompanied by these men, armed to the teeth he entered Constantine's cabin. It was noon and Constanting was dining then. Marie Cardouy, the French maid, was dining with him and they seemed somewhat amicable toward each other.

Cogia paused in the doorway and watched them a moment before speaking. Marie was drinking a glass of white wine which she had poured from a bottle and Constantine was about to utter some jest.

Suddenly the French lady pitched forward from her chair, her face turned pale and she fell to the floor. The half empty glass of wine fell with her and was splintered into a thousand pieces and the liquid flowed upon her dress.

Cogia sprang forward and lifted her in his arms and inquired what was the matter.

"I'm poisoned," she gasped, and fell back, dead, with a few convulsions, and lay on the floor as still as could be.

"You devil!" shouted Cogia, leaping to his feet and reaching for Constantine. "You've poisoned her!"

He snatched up the bottle of wine and attempted to force some of the contents down Constantine's throat, but Constantine was too quick for him and knocked the bottle out of his hand.

Before another man could do anything Cogia's men pressed forward and tried to separate them. Both were mad with rage and anger and were snarling at each other like two wolves over the body of the deer that they have slain.

"I tell you you poisoned her," panted Cogia.

"I did not," retorted the other.

"You lie!"

"So do you."

"Let me go," said Cogia to the man that was holding him, and shaking himself loose he made for Constantine before that person could do anything. He sprang upon him like a tiger and had thrown him to the floor before the astonished sailors could prevent him.

Constantine was very nimble and probably the stronger of the two but his strength availed him little when that fellow had gotten him down.

Cogia closed his hands upon the man's throat in an iron grip and would not let go. Many hands were tugging at him but he held on with superhuman strength and was slowly choking his enemy to death.

Constantine gasped and his face turned pallid. With spasmodic, maddened strength he strove to unlock those iron fingers but he could not, and finally he fell back, and his eyes closed.

Cogia thought him dead and loosened his grip and suffered his men to pull him to his feet.

Almost before he was fairly through Constantine leaped to his feet and made at him like a lion. Driven to the end of his resources he had at last feigned death to escape from his foe's clutches.

Cogia staggered back and would have fallen had his men not caught him and held him upright.

It required three men to hold Constantine back for he was terribly angry and would have killed him with his bare hands.

"Let me go," said Constantine, struggling to escape from his captors.

But they knew better than to allow him to escape and did not do so. On the contrary they began to bind him with ropes. Then he shouted for help and his own men came running into the cabin and a fight ensued between Cogia's men and Constantine's sailors, which ended in a victory for the latter. Cogia was bound and so were his men and they were all taken on deck, Constantine accompanying them.

By his order they were stood up in line and Constantine addressed them thus:

"Your Captain, Cogia Dagh, broke into my cabin just as the woman who was to have been my wife fell dead. I do not know what has killed her, but I think that her wine was poisoned. Who poisoned it I do not know but I strongly suspect that it was done by Cogia, who doubtless intended it for me.

"However, this lady got it in my stead and she is now dead, lying on the floor in my cabin.

"After that Cogia rushed upon me and tried to kill me but was frustrated by my superiority.

"Now you behold him a prisoner. What should be done with such a wretch?"

"Death," replied Constantine's sailors in chorus. "He deserves death."

"I know that perfectly well," said Constantine, "but I mean to give him a chance for his life. He must fight me now in a duel. As he is the challenged person he has the choice of weapons."

"You do not deserve the honor," said Cogia, haughtily, "but I will fight you if you so ordain. I choose swords as weapons, for they are the weapons with which gentlemen fight and murderers, too, though they sometimes prefer to do their work with poisoned wine."

Constantine ignored the insult, though his face flushed, and told a man to fetch a couple of swords.

"Why cannot we fight with our own?" said Cogia.

"Because the swords we wear are scimitars, and as our quarrel is over a French woman, it is fitting that we fight with French weapons."

"I admire your taste," said Cogia, "but you are not a true Turk."

"We will soon know which is the truest Turk," said Constantine bitterly.

His men released Cogia just as the man returned with the weapons. They were long and straight and not unlike the rapiers of the seventeenth century, save that their flanks were broader. The hilts were straight and were of silver.

Constantine carefully selected one and Cogia took the other, though with misgivings as to the genuineness of the steel. He had no time to test it, however, for Constantine had tossed aside his cloak and was motioning him to do the same.

Cogia did the same and grasping the sword firmly crossed it with his antagonist's in true duelling fashion. He did not know what was to be the outcome of the fight but he was ready to do his best. He firmly believed that Constantine had poisoned the French woman.

And now a word of explanation must be offered as to her death. Constantine had invited her to eat with him and she had accepted the invitation. Their conversation was somewhat strained during the meal until wine was served. Then they grew more confidential and became somewhat friendly.

Marie had happened to look toward the wall at that spot where the recess, in which the wine bottle was concealed, was situated. It was covered by a drapery and Marie began to wonder idly what was within.

She determined to find out, being of a very inquisitive nature, and was too impatient to wait until dinner was over. When Constantine looked away from her at something she had slyly slipped her hand behind the curtain and brought out the small bottle of poisoned wine.

Fancying that it might be better than that which she had been drinking, she poured out a glass and drank it. Just as Cogia had entered the room she had fallen to the floor, under the influence of the deadly poison which had at once taken effect.

And so it was come to pass that she had died by the very poison that had been intended for her lover, and perhaps you may think that it served her right for being the cause of such a quarrel between two good friends even though they were Turks, and corsairs at that. And so it happens in this world of mingled sorrow and joy that the person who is the cause of a quarrel receives his or her just punishment unintentionally from the hand of one of the wronged.

But after all she was not so much to blame. She had fallen into their hands and they had fallen in love with her and had been split asunder because of her, but she was not so much to blame for that, for they had loved her through no trickery of hers except her beauty, which was a thing she could not help. But strangely indeed she had received the poison intended by one of her lovers for the other, and because one believed that the other had intentionally poisoned her they were about to fight a duel to the death.

But perhaps it is best that a woman who causes so much trouble though not intentionally should die and be out of the way. Beauty is a gift of nature which may do both good and bad, intentionally or unintentionally. Those who do good intentionally are to be praised, but those who have done it unintentionally are not to be praised so much, and those who do bad intentionally are to be condemned, but those who do it unintentionally are to be pitied.

Constantine and Cogia faced each other, swords in hand, hate and rage on their faces, and the sailors looked in rapt attention, not daring to interfere.

Slowly and ceremoniously they advanced toward each other and bowed, then crossed swords and leaped back to their old position and the fight began.

Each was a master in his art and they were so evenly matched that no man could safely prophesy which would be the victor in the end.

For at least fifteen minutes they clashed sword upon sword and yet neither succeeded in touching the other. Then they both stopped for a moment and leaned upon their swords, eyeing each other furtively while perspiration trickled down their faces.

Suddenly a shout from one of the sailors drew the attention of all to what he pointed out. It was a number of ships half a mile away, bearing the standard of Italy.

These ships were coming toward them at full speed and the pirate crew saw at once that they were in pursuit of them. There were five of them and each carried a large number of cannon.

Instantly the two captains forgot their private quarrel and Cogia threw down his sword and running to the side of the ship leaped into the boat that was awaiting him, followed by his men, and was immediately rowed to his own ship which he found in a state of turmoil.

Both the corsair ships went forward at their hardiest rate now and every bit of canvas was up in the wind. They were assisted by a brisk breeze and though the Italian war-ships hung on behind most tenaciously they finally distanced them and reached Constantinople safely, seven days after the termination of the quarrel on board Constantine's ship.

Cogia believed to his dying day that Constantine was the wilful cause of Marie Cardouy's death, and Constantine never forgave him for the affronts he had made and the fact that he had made love to Marie.

Each was a master in his art and they were so evenly matched
that no man could safely prophesy which would be the victor in the end

It was a sad thing for two friends to be parted in such a misunderstanding and it would have been much better for both of them if the Spanish treasure ship had never existed, and they had not set out in pursuit and been so successful as to capture it.

And now my dear reader, the forgoing tale is what Mustapha Dagh read in an old manuscript belonging to his father which he had found in an antiquated iron chest which had been saved from the fire.

The day after the trial which had terminated in Abdullah's wonderful escape he had employed in looking over the manuscript. It was a confession made by his father, Cogia Dagh, and hidden away in this old box. It clearly revealed why Abdullah had hated him so much and the cause of the quarrel between the two families.

Of course it was not told in the way that I have told it and many parts that I have supplied were omitted. But Mustapha knew that there was more than one standpoint of view, and having viewed the matter from both standpoints saw that there were many parts that had been left out, and so supplied these. They are the same as I have put in.

After thinking the matter over a while he called Baber and bade him examine the manuscript and then give his opinion. Baber perused it very carefully and then gave an opinion that coincided in all particulars with that expressed by Mustapha.

"This is clearly a memoir made by your dead father," said Baber, "but he left out many things which he should have put in. For instance: The bottle of poisoned wine that Marie Cardouy drank was probably the same that the negro lad brought to Cogia's cabin. Evidently this view did not strike your father or he would have said it." Then Baber went on to cite a number of other details with which you are already familiar.

"Your view agrees exactly with mine," said Mustapha. "As both of us have hit upon the same things it is evident that they must be correct, or else this life is full of very strange coincidences."

"I have heard of many stranger coincidences than this," said Baber, smiling. "But, listen a minute, Mustapha, I have something very important to tell you."

"What is it, Baber?" said Mustapha, turning to him in surprise.

"The other night when I told my tale to you and your friends I left out some particulars that I am now about to relate to you.

"You must not be astonished at my tale, Mustapha, for it is perfectly true," and here Baber sat down and told it as follows:

"The night before the day in which I was cast into the shute I had a long talk with Ahmed and his sons and they revealed to me many things that they wished me to tell you. And these things are: that they are no relation of yours but imposed on you because of the strange circumstances which threw you and they together. Ahmed bade me tell you everything and I promised, but that night before so many people I hesitated when I came to this part of the tale and so omitted it. He also bade me take both the diamonds, which I did, and told me to give one of them to you and keep the other, as a remembrance. We parted with many tears and I promised to obey his instructions to the letter. Here are the diamonds." Baber drew them from his pocket and laid them on the table.

"Take your choice, Mustapha," he said, "I will take what you leave. Either will suit me."

The diamonds were so alike that Mustapha did not know which to choose but closed his eyes and putting out his hand grasped the first one that he came to.

Baber took the remaining stone and put it in his pocket.

"Now we will speak of other subjects," he said wiping a tear from his eye. Mustapha agreed with him.

"What do you intend to do about this Abdullah?" said Baber. "He has escaped, and what is worse no man knows where he has gone to. His ship has disappeared and no one seems to have seen it anywhere. However, sailors are busy people and soon forget that they have seen a ship in which they are not concerned. It may have either gone up the river and put off in some of the tributaries of the Tigris and then have been left aground or in some secure spot, or made a dash down the river for the Euphrates and afterwards the open sea, which is the most likely course."

"There is no telling where Abdullah has gone to," said Mustapha, shaking his head, "for he is a very eccentric man."

"Well, answer my question. What do you intend to do?"

"As soon as possible," said Mustapha, "I will start out to search for him and if I have to go to the ends of the earth I will get him and revenge the death of those men whom he killed, and who fooled me into thinking that they were relations of mine. I freely forgive them, and will surely revenge their deaths."

"But we do not know whether they are dead yet," said Baber. "They may be alive at this moment."

"It is hardly possible. Abdullah would not have delayed his wrath so long, and it would not have been possible for them to have escaped."

"Admitting the truth of what you say it is possible that they may have gotten away, for you say that it is hardly possible. Now hardly possible is not 'impossible' so your very words admit that there is a chance that they may have escaped."

"Your reasoning is good, Baber, but I did not mean exactly what I said."

"Then what did you mean?"

"I meant that it was impossible."

"But I have heard you say that nothing is impossible."

"You have a good memory."

"Perhaps I have, but that has little relation to what we set out to speak of."

"I said that as soon as possible I would set out to search for Abdullah. Will you go with me?"

"Of course I will. You may be assured of my assitance in attaining such an object. Though Abdullah may go the ends of the earth as you said, we will find him if we live long enough, and when we get him he will not escape us. I shall have no scruple at shooting the rascal on the spot if I ever see him again."

"Neither will I, but I think that shooting is too good for such a villain as he. Hanging would be better, though he is not worth the rope to strange him with."

"Well, we'll decide upon the death he deserves when we get him, and arrange it according to circumstances."

"Do you remember the message that the pigeon brought to your ship?" said Mustapha.

"Yes," said Baber, "no one could understand it."

"Here it is," said Mustapha and he took a tattered piece of parchment from his pocket and read the contents to his compere as follows:

"We if will we attack are the not ship able five to days rescue from you now jump if overboard and possible you. Have will no be fear picked answer up this by message our by men the. If pigeon we if cannot you attack have we anything will to let say. You ―――― know."

"Have you hit upon the explanation to it?" enquired Baber.

"Yes," said Mustapha, "after puzzling my head on it for many hours I at last found the solution. Beginning with the first word I read every second word to the end and what I found was as follows: 'We will attack the ship five days from now. Answer this message by the pigeon.' Then I began with the second word and read every third word to the end. By doing this I found the rest of the message, which was as follows: 'If we are not able to rescue you jump overboard and you will and you will be picked up by our men. If we cannot attack we will let you know.' I had to use the last two words together, and I suppose the blank was put there because there was no word to fit it.

"It is evident that this message was written by Abdullah and sent to the spies by means of the pigeon. Unfortunately for them the pigeon mistook me for one of them, and let me take the message away from it."

"You are very clever," said Baber, "and you would make a fine man to decipher old manuscripts and things like that."

"Come, I think that dinner is awaiting us," said Mustapha. "After dinner we will arrange our plans and talk them over."

"As you say," said Baber.

"What shall we do with the diamonds?" said Mustapha a few minute later as they left the room.

"Keep them as remembrances of our friends, the Begs," said Baber pleasantly as he entered the dining room and seated himself at the table at which the servants were depositing a quantity of food. Mustapha followed his example and they were soon eating a substantial dinner.

Chapter XXIV

When Abdullah Houssain, to whom we will now turn our attention, left the room in which the pasha and the others had been trying him for a very grave crime, he did so thinking that he had won a great victory.

He had anticipated beforehand the concentrated attention of all these when the cadi should open the packet and he had known that their attention would be so engrossed by this that they would not notice him in the least, so that if he could manage to get himself freed from the chains he would be able to escape.

When he got into the next room he muffled himself in a long cloak that he found there and boldly left the house walking past a couple of soldiers at the door as if they had not been there. They paid little attention to him and he proceeded down the narrow street which was almost deserted and entered another.

Finally, after traversing a labyrinth of these streets he reached the great gate at the southern side of the city and going there then passed Mustapha's house and soon reached the river where his own little ship was awaiting him.

He went on board and giving an order to the sailors went below to his cabin and threw off the cloak and laid down on the divan to rest. Being somewhat tired after his long walk, he soon fell asleep and did not awake till a sailor announced that dinner was ready.

He ate very heartily and then went on deck to look at the scenery. They were going down the river for such his order had been, and a light breeze was blowing which helped the ship along. Now and then they passed a vessel homeward bound, but the river seemed deserted.

The ship went at a rate of about three miles an hour and Abdullah estimated that they would reach the river Euphrates sometime the next day. When night came he went below and covering himself with a rug soon fell asleep and did not awaken till the next morning.

He ate breakfast and then went on deck to see how weather was progressing.

The river had broadened considerably and he knew that in a few hours they would enter the river Euphrates which he intended to ascend.

In a few hours they saw a much broader river before them and into this the ship sailed. Up this the ship went and when Abdullah saw that he was safely on his voyage he went below and laid down.

His thoughts were not very pleasant, and on the contrary were very bad indeed. He was meditating a murder by means of which he would get rid of Mustapha and that person's friends.

Finally he arrived at a definite plan of action and arising from his seat and going on deck told the sailors to start the ship back down the river.

In a few hours they entered the Tigris and sailed up it toward Bagdad. In a day or two they reached that city at night and Abdullah landed and went toward the city gate.

He walked past many people unnoticed and was able to listen to their conversation. Most of it was about him and he knew that the talkers would not have been so unexcited had they known that the object of their conversation was so near them.

Going through the city he finally arrived at his own house and entered. He gave an order to the servants though they showed some surprise at his return, and then went to his own room.

He seated himself at the table and began to write a letter, carefully disguising his own handwriting. Suddenly, while occupied with this, a servant entered the room and announced that a man wished to see him on very important business.

Abdullah threw down his pen with a muttered imprecation against all visitors in general and then harshly ordered the servant to show the fellow in.

The servant left the room only too glad to comply and Abdullah turned to the letter that he had been writing with a scowl on his dark face. Scarcely had he written a line when a man entered the room and bowed to him.

"What do you want?" he said, showing an inclination to return to his work again.

"I should be much obliged if you would lock the door," said the stranger.

"Why should I?" asked Abdullah. "We can transact our business just as well if it is open."

"I want you to close it," said the man.

"Pray tell me your reason," said Abdullah. "You are very insolent," he added with a frown.

"I have heard you make that last remark before," said the visitor, throwing off his cloak and seating himself on the divan.

"Then you know me," said Abdullah. "Who are you, anyway?"

"I'll let you know when you lock that door," was the stern reply. The fellow's voice sounded forced and unnatural, and Abdullah thought that he must be feigning it, for fear of having his real personality discovered.

He locked the door though somewhat unwillingly and turned to the man again.

"Now tell me your name," said he, throwing the key upon the table.

"Akmat Beg," said the man, in his real voice.

Abdullah started aback as if a thunderbolt had struck him.

"Akmat Beg?" he asked.

"That is my name," said Akmat, throwing off his turban, the wig beneath it and a mask that had covered his true face.

"What do you want with me?" asked Abdullah, trembling.

For answer Akmat picked up the key, slipped it into his pocket and said:

"I have come here to end your evil days."

"You dare not kill me," replied Abdullah. "My friends would never rest until they had gotten you."

"And what would they do with me if that unfortunate event should happen?" asked Akmat.

"Give you the death which you and your comrades were to have met but escaped by some miracle," replied Abdullah.

"You may threaten and fume and fret all day long," said Akmat. "But you will not frighten me in the least."

"What will you do with me?" said Abdullah.

"I told you that before," replied Akmat.

"Oh, I remember, but how will you kill me?"

"Shoot you," said Akmat, pleasantly.

"I shall call for help," siad Abdullah.

"If you do you will fall dead before your voice has ceased echoing."

"What if I do? You will die. That at least will be some satisfaction to me."

"And if I die I will have the satisfaction of having your soul as my companion in Paradise or the other place, I suppose."

"Probably you will. It seems fated that we should meet after."

"And perhaps we shall not meet in the hereafter. After all your deeds, Abdullah, I scarcely think that you would hope to spring into eternal bliss in the Mohammedan Paradise. You have been a Fire-Worshipper and therefore cannot enter the heaven of all good Turks."

"But a man may worship two gods if he please," said Abdullah.

"Perhaps he may, but Allah does not allow such people to enter the Paradise which is intended not for infidel dogs, but for those who are righteous and have faithfully adhered to him."

"But cannot there be two heavens?" said Abdullah. "The Christians and the Buddhists have their hereafters as well as your Mohammedans, so why may the Fire-Worshippers not have theirs?"

"Because they are mere idolaters and bow down before images of wood and stone," was Akmat's stern reply.

"But," argued Abdullah, "so do the Buddhists. "They bow down before the image of Buddha."

"We Buddhists," said Akmat, he himself being a firm believer in the creed of Buddha, "only bow before the image of one who once really existed, while the Fire-Worshippers worship fire and the image of one who is a mere myth, probably originated by some mad priest who wished only to delude mankind."

"That is a lie," answered Abdullah hotly. "Our god was a person who really existed."

"I did not come here to argue religion," said Akmat, thinking it high time to close the argument, "but to kill you. I have with me a vial of poison, a dagger, my sword and a brace of pistols. Which death do you choose?"

"Shoot me," said Abdullah, assuming an air of indifference. "When you shoot I will call my servants and they will make an end of you, as I said before."

"Very well, but I choose the method of shooting," said Akmat. "You have challenged me to shoot you."

"I did not know that there was more than one method of shooting," said Abdullah, who had now recovered his full composure and bravery. He was really a brave man, but the sudden entrance of Akmat had unnerved him so that at first he had felt fear, but this fear he had now overcome. He had already made up his mind to meet death as bravely as he could.

For answer Akmat walked to the large clock which was on the side of the room opposite to where Abdullah was seated and tied a heavy thread to the hour hand. Then, in a kind of bandage suspended from the wall he fixed one of his pistols, cocked it and tied the thread to the trigger, leaving it a little slack so that the hand would have to move several inches before it was drawn taut and the trigger pulled.

Akmat took the other pistol in his hand and approached Abdullah. "Would you kindly walk to the table and seat yourself on it?" he asked.

Abdullah complied, but only at the muzzle of the pistol. Then Akmat carefully bound his legs to the legs of the table and his arms together so that he could not possibly move them.

Abdullah was now sitting facing the muzzle of the suspended pistol, and this muzzle was directed at the center of his forehead and was only a few feet away. In about two hours the thread would draw taut and the trigger be pulled and Abdullah would be no more. It was a few minutes before he saw through the affair and then he sarcastically complimented Akmat on his ingenuity.

"I myself could not have done better," he concluded with a sneer. But he found that it was no joke sitting there facing that loaded pistol which would go off at a certain time. He began to get nervous and his face to pale. It was very ticklish work, he thought, and wished that Akmat would make an end of the matter. But the unkind Akmat showed no indication to render him such a service. On the contrary he sat quietly on the divan and watched the passing shades of fear as they went over Abdullah's face.

"What are you going to do now?" said Abdullah, turning his head and looking at Akmat.

"Stay here till that pistol goes off," said Akmat. "It would not do to leave you for you could easily get yourself out of the way if I left the room. You could duck your head a few inches and the bullet would do you no harm. I intend to stay here and see to it that you escape not so easily. If you duck your head again like you are doing now I will make you swallow this poison which does not do its work for twenty-four hours. I'll warrant you that you will then prefer to face that pistol rather than endure the slow but terrible effect of the alternative that I offered you."

"Perhaps I would," said Abdullah. "It would be more nerve-racking to swallow poison and not experience the effect until a long time afterwards than to face a loaded pistol which would go off in two hours."

"If I were in such a predicament as yours," said Akmat, "I would surely do so. To die a thousand imaginary deaths as you will is not as pleasant as dying one real one, which ends the matter for all eternity. Your evil deeds have brought this fate upon you, and I have been chosen to see that it is carried out. I am disposed to be talkative, and as you are to die so soon I have no objection to exchanging confidences with you."

"You mean by that," said Abdullah, "that I am to lay all my misdeeds before you while you give me the history of your past life in exchange."

"Exactly," said Akmat. "I will begin by telling you how I and my brothers escaped from your prison."

"Very well," said Abdullah. "Go on. I am not at all adverse to hearing so intresting a tale."

"Then here it is," said Akmat, and he told to his enemy the following story.

"There was, among your servants in the Temple of the Fire-Worshippers, an Afghan who was to bring food and water to me and my brothers and father and the captain and Mustapha. He told me that he was not a member of the society and that he abhorred it and had he known what he was attaching himself to would not have been in your employ. However, he had been poor and the wages you had offered him are very tempting, so he had sold himself into your employ as a slave for seven years.

"These seven years were at the time almost passed and he told me that the day after our intended deaths would be the one on which he was to be liberated. He told me that he would smuggle my friends and me out of our prison if we could persuade you to delay the execution for some time.

"So you see now the reason why we begged for a delay when you called us before you to be thrown into the lake. Fool that you were, you granted our request and we went back to our prison rejoicing. Baber, who escaped by holding onto the ropes at the bottom of the chute, was gone and we knew that he had gotten away safely. With him he took the black diamonds which you hid in an iron box overhanging the lake."

"Did you give him these diamonds," said Abdullah, intensely interested, "or did he steal them?"

"We gave them to him," said Akmat, "telling him to keep one of them for himself and give the other to his friend Mustapha."

"Ah! I see it all now," said Abdullah. "Go on, please, your tale is very interesting."

"Next morning Youssouf Jan, your slave, dressed us in clothes of his own and led us forth from our prison unnoticed by your men and gave us a boat in which to row over to the mainland. He himself went with us and we landed near the mouth of the river Indus not long afterwards. While rowing to land we saw your ship leave the island and seeing us it pursued us to the coast. You came close enough to recognize us and shook your fist, and then sailed away."

"I did," said Abdullah. "What did you do then?"

"Went on board the first ship that passed bound for Bagdad and reached it the day after you did. We heard of your attempt to capture Mustapha, but did not visit him, and of your strange escape from your judges.

"We anticipated that you would do the very thing which people would not expect you to do, that is, to return to Bagdad. We haunted the landing-place disguised as Persians, and saw you land and go to your home.

"Then we arranged a plan to kill you, which is the one I am now carrying out. I was chosen as the one to execute it and came to your house not long ago. The rest is familiar to you."

"Did the Afghan come to the city with you?" asked Abdullah.

"Yes," said Akmat. "He is with my father and brothers now."

"Well, I suppose that it is my turn now," said Abdullah, sullenly. "If I tell you of my misdeeds you will only echo them to the world. But what is the use? I am to die soon and have a very bad reputation already. Why should I not add to that reputation and earn a notoriety that will cause my name to be remembered?"

"Why not?" said Akmat. "I would advise you to do so."

And so it was that Abdullah allowed himself to be fooled into telling to one of his enemies the tale of his misdeeds.

When he had finished the recital Akmat stroked his beard in silence. He now knew all he wanted to know about Abdullah and was prepared to be lenient with him. He deemed it no crime to slay such a murderer as Abdullah, but he hated to kill a fellow man in cold blood.

There was only a quarter of one hour of the two hours which Abdullah was to live now left and Abdullah had already suffered enough mental agony. So Akmat determined to take the lead from the pistol but he knew not how to do it. Suddenly an idea occurred to him and he determined to carry it into execution.

The two pistols which he carried were exactly alike, and the sling in which the pistol pointed at Abdullah was held, was very loose. All this fostered his plan.

He took the pistol which he held in his hand and walked behind the table on which Abdullah was sitting and silently extracted the lead. Then he called Abdullah's attention to something behind him and while Abdullah was turned around to look for it exchanged weapons with that in the sling.

"I don't see the picture," said Abdullah, turning around. It was a picture that Akmat had called his attention to.

"Here it is," said Akmat pointing to a small miniature framed in gold which lay upon the table.

"Ah, that is what you mean," said Abdullah, disgusted, and he turned about and looked steadfastly at the pistol, though his nerves were worn into shreds with the terrible waiting for a certain, but slow, death.

"Well, your career will soon be at an end," said Akmat.

Abdullah turned pale. This got in his nerves also and did not help his mental condition in the least.

"Don't speak of it again," he said, crossly.

"You will soon die," said Akmat, pretending not to hear him.

"Yes, I suppose I will," said Abdullah, seeing that the fellow continued to torment him, and knowing that he would only be adding fuel to the fire by retaliating. Therefore, he argued, the best thing to do was to stand it and say no more. After all, in ten minutes his misery would be at an end, and then Akmat could torment him no more.

During the ten minutes that followed he experienced all the torments of the damned. Akmat could not forbear telling him over and over again that he would soon die, and it was all that Abdullah could do to endure it. At the end of the ten minutes the pistol gave a snap, but no other manifestation and Akmat laughed.

"What a joke," he cried and went laughing out of the room, leaving Abdullah in a torrent of passion, which overwhelmed him for the moment. Anger, chagrin and relief perturbed his mind and it was a long time before he regained his tongue and was able to speak.

The unloaded pistol and the thread now drawn taut by the hand of the clock stared at him and he laughed with relief at his escape from the fate that he had escaped.

Then a remembrance of what he had told Akmat entered his mind and he shouted for his servants. They came crowding into the room and liberated him with their knives.

"Seize the man that just left this house," he said, and the servants poured forth from the room to execute his order. Abdullah followed them and was just in time to see Akmat disappear around the corner with half a dozen slaves in full pursuit.

Then he re-entered the house and sat down to await their return. In the meantime we will return to Akmat.

The slaves were not far behind him, but he was a good runner, and running past a house which protruded into the street, went up a small alley and the servants ran past in vain pursuit.

Then he slackened his pace and walked till he entered another street. By various routes he reached the Khan where he and his relatives had put up.

He entered the room that they were occupying and found them all there waiting anxiously for his return. At his entrance they besieged him with a multitude of questions and he had a hard time to quiet them down so that he could tell his tale without fear of interruption.

Finally he succeeded in doing this and then told the story of his adventure with Abdullah, going into full detail.

At the end they were convulsed with laughter at the joke and congratulated him on his success. All were horrified by the crimes which Abdullah had committed and plainly said so.

"Now what had we best do," said Akmat.

"Go to Mustapha, though I scarcely hope that he will receive us after the imposition we have placed upon him," said Ahmed.

"What you say is just," said the rest, and having decided upon this course they determined to take it that evening.

Supper was then eaten and they seated a while before starting out on their journey.

Chapter XXV

The servants who had set out in pursuit of Akmat returned to Abdullah, with their heads hanging down in anticipation of his anger when he should learn that his enemy had escaped, and the rebuke that would surely follow.

"Ha! You cowards, did you let him escape? Do you think that I employed you to let my enemies get away?" said Abdullah, shaking his fist and looking at the malefactors furiously.

"No master," they replied in chorus, "but he knew the streets better than we did and evaded us in some way."

"He did? Well, its my frank opinion that you let him escape. I shall have all of you bastinadoed to-morrow and discharged from my service. I know a man that wants to buy a number of slaves and to him I will sell you. He is a very unkind master and will soon make you lament that you did not obey my commands. Now leave my presence."

The servants had not another word to say in their own defense for it would have been more than useless to argue with Abdullah, so they entered the house and went straight to their own quarters, there to relate their misadventures to sympathizing friends.

Abdullah, in a brown study, his face suffused with anger and chagrin went to his own room and threw himself down on the divan in a storm of rage and began to think the whole matter over.

In the meanwhile several people who had observed Abdullah as he came out of his house into the street and the fruitless chase after Akmat by the unfortunate slaves, were speeding to the cadi to tell him of the man's return and bring soldiers to arrest Abdullah.

Abdullah himself knew that he had been observed and was now deliberating a final blow at Mustapha and an escape to his ship, intending, no doubt, to leave the country forever.

Murder was rampant in his thoughts, and certain murder at that. Finally he arose and dressed himself in the costume of a respectable Hindu of the middle class.

Then he smeared his scimitar with a kind of half-liquid poison and replaced it in the sheath. His dagger received a dose of the same mixture and the bullets in his pistols were dipped in the stuff.

Then he stole forth from the house, being very careful that he was not observed by any of the servants and at last reached the street which was now deserted. Everything was shrouded in darkness.

He carried a lantern and this lighted his way so that he would not fall. Knowing well the way to Mustapha's house, he had little trouble in reaching it about an hour after his start.

Walking boldly up to the door he knocked. It was immediately opened by a servant who bade him walk in. He entered and the servant flew to inform his master that a man wished to see him.

Then he returned to Abdullah and ushered him into the dining-room where Baber and Mustapha were eating their supper.

Mustapha arose and bade him be seated and eat supper with him, saying that his business could wait until the meal was over.

Abdullah complied with the request and ate heartily, even though he was in the house of his enemy. He determined not to kill Mustapha until supper was over and the servants had left the room. It would not be practicable to do so with so many slaves looking on, because they would seize him the instant he had done the deed and he would not be able to escape.

Suddenly a servant entered and informed Mustapha that five men wished to see him on urgent business.

"Bring them in," said Mustapha. Turning to Abdullah he added, "You see, sir, that I have many visitors. You would think that I would grow tired of receiving so many, but somehow or other I do not. I seem to take a joy in meeting people I have never met before and observing all their peculiarities both physical and mental. I take quite an interest in psychology and I can give anyone much information on that subject and concerning human nature."

"Strangely enough," said Abdullah, disguising his voice, "I also take quite an interest in those subjects. It is somewhat of a strange coincidence I may remark."

"Yes it is somewhat of a coincidence, sir," said Mustapha, "but here come the men that wish to see me."

Akmat, followed by the others entered the room and bowed to Mustapha and Abdullah. Abdullah turned pale, and was very much astonished. He scarcely knew what to make of this visit.

Mustapha half-arose from his seat and stared at them with astounded eyes, his fingers gripping the table as if it would have been death for him to let go. He stared at them in mute astonishment for a moment unable to speak.

Akmat half-smiled and advanced toward him, holding out his hand in friendly fashion, being unable to think of anything else to do. Mustapha seized it in a grip that surprised the one just mentioned, hardly knowing what he did.

Then he spoke.

"Be seated, Akmat," he said, "and eat supper with me. You can tell your tale afterwards."

Akmat seated himself and his brothers and Ahmed did the same.

Baber did not know what to do. His mind was in a whirl and so he leaned back and began to think it over.

"How did they escape?" was what puzzled him and he turned this thought over and over in his mind and observed it in all lights and from all sides and directions, fully determined to arrive at the solution sooner or later.

Mustapha was still half-dazed by the sudden reappearance of those who had been his friends and had imposed themselves on him as his cousins. He sat down mechanically and began to think it over as Baber was doing.

"How did they escape?" was the question that also troubled him as well as the sea-captain.

Abdullah was not perplexed by this, having heard Akmat's own explanation, but another question bothered him. "Why had they come to Mustapha's house?" he asked himself and the answer was always the same till he grew tired of it and resumed his eating.

Finally the meal came to an end as all meals do, and Mustapha forgot about Abdullah in his curiosity to hear Akmat's tale. The servants were dismissed from the room and Akmat began his story. Abdullah determined not to try to kill Mustapha until he had heard the purpose of the visit of the five Hindus.

Akmat told his tale from the time Baber had escaped up to the conclusion of the trick he had played on Abdullah. Mustapha laughed at this and Abdullah had hard work to refrain from drawing the poisoned scimitar and smiting him down then and there. But by a miracle and the aid of his strong self-control he succeeded in doing so and listened with outward patience to the remarks they made concerning him. These remarks were not very polite and they only added fuel to the fire of rage that was burning within Abdullah's breast.

Then Mustapha told his story to them and so did Baber. It was an hour before they were through talking and then Mustapha recollected his guest. Turning to Abdullah he said:

"Sir, I beg your pardon for my neglect, but as you see I was so interested in talking with some friends of mine who have passed through miraculous adventures that I entirely forgot you. I heartily apologize and beg a thousand pardons."

"One pardon is enough," said Abdullah, letting his rage reveal itself in his words and tone of voice.

Mustapha was astonished at this impertinent and ungracious reply and drew back, scarcely knowing what he should do or say.

Then Abdullah flung aside the wig that he wore on his head and his Hindu cloak, and drawing his sword spoke in his true voice:

"Mustapha Dagh, you are now about to die." He brandished the poisoned scimitar above his head and made for Mustapha, bent on murder.

Mustapha fortunately evaded the first blow and sprang aside, calling to his friends to help him. Baber drew his dagger and made for Abdullah but tripped himself and fell forward at that person's feet, his dagger grazing Abdullah's leg as it leaped from his hand.

A smile of satisfaction crossed Abdullah's face and he raised his sword and was about to strike Baber's prostrate form when Akmat leaped upon him from behind so violently that the went to the floor, but was immediately on his feet again, leaving Akmat sprawling about on his hands and knees.

The sword was still in Abdullah's hand and as he arose he struck at Baber who was on his knees and the sword went into his shoulder scarcely reaching the bone. The wound would not have been serious had it not been for the poison but this caused it to be fatal.

Abdullah then struck at Akmat but Akmat evaded him and leaping to his feet drew his own sword and was about to attack Abdullah and put an end to him.

Suddenly a sharp hiss pierced the air and all turned toward the door to see what the cause was. In the doorway lay an Indian cobra, which was crawling toward them, occasionally raising his swelling head and giving forth an angry hiss.

"It is Sehi's cobra," shouted Mustapha. "It has broken out of its cage and has come here attracted by the noise." Sehi was a Malay servant who kept a pet cobra which he had taught to dance and perform several tricks.

All of those in the room drew back in alarm, scarcely knowing whether to kill the intruder or drive it out.

Suddenly the reptile caught sight of Abdullah and its head swelled to an enormous size and it showed its venomous fangs and emitted a loud hiss. The smell of the blood upon the scimitar he held in his hand had excited its rage.

It launched itself into the air and sprang at him with another hiss, landing on his breast with such a terrific impact that he staggered and almost fell to the floor.

He recovered himself with supreme effort just as the cobra's fangs penetrated the skin and the venomous and deadly poison entered his system. He waved his sword and struck at the creature as he knocked it to the floor with his fist and severed the head from the body. His face was livid with excitement and a momentary fright and fear of death, and he almost grasped for breath, then recovered and brandishing his sword again emitted a brazen yell and made at Mustapha, fully determined to kill him.

"You shall die!" was his yell and he fully intended to verify the statement. Mustapha dodged under the table and the futile blow exerted its force upon that useful piece of furniture.

Mustapha came up on the other side just as Abdullah leaped upon the table. He had presence of mind enough to seize the table and overturn it with Abdullah underneath.

Abdullah's sword fell from his hand as he fell backward under the furniture and struck itself in the floor about an inch from the snake's head and stood there, quivering from the force of the throw.

Abdullah and the table on top reached the floor with a terrific crash but Abdullah was equal to the occasion and dragged himself from beneath the heavy piece of furniture, though somewhat badly bruised, and went for his sword before Mustapha or anyone else could protect him.

Waving it high in air once more he made a rush at the young Turk, but stopped in mid-air and uttered his death-cry. The poison of the cobra had taken quick effect, being so near the heart, and he fell to the floor, stone-dead, his eyes starting from his head in affright.

The poisoned weapon leaped from his hand and struck itself in the ceiling, so terrific was the force with which he threw it. He lay there in silence, his eyes closed, and gave one quiver before the wicked spirit parted from the body.

Then they knew that his evil career had come to its end and all clustered around his body, even Baber, who was bleeding profusely from his wound, the poison not having yet taken its effect.

Akmat then spoke as if addressing the body:

"During all thy evil life thou wert a serpent, Abdullah, in all thy acts and thoughts, so it is but fitting that thou shouldst die by a serpent's tooth."

He paused and turning to his comrades watched their faces in silence. They also regarded him. No one spoke, and a death-like stillness reigned in that room of death.

Then all turned to the corpse again and watched it. They could scarcely realize that their terrible enemy was dead and none thought that one of them was soon to accompany his spirit to the company of the shades.

Several servants peeped timidly in at the door and watched the silent group in affright.

Ahmed then spoke:

"My sons and my friends, this man who has been an enemy is now dead, by an accident which we must regard as the work of Allah. As Akmat says, it is fitting that he should die by a serpent's tooth, he himself having always been a serpent during his life, but still we must bury him though all he deserves is to be thrown to the vultures who would make short work of his corpse. We had best send someone to the pasha to inform him of what has happened and he will take care of the rest. In the meanwhile we will cover the body with a cloth, so that it will be ready for the bearers."

Scarcely had he finished this oration when Baber, who had been laboring under terrible pain since its beginning, threw up his hands silently and pitched forward to the floor, dead. The poison had done its deadly work and Abdullah's wicked soul had a companion on its journey to the shades of death.

He lay there on the floor beside Abdullah's silent corpse as still as a leopard watching its prey. Not a quiver moved his body but he lay quite still, not moving in the least bit.

Mustapha, who was the first to recover his senses, knelt beside him and turned the body over so that the face was uppermost. Baber's silent countenance was ghastly in its paleness and he had almost stiffened. The poison had done its work well.

All knelt beside the corpse in silence, knowing that it was quite dead. They at once realized that the sword must have been poisoned. Therefore it was of no use to try to make it breathe again. The blood flowed freely from the cut in the shoulder and stained the floor in little pools and streams.

Then Mustapha began to sob for his friend and the others followed his example. Baber had been a good friend to them all and they were sincerely sorry that he was dead.

In a few minutes Mustapha arose, having regained his self-control, and the others also rose.

"Farewell, Mustapha," said Akmat, and he and his brothers and father passed out of that room forever, leaving Mustapha in a torrent of astonishment.

"Sehi," he shouted, "come here for I have an errand for you to run."

The End.